THE SOUL QUEEN'S PROMISE

THE SOUL QUEEN SERIES

RIPLEY SHAINE

Modern Guard Publishing LLC
5900 Balcones Drive STE 100
Austin, TX 78731
rights@modernguardpublishing.com

Obsidian Quill is an imprint of Modern Guard Publishing LLC.
Visit our website at www.modernguardpublishing.com

Edited by Ripley Shaine
Cover art and design by Olivia Pro Design

Paperback ISBN **979-8-9990095-0-0**
Ebook ISBN **979-8-9990095-6-2**

Second Edition October 2025

For those who have walked through shadow—
Keep turning your face towards the sun.

Content Warning:

This novel contains themes that may be distressing to some readers, including grief, emotional trauma, fantasy violence, and scenes with mild romantic/spicy content that include implied coercion. Reader discretion is advised.

CHAPTER ONE

GRIEF washes over me, a heavy wave crashing into me and flinging me out onto rough waters. The pain in my chest ebbs and flows but never dissipates, as I sit in the home Sivan and I built together, the home for which we had fought. Soft tears trickle down my face while I sob silently in our bedroom, giving myself a few moments to fall apart in relative privacy. Memories whisper and swirl, beckoning my power forward, but the broken part of my heart refuses the call.

On the other side of the door, down the hallway in the small room Sivan and I took our suppers in, his family gathers in mourning, waiting patiently for me to slither out of my cesspit of grief. Sivan would most likely be overjoyed at the sight of our tiny cabin being overrun by his plentiful nieces and nephews. Sivan was the youngest of six, and also the first to die.

Losing a fated mate is a tragedy; all fae children grow up hearing the stories of the unimaginable pain that comes from two souls cleaving apart and being locked away from one another in separate dimensions. But Sivan wasn't my fated mate- he was my chosen one. A different type of pain altogether. The years we thought we had drifted away like sand in the wind, all our hopes and plans drifting along with it.

A hollow knock sounds at the door to the bedroom, and I hastily wipe the tears from my face. I had fallen to the floor while going through Sivan's clothing, lost in memories and whispers. Every inch of our bedroom is a reminder of his life; each moment I stay, a salted finger in the wound that is his absence.

I know I need to get up, to pull myself out of this grief. It has been weeks since Sivan died. Maybe a few months. Time has blurred together in one long dark night. Since then, I have gotten up each and every day, dragging myself out of bed with sheer determination. Then I prepare myself a meager breakfast, usually whatever leftover game from the day before and maybe an apple from the tree outside. Then, I see to all the chores Sivan used to: caring for the horses and stables, checking the food stores for pests, chopping firewood, and so on until the sun herself is nearly gone. Often, that tires me out enough that I take a quick supper before finishing the housekeeping and any other necessities. But a routine is not enough to erase the ache in my chest.

The silence in the house nearly drives me mad at times. Other times, visitors arrive, and the noise threatens to swallow me whole. I lose either way.

Today is important, however, and I force my legs into action, standing up slowly and forcing the blood back down into my feet.

As I stand, I let my fingers trace over our bed frame, the wood hand carved by Sivan. Memories of our love beckon me and power trails along my fingertips in response, but I quell it with a thought. Autumn tradition dictates that until the loved one's soul has departed to the Nocturnal Realm, the Under-Realm, those left behind are not allowed to use their powers to so much as light a candle. Still, the memories of the dead call out to me, whether I answer or not.

"Come in," I tell the knocker, while arranging the heavy green dress around me. Forest green, the color of mourning, interwoven with gold and silver strands to represent our marriage and unity. Even though the weight of the material threatens to pull me down, the fabric is soft and comforting. I stand proudly despite its weight, readying myself for my husband's send off to the gods with a calming breath.

"My dear, it pains me to ask, but have you chosen his attire for the ceremony?" Sivan's mother, Adeline, asks as she glides into the room. The long folds of her gown billow around her and settle on the floor. She's chosen a shade of green so deep that it looks black until the soft light streaming in from the sole window in the bedroom hits the fabric, revealing the green sheen.

Typically, I see Addie in reds and golds, the colors of her court. Colors that light up her face. Seeing her dressed in all green, in a formal gown instead of her usual linen pants and hunters' garb, or the occasional robe for ceremonies, sends a slight shock through me. A fae woman from the Autumn lands, she carries the glow of a rising sun with her everywhere she treads. That glow is a bit diminished with her grief, but a hint of her power glimmers over her smooth, dark skin. Adeline has always been the type of woman I aim to be. Strong and unrelenting in the face of a challenge. She and I were enamored with one another from our first meeting.

"Addie, please, you can call me by my name, and yes, he's already dressed and in his coffin." She never understood why Sivan and I chose to live out here, away from society in the Hollow Forest. Despite the name, I find the place a lush garden of tranquility, away from the demands of my birth and away from the expectations of others. Addie, a deeply devout fae dedicated to the old gods, nearly collapsed upon learning of my royal bloodline, and then nearly collapsed again upon learning I had rejected that bloodline in favor of marrying her son.

She clucks her tongue at me and comes over, brushing a stray tendril of curls away from my face.

"Your wild hair," Addie murmurs, her eyes brimming with sadness, then clears her throat. "Sivan loved when you had your hair like this," she says. Pain steals through my chest. Breathing in slowly through my nose and out through my mouth, I center myself. I must remain strong, steady, so Sivan's family does not worry about me. I can take care of myself well enough. The call of my power does not warp me so strongly that I cannot tell fantasy and reality apart from one another.

She presses a kiss to my temple and brushes a comforting hand over my hair. A better mother to me than my own. A few small, dejected sighs escape her. Though my own pain beckons a finger at me, threatening to pull me under, I push it aside in favor of the tasks at hand. The soul ceremony must be completed at sun fall, or else Sivan's soul may become lost and stuck in the Under-Realm. Autumn tradition had dictated all but my role in this. That was left up to me.

Addie readies herself, looking over her reflection in the dirty standing mirror next to the bed. I wonder, when she looks at herself with those piercing eyes, does she see all that I can? The shadows and highlights of a person's soul glow brightly in my eyes, an aura that covers all living things. The dead have more unique, darker energies. I can ignore it when I wish to, but while Addie has this moment with herself, I let her soul colors come into clarity. Darkness encroaches around the edges of her soul, expected after the tragedy we had endured. Sivan's death was not quick, easy, or painless. Some sort of disease, a plague the Autumn fae had never seen before. As the illness progressed, I contacted some of my more discreet friends in the Under-Realm, but they had little information to share. Though he was young and strong, his Fae blood could not heal him.

The day he got sick, I sent word for Addie immediately via hawk. The bird flew fast and furious across the Hollow Forest, to the village Sivan grew up in at the base of the mountains. Nisaba is neither large nor small, but somewhere in between. The Autumn fae settled there due to the protection the mountains and waterfalls surrounding the area provided. They built their homes out of packed clay and tree branches, building into the cliffs of the mountains, but had little contact with other fae on the continent. Addie was the first of the fae in Nisaba to travel out of the village, making her a legend among her people.

Not only is she a gifted healer, but she is well respected in her community for curing illnesses brought on by opening trade up with the fae and human populations previously restricted from crossing into these lands. For her exploits, Addie was blessed by the Goddess of Healing, Inya, increasing Addie's strength further. Hopefully, she would know what illness had overtaken Sivan. She came as soon as she received my message, even using teleportation magic to do so, at great magical cost to herself. In the end, none of it mattered, and Addie returned home, letting Sivan and I live out the inevitable.

I don't typically travel up to Nisaba myself- a dark haired, pale faced dark-fae woman among the golden, superstitious Autumn fae brings looks and questions that I usually am not in the mood to answer. As I think of Addie, our connection and her life, her soul's aura glows, and swells.

The darkness in Addie's soul crescendos with dark memories, the intensity of her pain causing them to play in a loop. But other colors reside there as well. Love, golden and pure shines brightly from the center of her soul, memories of her four daughters and two sons nestled tightly there. And there, twined amongst her cherished loved ones, sit memories of myself. My dark curls and pale skin swirl this way and that in the water-like echoes of Addie's memories, and I catch one in my minds-eye, watching vicariously.

Rhea's black curls swim around her face, barely contained by the small tie desperately holding the mess back. Flour dots her already pale face, and trails down her arms. They contrast with the deep bronze of my own skin, as we work in tandem on the balls of dough on the table before us. So serious, her face always guarded. When I first met her, it caught me off guard that Sivan would choose her. He was a deeply unserious boy, and that hadn't changed as he became a man. The Autumn Fae are known for being loud, boisterous revelers, so why would a dark fae be interested in our lifestyle? But in this moment, her face is soft, her eyes lit like a beacon of joy. She kneads dough with calm hands, and laughs quietly at a joke my eldest daughter, Koda, makes from her spot in the corner, eating scones while Rhea and I bake together. In these moments, I see her as she is. I see what Sivan sees. I wish she would let that light in a bit more, but I'll keep working on her. I hope she'll be comfortable with the rest of the family soon enough...

I fight against the memories grasp, swimming up and away from Addie's soul. A small sigh escapes me as I return to the moment, the love and adoration Addie holds for me stunning me into silence. Seeing myself in someone else's memory always feels peculiar but also light and uplifting-depending on how they see me. Addie's memory leaves me warm and tingly, and I try holding onto it as Addie clucks her tongue and turns away from her reflection.

"Being nosy again, are we?" She asks me, but she's not truly bothered. "I can always feel when you go poking about in my head, dear. It's not a bright place to be at the moment."

"I'm sorry, I know. I'll do better controlling it next time." Her expression darkens a bit, and I already know what she's going to tell me before she does.

"Rhea, your powers are getting stronger. I've told you for months now. You need to contact your family, or the Goddess Rhian—"

I cut off Addie's sentence with cat-like hiss, fury washing over me despite my respect and adoration for the woman before me. Grief and fury compete within me on a daily basis.

"Do not mention that woman's name in my home after all the spells and wards I've put in place to prevent her from finding it in the first place." The finality in my tone gives her pause. Addie purses her lips and looks into the distance for a moment before I feel her own power tugging at my core.

"There's nothing to heal here, Addie. I wasn't his true mate- my soul is intact; however, my heart might feel."

"Oh fine," she says in a motherly tone, fiddling with the amulet of healing tucked around her neck. She means well, but considering today is my husband's funeral, I do not quite feel like debating my powers or my grief. Addie turns and walks to the door, turning the knob before hesitantly asking, "Rhea...?"

"Yes, Addie?" I ask, my voice softer at the pure unadulterated pain in her own.

"Have you... have you, you know, felt him? His soul? Since he passed?" Addie normally asks me as little as possible about my death powers. They are antithetical to hers in every way, two sides of a coin that never meet. Souls, death, shadows, and monsters. The powers passed down my bloodline from the Goddess Rhiannon, Queen of Death, Souls, and the Under-Realm. My family thought I should be grateful, but I found Rhiannon to be a sanctimonious bitch with no interest in me other than finding out if my powers were greater than hers and how best she could control the growth of said powers.

I had in fact felt Sivan, upon his passing and for a few moments thereafter. It left me lifeless for an entire day; I laid next to his body, staring up at the ceiling as his soul fought for freedom from his lifeless body. Some parts of death are too macabre to share with others. Some souls are weaker and pass easily. Some try to hold on to their physical bonds. Most people don't genuinely want to peel back the veil and see what's behind the curtain of death. It creates more questions than it answers. It creates more fear than relief.

"Yes, Addie, his soul is free. The soul rites will guide it home to your ancestral resting place." Putting her at ease, while not outright lying, seems like the best course of action. Besides, I cannot lie very well. That's another problem with seeing people's souls laid bare before you. It erases the need for deceit when you see what others are capable of.

She cries out at my words, leaning against the door instead of opening it. Her brown hand rests over her heart, while she whispers prayers in the old language to her gods. Her vulnerability causes my eyes to burn and pain to lance at my throat. The trivial lie sticks in my throat, but I hold my tongue. Best she doesn't realize how much Sivan's soul struggled in the end. I wish I had not witnessed it myself.

"Thank you... Thank you..." She cries for a few moments longer before pulling a white handkerchief out of her bosom and drying her tears with it. The whole scene leaves me feeling as if something is stuck in my throat.

Then she arranges her ceremonial gown around her, the green once again swallowing her whole. Addie steels her face, her jaw growing taught as the mask of the High Healer slides into place. Her duty here is not only to her son, but to her people counting on Addie to see their souls and their families' souls to the afterlife when their time comes. Her control, their respect, are all absolutely crucial in their culture. The dark fae, my people, only let their masks slip when death comes. The Autumn Fae see death as an ending, a new beginning; something solemn and sacred. The Dark Fae see it as a time of revelry, to celebrate our transition to the next plane. It seems twisted that even in death Sivan's people and mine would differ.

"Rhea, the Promised-Queen of the Under-Realm, the Soul Savior and Shadow Wielder, as the High Healer of the Autumn Court of the Fae, we will begin the soul rites out front in ten minutes," she begins, her voice ancient and serious, "Do you accept your responsibility as soul guide for your betrothed and chosen-mate, Sivan Fieros of Nisaba, son of the High Healer of the Autumn Court of the Fae, and heir to his people?" Magic, ancient, and thick coats her words, its binding properties wrapping all that I am, my own magic, my soul, my center of being within their fiery grip, demanding I answer in honesty and with purity in my heart.

"Yes, I accept my responsibility as his wife and chosen mate, to guide Sivan's soul to the afterlife." Some fae add "provided they have earned their place" at the end of their acceptance. Addie asked me about it when we practiced the time-honored rights last week. I merely gave her a long, long look and shook my head slightly.

If a single god tries to deny Sivan his rightful resting place, or even questions his worthiness, I will burn their kingdom to the ground and laugh as I do so. We were only married for six short months before illness overtook him; before that, so much time was wasted waiting to sneak a moment together, fighting against the constraints of responsibilities, leaving my family. Sivan brought out the wild in me, something I needed desperately.

Besides that, he was so young, both of us only two and twenty. Time seemed infinitely stretched beyond us when we tangled our bodies together night after night, loving each other thoroughly and passionately, scratches and bruises lining our limbs. Sleeping through the days, fucking all night, and downing enough mead to kill a dwarf. Our honeymoon was gloriously spent doing nothing else in the small cabin we claimed on the edge of the Hollow Forest. The yard, a small clearing surrounded by forest, contained all we needed back then. When I was with Sivan, I was simply myself, a gift not often afforded to me then—and now. And when we finally tore our bodies apart, we spent the days exploring the forest, learning her secrets, and enjoying her beauty. It was the happiest time in my short life.

"Pay attention girl," Addie says solemnly, "Being a soul guide is a great and heavy burden. None of us knows what truly lies in another's soul, not even in marriage. But lead him through you must, no matter what you see." *I do,* I think, but do not dare say to High Healer Adeline.

"I understand," I say in the old tongue.

The magic finally accepts my answer, accepts my dedication as a sign I am worthy of the role of soul guide. Autumn magic washes through me, light and refreshing, completely opposite of my own. The taste of spring buds on my tongue and the scent of wildflowers breezes through the small room. A guttural moan flows out of my mouth as the power fully overtakes me, and I brace myself against its impact. It's not entirely foreign, a hint of it feels like Sivan, a bit like home.

"Remember Rhea, you now have only a few minutes to be outside. The magic will take another moment or two to settle. Adjust to it, let it flow over you, but be careful not to be pulled into its thrall or Sivan's soul could be lost in the soul stream..." *Not likely,* I think, considering my own powers.

The new power begins vibrating on my skin, sparks gathering on my arms, my legs, until my entire body glows. Addie watches over me while I bite my lip so hard blood trickles into my mouth. The light magic of the Autumn court electrifies my veins, combusting as it interacts with my darker, heady magic. A note of understanding shines within her hazel eyes. They widen for a moment, before she presses her lips together in a thin line, and finally opens the door, leaving me alone surrounded by memories of my dead husband as his ancestral magic flows through my blood unbidden.

But I am not any soul guide, or some weak child just discovering how power feels. I was born with the magic of the dead in my veins, with the magic of a death queen. I will master this too. I imagine the Autumn magic like golden tendrils unfurling through me, and my own as a dark intricate web. Carefully, seeing where my magic ends and begins, I untangle the light and dark strands from one another and force them apart. Once I master that and feel confident in holding each, I force the powers down to my hands: an orb of pure, golden sunlight in one palm, and one of impenetrable black in the other. *I am a Queen, even if I have yet to claim my birth right. And no one will keep me from guiding my mate's soul home on this blessed day.*

At that thought, holding each power ceases to be a struggle. I feel each of them, like a coil within my mind, a leash I can whip out at will. Smooth and comfortable now that I know how to access them. Magic tempts its user with promises and whispers of more, if one is not careful, so I do not drop my control altogether. Power limning my very being, I rise from the floor, a queen without a crown, holding my back straight and forcing an impassive look on my face. I let the two powers crackle like leashed bracelets down my arms, zinging as they glide along the floor, careful not to unleash them. Light and dark, together again.

The magic settles into my skin after a few moments, no longer a physically controllable thing. With that small thing conquered, I grab a few items I'll need for the ceremony: my mourning veil, a vial Sivan's sisters gave me, and a shadow orb for focusing my power during the ceremony. A thought hits me, and I also pull out my family dagger, hidden in a dresser, and sheathe it to my thigh. A slit in my dress will allow me quick access to the dagger if anything goes awry. Nothing wrong with being prepared, and besides, the ritual calls for blood anyways. That settled, the empty feeling returns.

Looking around the room, I realize what I have not been able to face: there's nothing left for me here. The dirty mirror, crumpled bed sheets, burnt out candles. Small traces of Sivan remain, but other than that, it's slowly being replaced by pieces of me. A part of me slips further into that black hole again as I leave the room behind.

CHAPTER TWO

SHUTTING the door behind me sends a familiar sense of foreboding through my body and soul, an echoing of power tingling along my tongue. The shadows in the cabin shimmer fervently, their whispers growing frantic and disruptive. Moments before, I was entirely sure everything was under control. But now? A ball of dread grows heavy and molten in my stomach. "Listen to the shadows," my mother used to tell me, over and over and over again. It is one of the first lessons the dark fae learn as children, especially those born with magic. One such shadow curls up along my spine, seeking comfort from whatever frightens them so. The unease grows as I count the small list of things that terrify shadows, each of them undesirable explanations.

"Rhea!" Koda calls my name from the kitchen down the hall. Shifting in her direction, I will my thoughts calm. I've gotten through every single one of my worst days so far. I shall get through this one too.

I stride into the kitchen, my posture meticulously cultivated, my very breathing timed. The shadows continue their watch from the eaves, watching over me like little dark angels. Koda stands by the sink, the small window above it open, allowing a cool breeze through the room. On the far wall, the hearth blazes, the stew simmering above it fragrant and inviting. From the direction of the front room, I hear Koda's children laughing and playing, small shrieks escaping them every so often. Like lightning, pain strikes the center of my heart at this moment, and all the future moments Sivan will not be here.

The world keeps moving on. Sivan and I are frozen together at the moment his life ended, stuck in time, our souls reaching for one another across the divided realms of life and death. Yet, the world keeps turning, the children keep laughing, our hearth keeps blazing, blissfully unaware that Sivan ever existed. Unaware that we ever loved each other at all.

Koda shifts away from the sink and her breath catches in her throat when she sees me, making an odd rasping sound. A strange glow encompasses her, side effects from the death magic, as her aura blurs in and out of focus. Is the death magic suppressing my own?

Koda's wan face reminds me: the worst part of being a widow is undoubtedly the pity. Though my skin is usually pale, circumstances have left me with deep shadows under my eyes, and for a while, there was no reason to go outside and greet the day, no reason at all to drag my weary bones from the bed. I ignore the fuzzy pull of her memories; ignore the way my reflection shines hauntingly back at me from her tear-rimmed eyes.

She remembers herself and forces a sad smile upon her face. Her eyes, green and flecked with gold like Sivan's were, roam over me. She wears a green dress, similar to my own, but lighter and looser, stretching around her pregnant belly. Her fifth child is due any day now. I was surprised the news of her brother's passing had not shocked her enough to send her into labor early.

Still, despite her condition, her hair sits neatly on her head in a perfectly braided coronet, the pointed tips of her ears peeking out around a few drifting locks. She appears glowing, and healthy, though sadness weighs heavily on her shoulders and face.

Rubbing her belly, she walks closer to me and embraces me in a warm hug. After a moment, I shift uncomfortably, and she releases me.

"You really should eat more," she says as she looks over me, "You're far too thin these days."

"I'm fine," I reply automatically. She ignores me and grabs a bread roll from one of the bowls nearby and shoves it into my hands.

"Eat," she commands, the tone in her voice leaving no room for arguing. Dutifully, I scarf it down. It's soft, warm, and fresh. She hands me a tankard of water without a word and I down that as well. Koda looks pleased with herself, rubbing her belly again without thought, and smiles gently at me.

"Five minutes left, Ri." She cocks her head slightly and adjusts a few of my curls, still trying to burst out from the confines of the single tie holding it back. "May the goddess bestow strength upon you." Releasing me fully, she resumes cooking, dicing brightly colored vegetables and grinding herbs in a stone dish. Sivan told me once that Koda always had the heart of a chef. Addie supported all of her children's desires and dreams, letting Koda wander across the seven kingdoms tasting dishes and discovering foreign spices. Koda let her heart and taste buds guide her way, until she met a gentle golden-fae male in the grasslands of Echosia, making a living serving food in a small tavern. She convinced the male, Irstin, to come along with her on the rest of her journey, and eventually to her home.

Koda and Irstin had been married nearly four years by the time Sivan and I married. A child for each year together. A blessing I am both grateful for, yet sorrowed by, as I will never come to know it. I watch Koda's back for a moment, as she twists and turns this way and that about the kitchen, adjusting the stew, cutting a fresh loaf of bread. When she turns back my way, she hisses at me, her face turning red. I wasted too much time this morning drowning in grief alone in my room.

"Rhea, you are running out of time. My mother is a patient fae but today is different. Difficult. Why are you still standing here? Go... go!" She waves her hands at me, urging me towards the front room and the little door leading outside. Since Sivan died, I've avoided that door. Using the cellar entrance when possible or avoiding leaving the cabin altogether. Today, there is little choice. The procession will begin right out front, underneath the canopy of trees, and march along the riverside until we reach the Standing Stones. The long walk is meant to signify the journey of Sivan's soul, but only I know that the journey is nothing like a hike through the forest.

Sivan's family decorated the space beneath the trees earlier today. Just his mother and sisters, as tradition dictates. Lighting thousands of fairy candles, releasing them into the air and arranging them with magic to look like the stars on the night of Sivan's birth. From birth to death, and back again.

They also draped soft fur rugs over some of the rocky ground for the parts of the ceremony that require kneeling. Some fae avoid doing this, saying death requires discomfort, but Addie said that Sivan wouldn't want any of us in pain when celebrating his life. He knew he was dying in the end, knew there was little time, and told us he wanted to be celebrated. To know he was loved and that his love left an impact. Not mourned in the traditional sense, but for each of us to look back on the memories we shared and know each moment counted. I wonder sometimes if he learned that from me.

The children ignore me as I pass by them, still playing despite the sadness permeating the household, so I say nothing as I approach the front door, a wraith with my green gown trailing the floor behind me. The door has a simple wooden frame, but the inner panel is beautiful hand-blown glass. Sivan was a skilled crafter in life. The whorls and patterns on the door were meant to represent our respective powers, dark blooming blossoms colliding with golden lilies. It catches the sunlight, sending it scattering across the exposed walls and rooms it touches.

Hesitation floods through me. It feels as if I take one step out of this door, then he is really gone. His soul offers little comfort to me, it but a small piece of who he is. Was. And that souls grasp on this realm grows weaker each day.

The glass flowers etched into the door catch the fading light of day, sending it shooting off in a million directions. I stare at them, contemplating what I am about to do, what I am about to experience. I will send off his soul and watch vigilantly as it crosses into the afterlife. The presence of his family will strengthen me, embolden me, despite the grief cracking through my mental shields. I will do this because I have to. Sivan was my chosen mate, and I will give him a soul yielding worthy of kings. A sense of pride rushes through me, a golden balm to my grief, that I can offer this one small thing to my love. I can do this.

Anxiety threatens my throat and chest. If I give into panic, I will have accomplished nothing. *Acknowledge it and let it go*. A mantra from my childhood trainings on meditating and learning how to control my power.

Focusing on each muscle in my body and forcing it to relax as I exhale a deep, long breath, I open the door, the glass sparkling mesmerizingly. I place a palm against the glass, as if it were Sivan's heart. My own heart aches, but the door reminds me: we created something beautiful here. Now, I have the future awaiting me outside this door. A future without the only love I've ever known.

CHAPTER THREE

OUTSIDE of the cabin, the atmosphere shifts immediately. Gone is the warm glow of the hearth and the comforting scent of spices in the air. Instead, storm clouds threaten in the distance, over the mountains. The sky churns, half dark-half light, and heavy clouds grow together. The shadows gather and cling along my arms, down my abdomen and legs, a relative suit of armor underneath my gown.

"Shh, shh, it's alright..." I murmur at the shadows absentmindedly, focusing on the events ahead.

Everyone else is already gathered together aside from Koda and a few of the children. Friends and family members bustle about the yard, but their faces blur past me.

Of Sivan's siblings, the second oldest and Sivan's only brother, Grigori, stands chatting quietly with the rest of the children a few feet away from me. Grigori is a taller version of Sivan, with a crooked nose from a brawl when he was younger, and a wave of messy brown hair on his head. Catching bits of the conversation, it seems he's going over ceremony etiquette again for good measure. The twins, Sienna and Orla, sit alone on a small wooden bench further away from the house, in the small clearing that serves as our yard. They're both slight, quiet women. At twenty-five, they still prefer each other's company over anyone else's.

Sivan's casket rests beside their feet, on a tall slab so we can easily pick it up when the procession begins. Grigori crafted it from a rare dark oak found deep in the forest. He taught Sivan everything he knew about creating something with his own two hands, about not relying on magic when beauty can be found in hard work. When the time came, Addie suggested we have a crafter from one of the bigger cities design the coffin, but Grigori insisted on making the coffin. He said it was the least he could do for his baby brother.

The lid looks like branches weaving together and climbing over one another, as if life is waiting for the right moment to spring forth and bloom. Other than that, the coffin keeping my husband's body secure is plain. Decorating it for the journey is a part of the opening ceremony. His family—our family—will add offerings his soul might need for the journey and Addie will bless each one.

"Rhea!" A bright voice pipes up behind me before something barrels into my mid-section. The two of us go sprawling into the dirt and leaves, my dress flying up over my head and exposing the fact that I wore pants underneath. The shadows on my skin buzz with excitement at the sudden action, but their sinewy bodies protect me from even so much as a scrape.

"Well, hello to you too, Brynn," I say calmly. If the schedule is thrown off, Addie can yell at Brynn instead of me. She laughs, and helps me to my feet, each of us composing ourselves and dusting off our dresses. The small moment lets me glance up and down, analyzing Brynn's appearance since I haven't seen her in a few weeks.

Her eyes are bright and merry, even surrounded by death. Brynn certainly inherited her mother's sunshine. Brynn is the only one of

Addie's children with their father's golden-brown eyes, and even now the look in them is undaunted. Her freckles stand out strikingly against her brown skin, like stars smattered across her face. A slight smile graces her lips, as she analyzes my appearance right back.

Her presence is like a balm on my weary and bruised soul, a bit of light in the dark. Knowing Sivan's death hasn't stolen her bright energy, given how close they were with one another, is another small thing that will guide me through this.

"Good, you're both here." Addie's voice pops up behind us, "And it looks like you're both on time as well." Her smile is one of an amused mothers rather than the stern healer she transforms into.

"I aim to please, ohmostbelovedmotherandhighhealer!" Brynn's words race by as she bows dramatically and deeply in her mother's direction. Addie simply rolls her eyes and looks at me instead.

"The men are all ready, though a few are grumbling about the storm. All the husbands and sons over thirteen will carry the casket behind you, Rhea, and then place it in the Circle of Stones. From there, you will start the ritual, and I will finish it after you release his soul. If no further explanation is needed, then we begin adorning his casket."

I shake my head, quiet so my feelings do not spill out of me. Everything will go perfectly. It has to.

"Alright then, ladies, let us join the others and begin."

We follow Addie across the small clearing, to the closed casket devoid of life. Huge woven bowls sit nearby, some filled to the brim with flowers in shades of purple and red. Others hold golden leaves and acorns. Smaller bowls contain salt, herbs, shells from the lake, and a few with items I cannot identify. Addie pulls out a small horn from the hidden pouch at her hip and sounds it off in three short bursts. A signal to all that the time has come. Koda pops out of the front door, her belly leading the way, with a gaggle of children at her feet, rushing them over to join the family. Grigori's group meanders over slowly, the other fae adults with him picking up their children and carrying them. Sienna and Orla remain seated, but this close I can see they have bits of twine in their fingers, long strings of it in red and gold. Each of them braids a section, before swapping it over, creating an intricately flowing design that one set of hands could not accomplish. They see me staring and Sienna clears her throat.

"Hey, Ri."

"Hey." Orla echoes softly.

"Hi. What are you making?"

"A talisman," they say in unison, "to watch over Sivan when you release his soul."

The twins inherited Addie's powers for healing, but their own went a few steps further. They cannot see death the way I can but... they can hear whispers and echoes of it. They can sense things about me that I'm not even fully sure of. Most fae find them creepy, but with their healing gifts many are willing to overlook their oddities.

I smile at their answer, a genuine smile. I have always been a little odd, too. My heart warms at their care for their brother, and they know as well as I do what lurks in the shadows. Anything that helps Sivan, I am all for.

"Thank you, Sienna, Orla. This is hard for me... but at least I will have all of you by my side."

"We have to finish it now," Sienna says. She looks at me, her eyes all-seeing and piercing, but says nothing else.

Orla merely nods her agreement, and they begin their pattern again. They might be older than me, yet I feel protective over the two women as if they were my own sisters. Maybe this is what it means to be a part of a family. Even with Sivan gone, Addie checks in on me constantly, if not more. Koda makes the several hour-long carriage ride down the mountain pass to see me at least once a week, even as her child readies itself to arrive. She fusses over me for a day or two, cooking and playing cards with me in the faelight, before returning on the holy day. The twins send me notes and letters, usually odd things. Last week, a small box arrived outside of my door (courtesy of magic) with a letter that simply read "don't drink." Inside the box was a small vial of dark liquid, filled with the strange small blossoms of an unfamiliar flower.

I asked them about it a few days later, when I made the journey out to the village on a whim, fueled by the note. What was it? Why would I drink a strange vial? Why shouldn't I? The questions swirled through my head for two days, the bizarreness of it all driving me mad. I took my horse, Astraea, and a small pack before we headed up to see the twins. When we arrived, the journey quick for my slender, nimble mare, I saw to it that Astraea rested with the other horses in the pasture and made my way over to the twins round home.

Spending time with the twins always leaves me feeling languid and happy. Their home grows up out of the ground, a half circle covered in bright open windows. Sienna and Orla prefer passing time with their hands covered in dirt, growing normal herbs and tea, but also medicinal plants and various exotic plants from around the world. Really, they could have sent me anything, but why send me something that says don't drink?

When I knocked on the door to their home, overgrown with small white blossoms and vines, neither of the twins looked surprised at my arrival. They took one look at me, looked at each other, and said, "come in!" as if they were expecting me all along.

We skipped pleasantries, Sivan's death still fresh in our minds, but Orla brought out a full tea service with snacks and we munched in silence for a bit. A comfortable silence between family members.

"So, what brings you out here?" Sienna asked. She's much more forward and direct than Orla, Orla always letting Sienna take the lead. Orla has her own opinions but prefers letting life pass her by quietly.

"The vial." I responded. What else could it have been? They had never sent me such a strange gift before; they would send me many after. But since this was the first, I needed to know the *why* behind it.

"What about it?" Orla said around a mouthful of cookies.

"Why can't I drink it?"

Sienna and Orla shared a look, their eyes dancing, then looked at me as if the answer was quite obvious. Sometimes, twin speak is really irritating.

"Because you will die if you do," they said in unison.

"Okay... why send it to me?"

"Why not?" They echo.

I knew any other information I managed to pry from them would be as useless as the first part of the conversation, so we spent the rest of the afternoon trading stories and chatting about the weather, before I returned home to stare at the vial.

I keep the vial with me everywhere I go now. Its color remains unchanged, whatever liquid the vial holds still as deadly as the day it arrived. I wear it on a simple chain, around my neck, as if a talisman holding me steady. I would never drink it, but having death near has always been a comfort to me.

"Rhea? Where'd you go? You've got that distant look in your eyes again." Brynn laughs at me, forever amazed by my ability to tune out anything and anyone, no matter what's happening around us. The wind blows a little harder, the baskets holding our decorations shifting in the breeze. "We need to decorate the casket and get going."

"Yes, of course, sorry." I say sheepishly, like I am embarrassed, but that's the furthest thing from the truth. The truth is I would tune out the rest of the world whenever I can, for as long as I can. Existing in the world of the living, surrounded by the dead, I live in the in-between. Cloaked by shadows, but never truly consumed.

We join the rest of the group, adorning Sivan's casket with bits of nature and love, until it looks like a tree in full bloom. The twins finish their charm and attach it gently to the center of the tree.

We monitor the storms' progress, as well as the sun's. Thunder rumbles ominously, the sky blotted out like an ink-stain. Something about this storm feels off. Even listening carefully with my fae ears, I cannot hear a single bird or critter rustling about. Usually, this forest teems with hidden life; birds squawk from high overhead, creatures rustle through the underbrush, and the various insects chitter away all day. But now, the forest is dead silent. The shadows on my skin buzz with something akin to fear.

As the storm grows, the shadows hide wherever they can: under trees and rocks, in the small well next to the horse shed, and more join the ones coiled around me, shrinking into my skin as much as possible. The air is pregnant with anticipation, as if the world around us is preparing. For what, I don't know. Tension prickles along my spine, a fleeting feeling, reminiscent of a feeling I've had before. Something from a hazy childhood memory. While I try to discern what this feeling reminds me of, lightning cracks across the clearing, frightening a few children nearby. Astraea in the stable whinnies nervously and the forest goes silent.

Addie clears her throat against the growing worry. It's natural to fear a storm. Even the gods cannot overcome nature. But we have a task at hand, one we cannot delay further. It's time to say goodbye.

"Take your places and let us be off." Adeline the Healer's voice booms around the storm, loud and clear despite the growing wind whipping through the tall forest trees. Her voice clears the spell the storm holds over us, and suddenly the clearing is a flurry of activity. While the men grab the casket, hoisting it up onto their shoulders, I take my place at the front of the procession. The loose curls of my hair flutter tumultuously in the wind, and I pull my mourning veil over it, securing it in place with a golden diadem.

The men take their place behind me ready for my signal. One of my hands grips the vial at my throat; the other hand grips the focusing orb. The rest of the siblings and family will follow behind us for the several miles we walk along the river path, guided by my voice and incantations, until we reach the Standing Stones.

Addie takes her place beside me, and we turn to face the rest of the procession together.

"Today we gather, blessed by two Goddesses, brought together by two clans, to celebrate the life of my son, Sivan, and guard his soul as he makes the journey to the afterlife. His soul guide, Rhea, the Promised-Queen of the Under-Realm, the Soul Savior, and Shadow Wielder, will begin momentarily and deliver Sivan to our ancestral home. Bow your heads."

We all lower our heads as Adeline begins the incantations of her Goddess, Inya, her voice carrying across the wind like a song. Inya, the Goddess of Healing and Water. The prayers reflect that, their melodic fluidity reminding me of ocean spray and loving arms.

Addie's hand searches for mine, and we clasp together, anchoring each other, right as I join my voice with hers, praying in the tongue of the dark fae. The language of my people is not fluid and melodic; it is harsh and haunting.

The wind laps at our clothes and hair, ripping the loosest pieces free as my prayers find strength. Still, the rain does not rend down upon us.

Soon, all of the fae in the clearing begin praying in unison with us, our voices winding up and up and up. Magic, thick and coy, fills the clearing as our prayers reach their mark; tiny glowing fae lights appear down the forest path. Our prayers come to an end, each of us blending our voices together until the very last syllable. Everyone looks to me, expectant. Anxiety creeps along my skin at their focused attention; it's been a long while since anyone expected anything of me. Or at least, a while since I knew they expected anything of me.

But this, today, this ceremony. Everything else fades from existence. I strip the world bare, down to shadows and spaces.

I begin to sing. Songs of mourning, songs of the dark fae, songs dark and ancient and cold. The children, too young and small to be pallbearers, begin pounding their small drums, the beat heavy and synchronous. My voice clear and bright, my feet move of their own accord. Left foot forward, now the right. Avoid that branch, do not let it snag your dress. After a few minutes, we begin passing the river. It is a small river, only a little wider than I am tall, but begins growing as we walk alongside it, the wind still ripping at our bodies.

The procession marches steadily behind me; I can feel their steps pounding into the worn dirt trail. I dare not look back. Instead, I continue my song, now more a steady chant, the long repetition already wearing on my voice. Faltering is not an option, so I continue, the procession a steady presence at my back. The sun continues her descent as well, the sky darkening even further with the impending storm. Here, deeper in the forest, up the mountain path, the trees stand even taller, blocking out most of the fading sunlight. Only from the way we came, down the riverside, can we see the setting sun. The darkness looms before us, a mouth yawning open, ready to swallow us whole, before the trees open up and out.

At last, we arrive at the standing stones, nestled in a small stone clearing on a rocky outcrop, surrounded by forest for miles around. One long, tall stone sits in the center of a circular clearing, two shorter stones on each side of it. Each one has a different Goddesses symbol etched into the top of it. The tallest bears the sigil of the Goddess Inya, three short waves with a leaf. The stone to the left bares the sigil of the Goddess Rhiannon, simply a skull. The last stone, on the right, bares the sigil of the Goddess Megara, a small fire. Three stones representing the three strongest of the seven goddesses.

Addie and I stand in the middle of the clearing, at a spot designated for us. No pillow or rug, at my request. I may prioritize everyone else's comfort, but a little discomfort will help me stay focused while in the soul stream. The men set the casket down in the center of the clearing, adjacent to the standing stones.

Everyone settles into their spots, and a hush falls over the crowd as I finish my song, and Addie ceases chanting at the same moment.

The sun's final descent into the sky marks the beginning. Magic mixes with the wind, sweeping through the atmosphere like a warning. The shadows watch over the clearing, whispering anxiously among themselves. Twilight creeps over the circle, slowly but surely.

Ignoring everything, blocking out all of the physical world, I plunge deep into my power, more and more shadows gathering around me. My power sings them a siren song, and I gather them all in my hands. Connecting to another's soul is different for all shadow-wielders; for me, I imagine a bridge of darkness. A bridge I will build, stone by stone, shadow by shadow, using magic and memory. Memories are a kind of magic on their own, and I have plenty to choose from.

Memories pour out to me, as I slip into the soul stream: Sivan and I lazing in the grass in the springtime, kissing each other hungrily; Sivan, shirtless, the muscles in his back flexing as he builds our bed, the sweat beading off his back; Koda and Sivan baking bread together in our kitchen; Sivan holding his nephew right after his birth, declaring how he could not wait to have children of our own.

Love and warmth echo back through the soul stream, and my power reaches out across the bridge as Sivan's soul answers the call. Memories flow back from the other side: Me, my hair unbound as I lounge in a field of wildflowers; Sivan proposing to me, a moon-bell flower in his hands; Me, content in a chair, engrossed in a book, fully unaware anyone is watching. Sivan's memories, responding to my own. My breath catches in my throat as I realize he is here. All that's left to do is finalize the connection so Addie can send him off.

"Sivan, my love, I am here. I am here to guide you home. I am here." My voice is a whisper of silk against the angry wind. I wish it were louder; I wish I could scream into the void, drag him back, make him stay.

Each memory strengthens the bond between us, and finally, Sivan begins to materialize in the clearing, his soul made corporeal through my power. His brown skin is as warm in death as it was in life, a flush across his cheeks. He's wearing leather pants and a loose tunic, like he used to on hot summer days. His hazel eyes shine gloriously, if a bit translucent, as he gazes at me from beyond, the look on his face unreadable.

Tears hit my cheeks, fat heavy droplets spilling out unbidden. Hot and salty, blurring out the world.

"My love," my voice rings out through the clearing. No one else can see his physical soul; no one else has been burdened with that gift, though I hear their whispers and curiosity as if a distant sound.

"My love," I say again, "I miss you more than words could ever describe. I have so many questions but first... do you understand why you are here? Do you know what is happening?" Some souls carry an awareness, even after death. Not all, but some. I had hoped and prayed, though those prayers went unanswered, that Sivan's soul would know me when the time came.

His form shimmers, but he smiles broadly, the same warm smile he had in life. Like the sun exploding, immeasurably bright. Relief spreads through my dark heart.

"How could I forget you, Rhea? After everything we shared?" There's a teasing lilt to his voice. Blood rushes into my cheeks at his words, despite knowing no one else can hear him.

"Do you want to say anything... before?" *Before I release your soul.* I can build this bridge only once, and after that, even without help he would eventually fade into the afterlife. It is much more pleasant if a soul is guided there, however. I can't bear to let Sivan face that darkness alone.

Sivan's soul walks over to me, his palm gliding over my cheek, a ghost of a touch.

"Dry your tears my dark little queen," his laugh is the same husky thing from my imperfect memories, "My time has come, but for you, there are many adventures to be had."

I scoff at that. "My adventuring days are over, now that you're gone."

"Don't say that. You are capable of so much more than you know. I can see clearly, on this side. I never thought you could ignore your birth right. I knew the time would come when we would face that together. Even if you didn't want your parents crown, you cannot ignore the fact that eventually you will become the Queen of Death." In life, Sivan never let me lie to myself. He held me accountable to myself, refused to let me ignore the parts of myself I dislike. I should have known death would be no different.

Splash. Splash. Splash. The first few drops of rain begin to fall. No one moves; we will do what must be done.

Addie's impatient voice reminds me I am not alone. The shadows screech discordantly around me, the storm driving them into a frenzy again.

"Rhea, dearest, as much as we want to give you more time, we must complete the ceremony. We've only got half an hour at most before he disappears."

Sivan smiles at his mother, though she cannot see it. "She always wanted the best for you, Ri." His smile falls, his eyebrows pinching together. He always gets that look when something bothers him.

"What is it?" My question comes out in a rush. We've got only a short amount of time before Addie will send him to his resting place. The clearing is nearly black now, aside from the almost fully set sun and the fae lights in the air. The light drops of rain have turned into a pour, filling up the clearing with mist.

"I need to tell you something. Something serious involving the Godde- "

His voice cuts off in a horrible, pain-filled scream as lightning strikes Sivan right in the center of his being and the world explodes into shadows.

The shadows swirl and scream and fight in a vicious cyclone of darkness and dust before a strange green light flashes, blinding me. My arms shield my eyes instinctively, and I see the shadows clinging to my arms have also gone. In fact, every single shadow clinging to my body is gone.

"SIVAN!" I scream against the explosion, against the intrusion, against the anger pouring out of me. "Sivan, please!"

I force my eyes open despite the pressure. I wish I had not.

Standing before me, a mirror of myself, stands the tall and lithe form of the Goddess Rhiannon, Queen of Death and the Under-Realm, Lord of the Shadows, Lies, and Bones. The sanctimonious bitch herself, in the flesh, ruining my husband's funeral. Her gown sweeps the stone floor, midnight moss, a mockery of a mourning gown; the top is indecently low cut, sweeping to her navel. Her black curls are arranged in a half up, half down mass that writhe around her like snakes. No- not just her hair.

Shadows coat every inch of her cream white skin, blackness writhing in and out of her hair as it pleases. Her moonstone eyes glow green with her power; a line of kohl around them makes her look sultry and dangerous. Her cat-like grin is painted red. As are her nails. Which I notice, because those poison red nails are attached to hands that hold a leash of shadows.

She leashed my husband's soul with shadows.

Anger pours off me in waves. Grief had felt unending, as if I would die. As if my heart had ceased beating the moment Sivan's had. But... now? Grief is placid. Grief is a calm lake with a fresh breeze on a light summer's day. Grief is nothing compared to the chasm of rage that seeing Rhiannon leash my husband unlocks within me.

My power opens up before me, a gaping maw, a leap into a volcano. White hot, the opposite of the darkness I am accustomed to. This is the sparkling power of the autumn fae, still connected with my own, creating something new. Something that can give me an edge.

"Get your hands off of my husband." My words come out with an icy chill that only causes Rhiannon to smile even more. My face twitches with disgust but I am careful not to move, to slow down and think, observe, listen to the shadows. Clearly, they were warning me about her arrival. What else might they tell me?

"Or what, deary? I thought the little shadow princess was all grown up now." She cocks her head, her feline eyes narrowing. "At least, that is what you said when you left your parents last year."

"Get. Your. Hands. Off. My. Husband." My patience thins, the words coming out through gritted teeth.

She goes on, my words bouncing off of her, a peasant to a queen, a queen to a god.

"You know, my pet, if you had come and trained with me when I asked you to, none of this would have happened. You would have the power you so desperately crave right now, and your husband would have lived."

My entire world narrows to Rhiannon. To her words. The implications.

"What did you just say?" My voice is a harsh whisper.

"Oh, dearest me, what did I just say?" She winks a conspirator's wink at me, as if we are buddies jesting over a few pints of ale. "Let me be clear."

Her demeanor morphs and changes, her face becomes taut and drawn, the shadows around her swirling violently. The temperature plunges a few degrees, and a violent shiver runs along my spine.

"Since you refused my gifts, I took it upon myself to remove the problem. Have you heard of The Immortal Plagues? I suppose not, since, well, here we are." She gives an unapologetic shrug. "Look at it this way: now you can join me in the Under-Realm and begin your training. If you do, I promise to restore Sivan's soul for you. With a living body, as well."

A deadly calm floods my veins, and I look at Rhiannon through dead eyes. The only thought that enters my mind is the whisper of an old, dark fae vow. Ancient shadows guide me as I draw my dagger from its sheath, slice my palm open, and press my bleeding hand against the ancient standing stones. My vow spills into the earth, binding me to the three goddesses—Rhiannon's sisters, witnesses to my unbreakable promise. My future sisters.

"Unleash my husband. Now. And I might consider killing you quickly."

The air thickens as I reach for my shadows—my birthright, my power—but the moment they slip from Rhiannon's grasp, they wither. A phantom wind howls around us, and suddenly, my own magic recoils, shuddering like a wounded animal. The standing stones groan, pulsing with her energy. She barely moves, yet I feel her magic seep into my bones, cold and slow, like a hand gripping my spine.

She isn't just strong. She is ancient.

The drugs are wearing off; the ceremony should have been completed by now. We were supposed to gather around the fire pit afterward, sharing memories, eating, drinking, refusing to let grief steal our night.

Now, none of that will happen.

Rhiannon tilts her head, the candlelight catching in her black eyes. Not even a flicker of fear.

I step forward. She lets me.

I press the advantage, intent on showing her just how little I have revealed over the years. "Capitalize on an enemy's surprise—especially when they might be stronger than you," Asher's gentle but firm voice reminds me from deep within my memories.

Before I left home, my parents instructed their Captain of the Guard, Asher, to train me. They saw my strength early, my power over the shadows, and knew what it meant. My mother obsessed over it, convinced it would secure her dominance in the world—as if being a Fae Queen wasn't enough. She summoned tutors from every continent, forcing me to spend hours mastering shadowcraft and combat. Asher was the only one worth remembering, as he spent more time with me than any other fae, even my own family.

Rhiannon named me her heir when I was just a babe, recognizing the kernel of power within me. But she never saw its true depth. Power manifests differently in everyone. She fixated on that kernel, visited often to gauge it. My parents, as cunning as she, saw what she did not.

Unlike most dark Fae, my mother's magic is weak—limited to reading cards and glimpsing fractured futures. My father is magicless. But they knew Rhiannon would crave my power. So, my mother trained me to hide it. In hidden shadows, my childhood was relentless: training in the royal graveyard, speaking to my ancient, deceased kin, summoning shadows, pushing my body to its limits. Asher was the closest thing I had to a friend. I wasn't even allowed to have a pet. And then, I met Sivan.

While I wasn't allowed much, my parents gave me the freedom to travel and explore since my magic was more than capable of handling any bandits or ill-intentioned travelers. One evening, I had traced the dirt pathway that led out from the gardens surrounding the castle, into the small forest that bordered the castle walls. Hidden there was a small glade I liked to visit often, complete with a warm pond fed by a spring. Never had I ever seen another soul there, so I was caught off-guard by the sight of a man's naked shoulders as he rose from the water. To my chagrin, I stared. And stared. And stared. For so long, he turned around and caught me, a slight look of astonishment on his warm brown face. It quickly turned into a big, free grin and I blushed knowing I was caught.

Sivan saved me from drowning in my parents' darkness. Sivan gave me a voice when they tried to mold me into their private shadow-weapon. And though I waited, and I learned, I never stopped dreaming of a world beyond their grasp.

And now, all of that has led to this moment. This promise. This fight.

I step forward again, voice cold. *"I said—"*

A flick of Rhiannon's fingers.

It's barely a movement, but it hits me like a blow. Shadows whip around me, tightening like a noose, and suddenly my own magic is turning against me. I try to summon the darkness back, to make it obey, but it twists in my grasp, writhing like a serpent, unsure of who its master is. A sharp, searing *crack* echoes through the space. My knees buckle. Rhiannon watches, bored, as if I'm a child throwing a tantrum.

I push through the pain, straightening. I have trained too long, endured too much, to fall so easily.

But then she smiles. That smile means something.

She's holding a secret. But what? Does she suspect the true extent of my power? Or is there something else? I slow, unsure of myself, but a moment is all she needs. She relaxes her grip on the leash, and Sivan's soul sighs in relief on the ground.

"You see, I have your husband's soul completely in my thrall currently. If anything were to happen to me while I hold this leash of shadows, Sivan's little soul would be lost... forever. Irretrievable even to me, I'm afraid. So, again, think twice before making rash decisions."

Her red lips twist into a savage grin. The sight makes me go numb with anger. My face twitches, my throat convulses. This gown feels like it's suffocating me.

None of the Autumn Fae have said a word this entire time. Even Addie.

They all sit in their spots, staring. Silent witnesses as I make a solo stand for Sivan's soul. All of them, too small in the face of the death goddess. What is a handful of healers against death herself?

"Rhea," a small voice from beside Rhiannon cuts through my doom, "look at me. I have one more thing to tell you."

My head turns to look at him of its own accord, my body a puppet on strings, each movement stiff and jaunty.

"You are my whole heart," he begins, "but it's not enough to just dream. You have to act." His eyes have the look of finality, his words confuse me. And then, I know. Like I knew he was dying. The realization should not hurt me as much as it does; it's what we came here to do after all.

Slowly, so slowly I hope Rhiannon cannot feel the tug of my power, I begin to break down the bridge I had built to reach Sivan. The memories fade with time anyways, getting weaker and weaker. I hurry along, loosening stones, tearing them down, until the bridge is broken down the middle, Sivan and I standing on opposite sides. It feels as if tearing out another piece of my soul.

"You will understand later." His ghostly form mouths the words to me, and I know them as he does, despite his quickly fading form. Tears roll down my face hard and fast, lost in the wind and rain, as Rhiannon roars, her tether to this realm damaged.

I turn away, unable to watch the love of my life fade into the soul stream without the proper rites, and face Rhiannon.

She seethes with anger, and I think *good, we're a matching set, like always.*

"I promise this to you, Queen Rhiannon: I will come for my birthright. But only after I drag my way down to the Under-Realm and rip the crown from your head. I will kill you for what you have done, I will erase you from history. No one will dare speak your name again, after I finish with you."

I see a flicker of fear reflected in her eyes, her shock at my words clear across her face. She quickly regains control of herself, her face smoothing out like a stone. Her moon-bright eyes go impossibly paler, and she begins to murmur... something. I stalk towards her, intent on achieving at least one blow against her. Too late, I see the hints of magic gathered around her in the air, and before I can react, Rhiannon vanishes from the clearing.

"Ta-ta for now darling," her voice is a quiet chuckle left behind on the wind, and I am left with the feeling I have yet to win anything at all.

The shadows and green mist are torn away and abruptly replaced with a rolling storm, the scent of pine and dead leaves washing over us. The storm grumbles quietly overhead and the rain falls in a gentle pattern. The unnatural quality of the storm completely gone, as if the weather itself feared Rhiannon.

The insects and animals return, the sounds of the forest creeping in slowly, as I come to terms with what just happened. Every fae in the area is dead silent, staring at me, their faces wan. I do not know where to begin, what to say. I have gone completely numb, my failure and shame apparent on my face. Even my own shadows are still, as if they can sense the abrupt shift in mood. Koda and Irstin hold each other and their children, weeping unabashedly. The twins hold each other's hands silently watching. Grigori stays kneeling at his spot, head hanging low. Even Addie stands there limply, her bright warmth dimmed. And then there is Brynn- wonderful, sunshine filled Brynn.

Brynn is the one who breaks the shocked silence, as only she can.

"So…. Attempted murder and dramatic vows aside… I'm starving. Let's go eat some stars damned stew."

CHAPTER FOUR

A few of the men stay behind to burn Sivan's body and offer their private goodbyes. The walk back to the cabin is filled with an awkward, terse silence. Brynn tries interjecting comments here and there, ranging from how quickly the sun set, to how pretty the night blossoms look in full bloom, but too many unanswered questions linger in the air. Rhiannon disappeared far too easily, and now I have to take the fight to the Under-Realm, where I have never before been. Much easier said than done.

Most of our friends and family leave right away, making excuses as to why they cannot stay the night. Addie hugs each and every fae that came, while I stand in the kitchen staring at nothing, wishing the noise and the needs would disappear. Finally, only the core family remains, and we nestle ourselves into the kitchen and living room. I find Addie stealing glances at me as I fill bowl after bowl with stew for the family, but she keeps her mouth shut, she keeps her questions to herself.

At last, everyone else digs into their food, while I make a bowl for myself, buttering a bit of bread to go with it. Only the sounds of the crackling fire and spoons hitting bowls fill the room. The first bite of stew is heavenly, the gamy flavor filling my mouth and pairing perfectly with the spices Koda used to flavor it. Keeping my mouth busy with food also seems a perfect way to avoid any questions until I am ready to speak.

But, really, what can I say? We had one mission, to send off Sivan's soul gloriously, so he could rest with his ancestors. Now? What am I supposed to do? I was full of fire and spite when Rhiannon spewed her vitriol at me. She killed Sivan. She directly caused his death with the, what did she call it? The Immortal Plagues? My head spins with all the new information and the urge to take a very long, very hot bath overcomes me.

"Rhea, I know whatever happened back there was a lot... but when you are ready, I'd like to discuss your plans." Addie's head pops up from her own bowl, her words careful and low.

Of course, everyone else thinks I have a plan. When I threatened Rhiannon, I felt like I knew exactly what I was doing. The truth is, Sivan made all of our plans. I have always lived day to day, hoping I would find something to hold onto. For a long while, that was Sivan. Maybe I have let myself grow too dependent on others. Maybe this is a test, albeit one with dire consequences if I fail. One thing is certain: I have to do something. I cannot let Sivan's soul fade into the soul stream. And since the Queen Bitch of Death herself held his soul, maybe it would not fade the way we think.

Addie is waiting for me to say something, anything, and I say the first thing that comes to mind.

"Of course, I will. But first, I'm going to take a bath."

I ignore the shocked looks on everyone's faces, and before I trudge to my bedroom, I tell them, "Sleep wherever you like. There's blankets in the chest up front for the children, and the spare bed is made for whoever wants it."

I leave them with that, any words they speak reaching deaf ears.

* * *

My favorite thing in this world is a hot bath. When Sivan built the cabin, he asked me if there was anything specific I wanted, and my answer was a nice bathing room. The rest of our home could be as simple as he liked, but I wanted a private bathroom. While we do not have plumbing in the Hollow Forest, magic solves that problem quite easily. Within minutes, I have a piping hot bath in my large circular tub. My eyes scan the various jars and vials of scents and oils I have, debating which one to choose. Simple decisions are all I can manage currently.

My hand picks out a few items absentmindedly, and I look down, realizing I have chosen a jar of Sivan's: sandalwood and amber. Fresh and masculine. I add the liquid to the tub along with some salt to ease the ache in my bones. Another reason the dark fae utilize their powers carefully: using large amounts of death magic results in exhaustion. The more you use, the longer the effects.

The steam and relaxing scents become impossible to resist, and I slip all the way down into the tub, letting the scalding water wash over me, all the way up to my nose. Under the water, the world looks murky, sound slows and quiets. I can think more clearly, with everything else blocked out. My breath slows and calms. My body floats in the hot liquid. Here, away from sight and sound, my brain quiets enough that I can plan.

The first thing I need to do is speak with Inya. Of the seven goddesses, she is the most easily accessible to me. Tomorrow, I'll take Astraea and ride to Nisaba. I need to ask Addie for permission to enter the Goddesses Sanctum, but I am sure it will be of no issue.

There I can pray to Inya and ask for an audience. If she grants it, then I can ask for her help, or at least for some information. Of all the goddesses, Inya is known for being the fairest, though she likes playing games. Not all of her help is helpful. It might be that she wants me to earn her help or that I will need to amuse her in some way. I've never asked the goddesses for help before. I loathe to do it. But there is no risk too great when it comes to Sivan. I would climb Mount Horn itself, the highest point in Halcyon, or cross the great sea to Echosia with naught but a small dingy if it meant Sivan's soul would finally have rest.

Depending on what Inya tells me, I have a few paths forward after that. But it all centers on Inya.

Long wet strands of my hair float in the water, tangling around my body. While I think, I brush through it absentmindedly. If I cut it all off, then Rhiannon and I might look a little less alike. Her face is a little rounder than mine if you look past the dizzying beauty, and her skin lacks a single freckle or mole, transformed when she descended and took her place on the black throne. Becoming a goddess fills you with magic, removes any blemishes or imperfections, amplifying everything you are.

I'm not sure how long I've been bathing for, but it's long enough that the water cools, the bubbles dissipate, and worried knocks start coming from the door. Sigh.

The knocks continue, quick little raps that let me know it's Brynn knocking. Water sloshing, I get out of the tub, pull on my soft robe, and throw the door open in Brynn's face. Her hand halts mid-knock.

"What are you doing tomorrow?" I ask her, my hair streaming rivulets of water onto the floor.

"You're soaking wet," she says with a laugh, "And you're worried about tomorrow?"

"Always. But this is important, can you travel with me to Nisaba tomorrow?" Brynn and Sivan were the only two of the siblings that did not live in Nisaba. Now, I guess it's just Brynn, though I know she keeps simple lodgings in town for when she visits her family. She's the only one I would trust to come on this journey with me, but she runs a small flower shop, and I don't know if she can abandon it for a few days.

"Absolutely." She says it with no hesitation. Reassured. Confident. In control. One of the things I admire the most about Brynn is how positive she is, no matter the odds.

"I'm not sure what all I'm about to do, but you heard what I said to the bitch queen. If you start this with me, I don't think there's any going back."

"Rhea, you're my sister. I know you didn't grow up with siblings, so you might not completely understand this, but that means I'm not going to abandon you. No matter what. I don't care if Sivan is dead." I flinch at her words, but she continues on, unbothered.

"If you're going to hell, then I'll follow you there." Her eyes blaze with determination and something else. Love? Gratitude? Friendship? Some combination of all three?

"I think the Under-Realm might be a bit worse than hell." My attempt at a joke. Inject the situation with some humor, because the truth is I am unsure what killing Rhiannon really means. Her power will automatically transfer to me upon her death. I will become immortal, essentially. All my life, I yearned for a simpler life, without the expectations of titles or godhood weighing on me. Training with Rhiannon was out of the question when I was a child, and as a result, I am ignorant of what being a goddess truly entails.

Why would a new goddess even be born? Once a god, always a god...
right?

Brynn's face grows serious, her lips pursing together and eyes
darkening.

"I mean it, Ri. Sivan and I talked a lot about what it would mean
for you to become a goddess. Some destinies are unavoidable. This
day would always come about, in one way or another. You need to
decide: will you spend your life as a grieving widow? Shuttered in
darkness until your own shadows come to claim your soul? Or will
you finally accept your birthright? A birthright that many other fae
would squander or use for vicious means. I'm not saying this is
ideal, I know you truly do not want this power. But you have the
opportunity to use your power for good. As a goddess, you could
bring Sivan's soul back, you could set him free. Everything would be
alright again."

The news that Brynn and Sivan talked about my powers, my
birthright, before his death shocks me more than it should. Before
Sivan died, my life was made up of little boxes, segments divided up
and measured. The parts found wanting, left behind and forgotten.
That is no longer an option.

"What are you saying?" I ask.

"I'm saying, I will pledge myself to your future court. I'm saying
that I will help you gain the crown, however I can. I'm saying I
believe in you. So, yes, I will go with you tomorrow. I will go with
you wherever you trail after that. All I ask is that you send Sivan's
soul to rest."

I don't know if I can do it, I don't know if I can pull it off.
Rhiannon may very well kill me. The surety blazing in Brynn's green
flecked eyes sways me a bit, but the confidence in her voice is what

leads me to say, "Okay." Words seem inadequate in the face of her overwhelming belief that I will succeed. Looking in those endless eyes, so much like my late husbands, I almost believe in myself.

Brynn smiles a self-satisfied smile before her eyes trail down to the floor where the water dripping from my hair has created a small puddle. She cocks one eyebrow at me and back down at the water, as if to say *great, but you need to take care of that.*

I sigh; my energy depleted.

"Well, if you're to be in my court, can you help me with something?" Brynn looks eager at my question, her bright eyes shining.

"Of course! Sisters, remember? What do you need?"

"Will you help me dry my hair?"

CHAPTER FIVE

WE get up early the next day, eager to fill the rest of the family in on our plan. We also need to pack supplies, since we will be riding horseback, while everyone else returns in their horse drawn wagons.

I especially want to leave early, so I do not have to watch the family go through Sivan's things and divide them up amongst themselves. I told them they could; they are just objects after all, and I already have a small pile of shirts and trinkets set aside for myself.

I pull on thick leather pants, outdoor boots, and one of Sivan's tunics which I tuck around me using a belt. The belt has a few spots for tools and such, and I tuck my dagger into one of the notches. My hair hangs in a long braid down my back, some of my curls already escaping their confines due to the unusually hot and humid day. No jacket will be needed today, but I go ahead and put one in my pack for later.

Brynn is already in the kitchen by the time I make my way there. She sits on a stool, chatting casually with Koda, sipping hot liquid from a mug. Koda has a plate full of food in front of her when she sees me enter the room and a disappointed look crosses her face.

She starts to stand again when I wave her off with my hand and a short laugh.

"Don't get up on my account, I can feed myself. You rest up and eat, especially after all that cooking you did yesterday." Koda works too hard at taking care of everybody else, but with her baby due any day now, I would blame myself if something happened to her. I busy myself by piling eggs and bacon on my plate then realize Koda has also prepared a huge helping of hash browns. My mouth waters and before I know it, I shovel a huge amount onto my plate as well.

I sit there with Koda and Brynn, consuming forkful after forkful of food. When I am finished, the plate empty and gleaming, the two simply stare at me.

"What? Did I get some on my face?" I wipe frantically at my cheeks with a cloth napkin, but the two of them shake their heads in answer.

"It's just nice to see you eating so... heartily." Koda says tactfully. Brynn nods her head around a mouthful of her own hashbrowns. I have lost my appetite a bit since Sivan died. The food sours in my stomach at the thought. It's been only a few months since his death, and yet already I am moving on. Is this how it starts? I can eat again and a few months more will go by and then what? Will I even remember what he looks like? Already, the sound of his voice fades from memory, the planes of his face blurring a little each day.

I choose to ignore her comment and move on with the day.

"Brynn, when will you be ready? I want to leave as soon as possible."

"I'm already packed and ready- just let me finish my breakfast first. I can have Tilly ready in about five minutes." She shrugs unapologetically and resumes eating at her slow pace. While she eats, I plan our route in my head. The ride will take us about two or three hours, depending on our horses' moods. Astraea can do the journey in two hours no problems, but Brynn's horse, Tilly, is cantankerous on a good day. The day is hot and humid, sweat already beading on my neck. The shadows are nowhere to be seen on a day this hot. I can coax them out with magic if I want to, but they deserve the rest after yesterday.

"I'm going to get the horses ready. Meet me outside when you're done." I stand up and stretch my legs as much as I can in the small room. Koda stands as well.

"Do not leave without telling me goodbye!" She says, and walks around me, picking a package up off of the kitchen counter and shoving it into my hands. "I made you rations for the journey. Be safe. We will see you in a few hours." Succinct as always. On impulse, I hug Koda, being careful with her belly. She squeezes me even tighter in return.

"Sorry! I'll see you in a while. You all be safe as well." Koda became protective after Sivan died. Checking in on me constantly. Mothering me, I guess you could call it.

She looks at me up and down. "You won't be coming back here, will you?

My brows furrow together as I ask her, "What makes you say that?"

"Just a feeling," Koda says. She's not quite at Sienna and Orla's level, but Koda's "feelings" often turn out to be premonitions. I'll keep what she says in mind.

Brynn finishes eating, wiping her mouth hastily with a cloth, before putting her dirty plate on the counter with a sheepish grin directed at Koda. Koda raises her eyebrows for a moment, then opens her arms to her sister. The two embrace, Koda presses a kiss to Brynn's forehead, before they release each other.

Koda bops Brynn's nose with a light finger before telling her, "Be safe, sister. Take care of that one," and then jerks her head in my direction.

"Aye, aye Captain Koda!" Brynn vows brightly. Koda tries to resist, but soon a grin breaks out across her face, every bit as bright and wonderful as Addie's smile.

Brynn and I leave, dodging Koda's efforts to provide us with more rations and promising we would send word soon if we gained more insight on our situation. Once in the stables, we ready Astraea and Tilly as quickly as we can and then mount them.

Brynn has her reigns in one hand as she smirks at me.

"Race?" she asks, her eyes dancing with mirth.

"You're on," I respond and immediately spur Astraea into action. We gallop between the trees on the path that will lead us out of the woods and towards the mountains. I hunch as close to Astraea as I can, rubbing her neck against the whipping wind. "We've got this old girl, come on!"

She snorts in response but goes just the smallest bit faster. Brynn and I have raced along this path many times in happier days. We have even wins and losses. Sometimes I feel like the horses let each other win, but I figure there's no point in asking them. Astraea flies over a fallen log, before bursting out of the tree line that serves as our end goal. We slow to a trot and a huge grin breaks out across my face as I realize we've won.

Brynn follows close behind, Tilly snorting her frustration as they slow.

"Good race," Brynn says in a sour tone. Her competitive streak knows no bounds.

The day cools a bit as we trot at a comfortable pace towards Nisaba, the mountains no longer looming in the distance but swiftly growing closer. Sweat beads down my back and neck from the humidity. We reach the halfway point and wordlessly decide to stop for a break. Astraea and Tilly snort happily and we let them loose in a small field next to a pond while we rest. There's no one around for miles, the only company the small berry bushes dotting the picturesque landscape.

"Oh, my stars, it's so hot," Brynn moans out loud, the first words either of us have spoken since the end of the race.

"Here's some water," I tell her while holding out my canteen, "We can rest for an hour and then get going." I settle myself onto the soft grass on the ground and eat some jerky from back home. Brynn takes a piece from me, and we sit there together, munching silently and watching the horses drink their fill. The field stretches on, as vividly green as a spring day. The sun glares down on us, our cheeks turning pink with it. Insects chitter in the background, a continuous drone. I'm about ready to suggest we take a dip in the pond when Brynn interjects.

"Do you know any self-defense?" Brynn asks.

"Just with daggers, for the most part. Do you?" I think we've talked about this before, so I'm unsure why she brings it up now. I realize I've never asked her the same in return, being caught up in Sivan and our relationship, and then when the plague came, none of us spoke much at all about anything besides how to help him.

"Yes. I've trained a lot actually. When I was younger, momma trained us with swords. Said even if we're healers at heart, there may come a time when we need to defend ourselves. Sivan never told you that?"

"We knew each other for so little time. Our wedding anniversary isn't for another few months. It seems like there's a lot of things I don't know. I thought we had all the time in the world, but obviously, we didn't."

"Can I be honest with you?" Brynn asks, her eyes searching mine, pinning me on the spot.

"Always." If we're really like sisters, then sisters owe each other honesty, right?

"Look, I love you, but you need to start taking this whole 'bitch queen' thing seriously. You haven't trained in ages, you let your grief knock you flat, and you refuse to accept help from anyone. That's not strength—that's stubbornness."

She crosses her arms, her eyes sharp but not unkind.

"You need fae backing you. You need to actually learn about the Under-Realm and how it works, because look—you can't rule what you don't understand. Have you even been there once?"

I shake my head.

"Exactly." She exhales, but there's no judgment—just concern. "I swear, I'm only saying this because I care. But you've spent so much time running from the training your parents gave you. I get it. I really do. But you can't just pick and choose which parts of your destiny you like. That's not how this works."

She squeezes my arm, her voice softening. "I know you're hurting more than you let on. But if you really want that crown, you need to be strong enough to hold it." Her words echo in my mind. I know Brynn is right; I really do. I've enjoyed my powers here and there, the ones only granted to me by the goddesses seed within me. But, I have yet to dedicate myself to overthrowing her.

The problem being that rumors aplenty have been told about Rhiannon and the malicious ways she treats her court and her courtesans. She rules over them with such a tight fist, none of them are even allowed to travel to other realms such as ours. How do we verify such claims of mistreatment if the only information we get is whispers from the shadows? I have felt the shadows tremble after witnessing Rhiannon slaughter one of her serving boys, for the crime of spilling a single drop of wine. The shadows recoil at the mere mention of her name. That, and the risk of her sifting to our realm when her magic notifies her someone has spoken about her. Brynn is right. I've never even been to the Under-Realm, but if I had, would it really make that much of a difference?

"Let's focus on getting to Nisaba for now. Inya will respond to us, I'm certain, and then we can plan. I hear you; I trust you, but we can't do anything before Inya confirms a few things for me."

Those wide eyes search mine, her dark hair shifting over her face, looking for confirmation that I have understood her. She nods, and I hope I've done the right thing. If I am going to do this, I'll need the trust of the people around me. Brynn will be my second in command, I have already decided. I want to tell her when the time is right. If there's one thing I've learned since Sivan's death is that the timing may never be perfect.

"Brynn." I say, in a tone I hope comes across as royal and commanding, yet warm and personable.

She straightens from where she's slumped over in the heat, responding to my tone.

"Yes, Rhea?"

"I want you to be my second in command. Will you be my eyes and ears within the shadows? Will you guard my kingdom and all of its inhabitants as if it were your own?"

Tears rim Brynn's eyes, turning them even greener, but do not spill over. She bites her lip, trying to hold back the grin fighting to splay across her face.

"Yes! Absolutely... thank you! Do I need to call you 'your majesty' or something like that? You've always just been Rhea to me, but if you want me to show more respect, I understand."

A low laugh escapes me.

"No, please don't. At least, not for now. We can discuss the specifics later. I wanted to ask you now, before the adventure begins. Who knows what Inya will tell me? Where will her words lead us? I wanted you to know now, though, how much I value you."

Brynn was right when she said I never ask for help. I never have. As a child, it seemed like my needs were inconvenient for everyone around me. Too loud. Too bright. Too happy. Too girly. Too much. When I learned to tone it down, then it was the opposite. Too serious. Too quiet. Too weird. *Too different* were the unspoken words trailing after me everywhere I went.

This fight with Rhiannon could change all that. Maybe not erase history but chart a new course for those interested.

"Thank you," she says, her smile spreading brilliantly across her face, her freckles scrunching up with her nose. When her smile fades, she adds, "While you speak with Inya, I want to do some research in the library. See if there's anything about Rhiannon or in our history that could help."

"I know the basic histories, but a lot was lost during the Forgotten Years. It never hurts to check again, I suppose." The Forgotten Years were a period of ten years where all written works across Halcyon were burned. Librarians and story keepers all over the land were slaughtered, for what knowledge no one knows, but that knowledge died with them. The time frame is fuzzy, as this happened hundreds of years ago, but we lost an incredible amount of art and history.

"I know you do. But Nisaba just got a new librarian from across the continent. She lived on the island between Halcyon and Echosia. I think she said it's called Ancpei."

"What's her name?"

"Who?"

"The librarian, obviously."

"Oh..." Brynn goes quiet for a moment, her eyes moving back and forth, face twitching, and eventually her cheeks pinken. She looks at me, her green eyes filled with worry and begins chewing on her lip.

"You can't remember, can you?" I laugh and shake my head, my braid rustling with the movement. Leave it to Brynn to remember the name of a random city, but not the librarians.

"You can ask her yourself when we arrive." She says, spitting the words out, but there's no fury behind them. "I'm sure she would lo-ove to introduce herself to your royal highness."

"I'm quite sure she would," I say in a pretend haughty voice, before asking "Seriously, though, what is this librarian like?"

"Her name is Faye. She's a short little thing, with red hair and eyes like the sea. You'll have to meet her."

"Faye the fae? Really?"

Brynn laughs and shakes her head. "No, actually, she's a fairy." A fairy in Nisaba? The fairy folk usually keep to themselves, living in hidden forests away from the rest of the fae and elves inhabiting Halcyon. Fairies have the ability to transform into tinier versions of themselves and usually live that way, thousands of them able to colonize a forest simply by them being so small, the forest hardly even notices the fairies are there.

Even in full form, they are usually recognizable by their short stature and the whimsical glow on their skin. I've personally never met one, but Sivan once told me he met a group of young fairies when he was a soldier in the King's army. The group had come to the city interested in going from pub to pub and met the soldiers at one of them. Sivan said they were the most beautiful creatures he had ever seen, and that their mere presence was intoxicating.

"Interesting. Did she say why she moved to Nisaba?" The fairy folk are also known for causing chaos, spreading lies about the fae to the humans and so on. It's strange that one would settle in a small town such as Nisaba. The waterfalls surrounding the village are majestic and do bring in travelers, as does the beautiful monument built to honor Inya outside of her sanctum, but rarely do they permanently settle. Fairies tend not to stick around longer than they can down a few tankards of mead and copulate with some locals.

"I asked, but she gave a generic answer about Nisaba being rich with history. Really, you'll just have to wait and meet her." Very strange to me that Brynn is being so tight-lipped about this fairy librarian. She's usually the first to take up a bit of gossip and spread it around, but her smile is so wide and child-like, no one ever takes it to heart. She's got a mischievous energy about her at all times. Yet, she has little to say about Faye.

"Well," I begin, "I've rested enough. I'll gather the girls while you finish up." Brynn has barely touched her food. Too busy chatting about red-headed librarians. Bones pop and crackle as I stand from sitting for so long. Brynn is right about a lot of things. After we reach Nisaba, and speak with Faye and Inya, I need to start exercising and going through my training regimes again. Death magic is expansive, and I've barely dipped a toe into the lagoon of possibilities. Aside from that, there are many types of defenses I can learn. I can use a dagger well enough, but that requires getting up close and personal. How do I prevent someone from reaching me? Of course, most fae are unaware that I am a fae princess. I left home nearly a year ago now; my parents sheltered me so much before that, there are very few who know what I look like. That may be to my advantage.

Questions pound around and around in my mind until my head grows weary with it. Reaching for Astraea and Tilly's reins, I block the questions from my mind. One step at a time. One day at a time. Just like after Sivan died. I lead the girls over to Brynn, who thanks me with a wild grin on her face, looking well-rested and springy. I envy her easy nature and brightness. Not only that, but her happiness pours out of her, much like Sivan's did him. It draws me to her but also feels like being stabbed each time I see her eyes and smile. The ghost of Sivan will follow me for a long while.

The light in Brynn's eyes dims a bit at the look on my face.

"Is everything alright?" she asks, voice thick with concern.

I nod as convincingly as I can manage. "Everything's great. Let's get going. We can't waste another moment if we want to arrive with any daylight left over."

Brynn looks hesitant, as if she doesn't fully believe me. She doesn't say a word though as she gracefully ascends Tilly and sits in the saddle, reins tightly in hand. We spur our horses into movement, deciding a steady trot will see us through the rest of the journey, the silence between us laden with apprehension. Neither of us speaks another word. The sun begins falling, the three moons replacing her high in the sky, and finally we reach Nisaba as the stars begin dancing with one another.

The small city rises up out of the mountain, moving ladders and bridges rising high into the sky. At the back of Nisaba, monstrous waterfalls plummet from Mt. Horn, into the valley below, before flowing out to the lake on the other side of the city. Tales of monsters making their homes in those deep waters, or in the hidden caverns dotting the cliffsides, come to mind as I gaze upon the force of nature. Those falls are visible from every point in the city, a reminder of the awesome power of the goddesses. At the very top, reachable by ancient stone steps only, sits the Goddesses Temple and Sanctum. Nisaba, the City in the Sky, beckons us home, the scent of pine and fresh water welcoming us.

Each time I've visited, Nisaba has grown more and more as word reaches other villages of Nisaba's prosperity. A small rush of happiness goes through me on arriving here, and I realize my power to see auras is slowly coming back as well. Arriving at night is fortuitous as well- Inya is said to love the night and all its creatures. Hopefully, that means even a death queen such as me will be welcome.

Brynn and I absorb all the scents and sounds of the city as we lead our horses to the stable. I press a few coins into the stable boy's hands as we leave. He's a small elf boy, with delicately pointed ears and swirling tattoos of vines all over his face. His aura glows with the rich and changing hues of a child.

Fairy librarians, Elven stable hands. There's been an infusion of diversity in Nisaba since I last arrived. It's beginning to feel like being back in the Dark City, the capital of Halcyon, Darrid. A part of me loves it. Another part... Another part shudders in the wake of the ever-changing world, moving on without my husband, dragging me along with it.

I give a deep sigh as we leave the stables then tip my head back to watch the moons and bask in their cleansing light. Brynn gives me a long look before saying, "out with it." We're silent for a moment as we navigate the cobblestone and dirt pathways of Nisaba. Magic weaves itself through the very air of the small city as we pass vendors in tightly packed corridors selling trinkets and local foods.

"He would have loved to see this," I respond waving a hand towards the chaos and revelry of the night market, "He would beg me to describe the auras of those around us, what their colors revealed about them." Grief, white and hot and blinding, encages my heart. Through it, Brynn reaches out and grips my hand. Her own is smooth and warm and grounds me.

Brynn smiles gently and gives my hand a squeeze. "Tell me then. What are the auras around us like?"

Her calm voice is like a night kissed breeze—refreshing. A hand reaching out, offering support. I have to take it.

As we wind our way through the city, heading towards the courtyard that leads to both the healers sanctum and library, I describe the auras of the fae around us: the deep blue of a Autumn fae woman selling healing tisanes and tinctures, indicating a profound peacefulness and satisfaction in life; the rosy pink and yellow swirls of a young couple—an elf and a fairy—just beginning to fall in love. Brynn listens carefully to each description before creating a backstory for strangers we'll never meet. Before long, she has me laughing freely, and the ache in my chest ceases once more.

The courtyard is nearly in sight when I stop short, forcing Brynn to stop as well.

"What?" she barks out as the force of our still-held hands causes her to skip a few steps lest she fall on her ass. I'd laugh if every instinct in my body wasn't telling me to run, to protect Brynn, to hide. The shadows in the area freeze as well, not even a titter coming from their sinewy bodies. Then—out of the corner of my eye, I see a dark flash of green. I turn to see the source, but the flash is gone.

"There—in that alleyway," I say pointing to where I saw it, "I swear I saw a flash of an aura." Brynn stares at the empty alleyway, a frown forming on her golden face, her eyes scanning what little is visible from here.

She begins walking after a moment, pulling me along with her. Her voice remains casual, if a bit tight.

"Whatever it is, it's gone now. Now, come along. We're losing moonlight here."

The long, long steps of the sanctum come into view, their stone disappearing into the mist from the waterfalls. Brynn and I walk to the base of the steps together, navigating our way through the throngs of fae milling about and then she releases my hand and hugs me tightly.

"Be safe," she says as she squeezes my shoulders, "I wish I could go with you."

"Don't worry over me," I tell her, "I'll tell you all about it. And I expect to hear more about this Faye."

With that, she spins away from me with the grace of a dancer, and heads towards the library of Nisaba, a light bounce in her step.

"Now, it's just us old friends," I murmur to my shadows as I mount the first few steps to the sanctum and begin the several hours long ascension to face my destiny.

CHAPTER SIX

THE air chills as I climb the steps, higher and higher into the sky. Water sprays me continuously from the falls, but after the first thousand steps, I am grateful for it. Despite the chill in the air, sweat beads down my back. The muscles in my legs quiver around step two thousand. Each draw of air burns my lungs. The three moons, named after the three original goddesses, Ronin, Inya, and Megara, stare down at me reproachfully as I pace myself. The hike gives me time to think, and I find myself thinking about the goddesses as I eye the moons right back.

The death goddess has always been the only one to reincarnate. Before Rhiannon, there were two other women who made the descent to the Under Realm. I never cared enough to ask why, but now I guess I should have. All of it is my responsibility- I tried to ignore that for so long, a princess running away, dreaming of becoming the pauper. Fate cares little for my ideas of what life should look like. Deep down, I've always known that eventually, I would have to face Rhiannon, one way or another. If I had gone to her of my own free will years ago, none of this would have happened. Sivan might still be alive, blissfully ignorant that I ever existed. The very thought saddens me irrevocably. Magic tingles along my skin, the most active it's been since drinking the ritual potion yesterday. Apparently, Addie did not know the brew would affect my death magic for so long. Maybe the potions effects were too similar to my own skills.

I take a sip from my waterskin as I walk, only a few thousand steps from the top now. The tip of the sanctum peaks out from the top of the steps, the blue stone shining brightly in the moonlight. Long, tall gleaming columns hold up the domed roof of the sanctum, each overflowing with luscious vines and vibrantly colored flowers. The smell floats over, and before I know it, I'm letting out a sigh of appreciation. The floating gardens of the sanctum are widely renowned for their beauty, but I had forgotten all about them, so focused on reaching Inya and requesting her help. As I reach the top of the steps, the statue of Inya comes into view, etched in stone. Every part of the statue looks as if it should be in motion. I wonder how it compares to the real goddess.

A priestess glides forward, coming from seemingly nowhere, wearing flowing blue robes and a diadem of the three moons over her brow. Her braids flutter in the slight breeze, the moonlight illuminating her, filling her from the inside out. She glows with that light, her movements languid and feminine as she moves before me. Her dark arms and skin are painted golden with symbols I don't recognize and her smile breaks across her face like dawn.

"Hello, welcome!" she chirps in a bright voice, and I falter. Her voice doesn't match her exterior; I thought priestesses were quiet and pious.

She continues on, ignoring my reactions, "Are you Rhea? High Healer Adeline sent word ahead of you. She was right when she said you'd be hard to miss! Are you tired from the journey? Do you need water or rest?" This high up, I strain to hear her over the roaring waterfalls, but she seems used to it, trudging on ahead and leading me through a maze of gardens.

"No, I'm quite alright. I'm here seeking an audience with Inya, and I'd like to get right to it. Oh, and you are?" My voice is tired, weary, but I want to get this over with.

"How silly of me, I forgot to introduce myself again! I'm Katya, Adeline's protégé of sorts. She's training me to replace her one day, since none of her own children are interested." She says the words with a shrug, as if embarrassed, but I think nothing of it.

"Pleasure, Katya. I apologize for being curt, but time is of the essence. Perhaps you can show me to the inner sanctum?"

"It's fine. I'm used to it, being around Adeline. Yes, I'll take you there now. The inner sanctum is even more beautiful than this," Katya says gesturing around, her dark eyes unfazed by the unreal beauty surrounding us. As we watch, moonbells bloom beneath the hazy moonlight, the spray of the waterfalls wafting their scent over to us. I'd love to take a moment and breathe it all in, but maybe Brynn and I can come back up tomorrow, make a day of it. Besides the sanctum, there are the gardens to explore, caverns and overlooks to view the waterfalls from. Sivan and I never came, always spouting one reason or another why we were too busy. And now we will never get the chance.

Katya and I make our way through the sanctum doors, the large blue stone opening without our intervention. Inside, the ceiling rises high above, with a round skylight in the center. The light from that point falls in a perfect halo, until it settles above a large statue of Inya, holding jugs on her shoulders, her robes half open. Plants cover every surface visible here in the main room, far more than I know the names of. The floor looks hewn from the mountain itself, and small rivers of water slide along the floor in a spiral pattern, until they disappear, branching off into another room.

As walk, we pass other priestesses, each dressed in a similar fashion as Katya. Katya points each one out to me, introducing us as we pass them, but their names and faces ease from my mind instantly, until finally we land in front of a set of double wooden doors. Katya reminds me a lot of Brynn. Maybe everyone else in this world is that way. Full of sunshine and hope for the future. Have I ever been so full of light? I don't believe so. I was born cradled in shadows, with the mark of a goddess.

"Well, here we are." Katya says with a bright smile, one hand resting on her arm. "Beyond these doors, lies the Goddesses inner sanctum. No one besides Adeline is allowed in, with the exception of you. The rest of us have yet to earn the privilege." She says the words without malice. "Go on in, do what you must, and I'll be waiting in the front for you." With that, Katya turns on her heels, her braids whipping around with the motion, and bounds away, leaving me alone.

When my palm makes contact with the wood of the door, power rushes through me, deep and true. Interesting, the doors were sealed with death magic. What would the Goddess of Healing and Water need with death magic? The door pushes open easily enough. As I pass the threshold, magic tingles along my skin. I find myself in a large, opulent room. White and blue tiles make up the floor, every other one adorned with a flower motif, as well as the walls. The glass ceiling reflects the night stars down onto a large, square pool of water. Steam lifts up from that pool, beckoning me to come for a swim.

Beyond the pool, a large mural covers the back wall, depicting three women in battle: on the left, a woman with olive skin, and a long brown braid wearing leather armor raises a bow to the sky, her flaming arrow flying through clouds; in the middle, a curvaceous woman with warm brown skin and flowing hair, lifts her hands in an arc to the sky, light pouring from them; finally, on the right... me. Or a woman that looks identical to me. It must be Rhiannon. Her black curls float angrily around her, shadows warping her body. She's caught in motion, shadows ready to pounce. The three goddesses surrounded by enemies. I do not recognize the mural, the location, or even the twisted looking enemies they're fighting.

In front of the pool, a long pole sits with a note atop it. I walk forward, eager to read it and figure out what to do to call the goddess. Scrawled in neat, precise handwriting, the note says, "Remove your impurities and enter the pool to receive the Goddesses Blessing." Addies handwriting. None of the other priestesses have been allowed in the sanctum yet, so she must have left this here for me. Removing your impurities is simple enough.

I strip the riding leathers off of my body, and peel my tunic off, carefully folding them and leaving them in a neat pile on the stone floor with my other belongings. My hair, I leave bound in its braid, though I'm sure it looks worse for wear after the ride here. The room is humid and warm, even without my clothing, so the nudity bothers me little. The sanctum is quiet and peaceful, aside from the sounds of water pouring into the pool from the little rivers I saw earlier. Using the big stone steps, I descend into the turquoise water. The water is hot, easing the ache from my bones and worries from my mind. Languidly, I move deeper and deeper until I am standing in the center of the pool, water up to my neck.

"Ahhh..." a small sigh escapes me, and I nearly struggle remembering why I am here. Coming here directly after the ride was potentially not my best idea, but how was I supposed to know Inya's super-secret inner sanctum would be the most luxurious bath of all time? I wonder if Brynn knew. Addie certainly should have prepared me. Unless this is a test. As if I cannot resist the lures of a hot bath.

I slip my head under the water and push myself to the bottom. There must be a hot spring here for the water to be so warm unless this is the might of Inya's magic. Sivan would have loved this. He loved going on adventures and trying new things. Thinking of him conjures him in my mind; remembering those deep green eyes sends shockwaves of pain through my heart. Mixed in with the pain is rage, black and sinuous. Rage at Rhiannon for taking him away from me, rage at myself for not being able to save him. It is all consuming underneath the water, with nothing to distract me. I allow my body to float back to the top, tired of the ceaseless pain and hunger within me.

As I am coming up, a low and sultry voice says from behind me, "You look as if you're enjoying yourself." It startles me enough that I inhale some of the water and begin choking on it.

As my breathing rights itself, the voice laughs and I turn, outraged, and am met with the glowing body of the Goddess, Inya. She sits on the side of the pool in an outrageously large clam shell, the curls in her hair covering her luscious curves. Her body appears to be made out of water, her very movement liquid and easy. Her skin is smooth and dark, despite the swirling, and other than the magic, she looks like any other fae in Nisaba. Any other blindingly beautiful fae in Nisaba. She watches me analyzing her, patient and bemused.

She cocks her head at me, her grin feline, and asks "Do you like what you see, darkling?" Her voice is full of sensual promise. Inya is also known as the goddess of hearth and home; many fae pray to her on matters of fertility.

"I meant no disrespect, Goddess. You are exceedingly beautiful, and I've only met one goddess before. Thank you for appearing before me." I bow my head as graciously as I can without choking on the water again, not wanting to piss off yet another goddess. She descends from the clamshell into the pool and rests in front of me, not much taller than me, though her presence is commanding.

"No disrespect taken, Daughter of Death. My body is made for mortal eyes to gaze upon and weep. Or enjoy. Whichever I see fit." She laughs brightly, "However, you did not come here to enjoy my body, now did you deary?" Her tone takes on a motherly light, goading and fresh.

"I have come to seek your assistance, goddess, and I beseech you to listen to my story."

The glow in her eyes shifts from bright spring wells to stormy seas. Her magic thickens the air around us and I can feel her magic reach out to mine, tasting it, weighing it.

"Yes," she muses as her eyes roam over my body, "I am witness to your pain. Your magic is quite strong as well. Evenly matched in horror and heartache. Your soul is dark in color, but ripe with promise."

"You can see my soul?" I ask, my tone light, "I thought that was dark fae magic? Or bound to the Under Realm?"

The goddess laughs again. It reminds me of an old saying about the goddesses laughing when the faery make plans.

"Oh, child, there is much the fae do not know about our powers.

The other two wished it to be so. We can all see the fabric of souls, but what we can do with those souls varies greatly." She does not elaborate on what those powers do. It feels intentional.

Inya glides closer to me, her hips swishing as she does so, the water moving easily around her silent steps. This close, I can see her eyes are like turbulent seas, her monstrous magic reaching unfathomable depths. She puts on a flirty, friendly exterior, but I must remember she is a Goddess as well. If Inya wishes, she could crush me with that magic in an instant, like a flame snuffed out by a rogue wave. Here, and then gone in an instant. She gazes back at me, her eyes piercing through to my soul.

"It sounds like you have gone through great sorrow for a fae so young. But, what can I offer you that you cannot accomplish yourself? You are the daughter of death; souls and resurrection are your expertise not mine. I cannot heal a fae after death. There are limits to even the trio's power. So, what may I ask, do you think I can help you can accomplish?"

"I need information," I say tight-lipped. Her grin turns wicked. My breath lodges hard in my throat at the arch in her brow and the glint in her eyes. "I will do anything in return for it."

"You should be careful promising anything to a goddess deary. How about you ask your questions, and then I tell you the cost of the answer. Does that sound like a deal?"

One must always be careful when entering into deals with fae, especially one with tremendous power such as hers. A lot of the old ways have been forgotten by the fae public at large, but the dark fae have not forgotten. A weakness can be exploited, even one you are not aware of. My wording needs to be precise. Inya is right that I should be more careful—I cannot let my grief turn me stupid.

"I agree that you will tell me the cost after I ask my questions, *and* that you will allow me the opportunity to refuse or accept the cost before you answer." Inya's grin grows even wider, looking supernatural and off-putting. The look a snake might give you before swallowing you whole.

"Someone's trained you well deary. Very well, I agree to your terms. Ask your questions."

"First: what are the immortal plagues and how do you cure them?" Inya's face goes ashen at my first question and her mouth opens slightly, a silent "oh" on her lips. She shakes her head slightly.

"Where did you hear about the immortal plagues?" She asks, her lips a thin line of disapproval.

"Rhiannon. She heavily implied she used them to kill my husband."

Inya shakes her head again, more agitated this time.

"That stars-damned bitch. We agreed to never speak of them. Yes, I know what it is. There is no cure. It is the worst death one could offer a creature. If that idiot used the immortal plagues to kill one man... then many more fae may be in danger."

"You still didn't tell me what it is. Or what the cost for answering that one might be." The pool of water around us vibrates violently, sloshing out onto the tiled floors surrounding it. The temperature creeps up slowly, bordering on painfully hot.

"There is no cost!" She spits out, "This is more serious than a youngling like you might understand. Do you know the history of Halcyon? How Rhiannon, Megara, and I became the three most powerful goddesses?"

"I know what very little is left in history books. The three of you were knighted the trio by Prince Halcyon, several thousand years ago as thanks for your help during battle."

"And?" Inya's blue eyes search mine, her impatience clear.

"And nothing. That's all we know. There was a lot of history lost during the forgotten years." A knowing glint shines in her eyes. She would have lived through those years.

"The truth is much more complicated than that," she sighs heavily, a strange ancient sound.

"To me, those years are not forgotten at all. During those years, the fae, elves, fairy folk, and all creatures of the land fought in an unending war. The enemy was so mighty, that the Under-Realm sent demons and monsters to our realm to assist in the battle, convinced the enemy would not stop at the faerie realm. The King of the Under-Realm, Prince Halcyon, fought on the battlefield for endless days and nights. Near the end of the battle, the Prince saw Rhiannon slaying the enemy and the mating bond clicked into place for him. They wed, he made her his queen, and we named the country in his honor." Inya takes a deep breath, her troubled eyes hazily focused on the water below us.

Inya is being extremely vague, especially about an enemy supposedly strong enough to destroy realms.

My tone is laced with frustration when I ask, "who was the enemy? Where did they come from?" *And what does any of this have to do with the immortal plagues?*

Inya chews on her bottom lip, as if debating what to say. She slowly lifts her eyes to mine and says, "I cannot tell you."

"Can't, or won't?" I ask. The tranquil room no longer feels

welcoming or relaxing. Pressure builds within my veins. I feel as if I stand on a precipice; one strong gust of wind, and I will tumble down, down, down.

"I am.... Prevented from speaking of such things. There are forces stronger than even us gods. You will learn one day. However, I can tell you about the Immortal Plagues. They were a weapon created by beings from another realm. There were four different plagues: Victorum, Bellum, Esuries, and Inferus. Each one kills in a different way." Her voice is harshly above a whisper, as if the words themselves might cause those plagues to come sweeping in at any moment.

The burble of water roars in my ear. Useless. Useless. Useless. How does any of this help me?

"Can you tell which plague killed a person by the way they died?" Inya eyes narrow at my question, but she answers me anyway.

"Yes. They would have dreams, with symbols in them. And their symptoms would be unique depending on which plague they were afflicted with."

"My husband... Sivan... before he died, he hallucinated due to his fever. He told me he saw a man riding a black horse, a scale in his hands. After that, the illness worsened. No matter how much sustenance he had, he would beg for more. Eventually, despite eating regularly, he became emaciated and gaunt. The light slowly drew from him. At the end, his sanity had left him. He looked more like a wild animal, rather than the strong fae he had been in life." I do not wish to relive those last moments with him, but if Inya can tell me what caused his death...

Inya's face pales and her eyelids flutter closed. Her eyes move rapidly behind them. The water in the room grows even more turbulent, great big waves crashing into the tiled sides of the pool. A monstrous breeze sweeps through the room yet touches nothing. Inya's body begins glowing, the light within her expanding until it forces my own eyes closed. She chants in a language I do not recognize, an ancient unyielding voice coming from within her. Just as suddenly as she starts, she stops. The room stills immediately. The pressure within me continues aching and throbbing.

"Esuries," she whispers, "It can be no other than Esuries. The hunger and the horsemen are shrouded in my memories." Inya growls, her nose scrunching up tightly in the center of her face, her teeth bared against the unforeseen foe. "Rhiannon is an imbecile if she thinks she can simply unleash one and have that be the end of it."

"Well," I take a deep breath, "That's actually the second part of why I need your help. I want to kill Rhiannon and take her crown. And I would like your assistance to do so."

"Oh?" The goddess asks as if this is an everyday occurrence. I stare at her, my eyes searching hers, not letting up for a moment. Her face remains impassive, regal. Like the ocean, deep and mysterious, Inya reveals nothing.

"Please..." I say, near to begging, "The Goddess of Death has stolen my husband's soul. All I want is to see his soul to his ancestral resting place. That's it. Please, help me."

Inya cocks her head again, an eagle sizing up its prey, and contemplates my words.

"You do not beg, ever," she says, her voice carrying through the room like ocean spray, "You are a queen in your own right, you answer to no one." Inya rotates her head in circles, then her arms and legs as well. "I will grant you a boon, as well as a parting gift that will be beneficial to you on your journey. In return, you will owe me a single favor of my choosing in the future when you have taken your crown..." She smirks, sizing me up, then adds "...sister."

Inya confuses me. She exudes sultry confidence, acts as if she could ruin my day at any moment if she so choose, yet her words seem helpful... kind? Warm, even. Her wording seems fair, for the most part, and having another goddess as an ally, even for a moment, seems worth it to me. I almost wish Brynn and I hadn't separated- she would know what to say.

"Very well, I accept your boon and your bargain," I say and stick my hand out, waiting.

Inya looks at my hand with distaste and says "That is how humans seal deals darkling. Come closer," before grabbing my hand and pulling me into an embrace. Inya's body fills with light, spilling out onto me, and water swirls around our bodies, encasing us in a perfect bubble. Inya's entire body turns into water, and she leans in and kisses me. Her watery tongue fills my mouth, and I go slack with shock, but the kiss lacks sensuality. Despite the raging current around us, the kiss burns, hotter and brighter until I feel it settle on the back of my neck. The water settles as well, easing us down back into the pool, as if nothing had occurred. My hands lift to the back of my neck, where Inya's magic has burned into it. If I looked, I'm sure I'd see her symbol etched delicately into my skin. In ancient times, fae marked their bargains upon one another, but I've never seen anyone do it in my lifetime. Contracts and faith seem a better solution than mutilating oneself for a favor.

"You are lucky. A vision has been granted. Listen carefully, as I can only see a vision once, and then it is gone away with your memory." She backs away from me, the water swirling around her, until she is centered under the skylight.

She lifts her hands towards the sky, water swirling up her arms, much the way my shadows do mine. Soon, she is lost in the typhoon, the water spinning around and around her voluptuous body. A voice, ancient and cold, comes from within the cyclone of water.

"Daughter of Death, the Wanderer Between Realms. Your time is near. You must find the queen who started it all."

Inya's body convulses, the water pulsating in and out of her throat, choking off her air. A different voice emerges from her, this one a night laced whisper.

"*Find us. Destroy them. See the truth free.*"

Inya's body seems as if a ship's bow about to break in half. She contorts unnaturally; my own body shivers at that ancient dark thing controlling her. Gone is her fluid movement and natural grace.

Inya rises higher and higher towards that moonlit skylight, her body bent in half. All at once, the air stills, she ceases, and plummets back to the water. I cannot see her as the water explodes around her from the impact. The shock of it all takes a moment to register, and then I am rushing forward, water sloshing violently around me, the air colder than death.

"Inya! Inya, please!" I scream, my shadows threatening to release around me, but I fight for control over them. Shadow and water alike blind me as I reach into the water and pull Inya out in rough halting movements.

She sputters, coughing up water and light. "I'm fine, darkling," she calls weakly from where she rests in the water. "I've had a premonition," she announces once she has control of her breathing.

I stare at her, incredulous that one of the three would be defeated by her own element. Inya notices my gaze and scoffs in between vomiting up water.

"It's effortless for you to assume me infallible, but my dear, even the three goddesses cannot overcome the elements."

Inya's gaze softens when she looks at me, soaking wet from the turbulence and exhausted from the days travel. "Go to the shadow market. You will find that which you seek and that which you do not. Fret not, trust the stars, and you will see your way to the crown." She rises slowly as if adjusting to her body again. I motion to help her, but she waves me off. When she stands, she snaps her finger and both of us are completely dry.

"Thank you, Goddess," I say demurely. My emotions have gone numb, and I am ready for a warm bed. Inya does not speak, but motions for me to follow her. We rise up out of the pool, still dry by Inya's magic, where I dress in silence. Inya's clothes magically appear on her, but of course she does not extend that courtesy to me. Her gossamer gown seems fit for a ball, with long trailing strands of blue at the bottom and a bodice with whorls of green and blue, like seafoam. Her blue strands are coiffed and curled on the top of her head, shining against her bronze skin. I feel unbalanced next to her in my worn leathers. Her eyes devour me like a kraken.

The prolonged silence nearly has me walking out the door without another word, but Inya finally speaks, her voice rasping a little.

She says, "I promised you a parting gift, did I not?" She holds her hands to the sky again, but this time a small pouch appears between them. She hands it to me without a word. The pouch is made of dark, soft velvet with silver waves sewn into it. The string holding it together comes undone easily to reveal a dark grainy substance, glittering faintly.

"Traveling salts," she says, "Take a pinch and think of where you want to go, then throw it down at your feet. Use sparingly."

The gift makes me suspicious immediately. That, coupled with that freaky premonition, means Inya is hiding something from me. What does she get out of helping me?

I examine the salts before asking, "Can I use these to get to the Under-Realm?"

She smiles at me and shakes her head. "No," she says, "But your friend will have the information you seek. Beware of the fairies." I tuck the salts into my traveling bag. Inya offers no more information; it feels like it's time to leave.

"Thank you, goddess." I bow my head deeply, not wanting to piss her off with impoliteness.

Again, she waves me off. Maybe she is different than Rhiannon. It will be a long while before I can trust her, either way.

"I find myself enervated. See yourself out deary." A wave builds from the pool, and plucks Inya from the floor, cocooning her on a gentle bed of water. The tile on the left wall opens up, seamlessly hidden, and the wave rushes her out of the room, tile closing behind them.

The sudden silence engulfs me, shadows pulse beneath my skin. The pressure will keep building until I use my magic again, but a part of me cannot bear to touch it.

"Not yet," I croon, the shadows writhing, "I'm tired now." They calm a bit at my words, but I'll need to access my magic tomorrow before something happens.

I head out the way I came, ignoring the priestesses bustling about in the moonlight. Down, down, down the steps, through the square until I find myself in front of Brynn's home at the base of Nisaba. Tired. I'm so tired.

I barely remember opening the door, much less seeing Brynn, before I fall into Brynn's soft, feathery guest bed and sleep finally washes away my grief, pain, and confusion.

CHAPTER SEVEN

THE smell of bacon frying pulls me from my slumber. Sleep seems like the only time I can escape my grief, but the smell of Brynn's cooking does the trick as well.

Birds chirp outside, their songs bold and unbothered, while sunlight cuts through the window, far too bright. I blink against the glare—it's way past breakfast. The scent of coffee mingles with the bacon and my stomach groans. I'm lying face down on the bed, fully dressed in yesterday's clothes. The heavy sleep weighs on my eyes. My tongue is rough and desiccate in my mouth. I drag myself from the bed, a relative zombie, and stand aimlessly in the room.

The last time I was here was with Sivan. We were the only guests Brynn allowed- her other siblings teased her mercilessly for being untidy. Sivan helped her decorate it, designed and built the furniture for her. The walls used to be a soft brown color, but it seems Brynn has papered them with a delicate pink floral color since I last visited. The furniture looks new as well, and the bed sheets are a different color. I wonder when she changed it. Why? Why did she change it? The sight digs at something in between my ribs—half sorrow, half relief.

Brynn's voice, bright and carefree, floats in from the kitchen, drowning out even the birds.

When I enter the kitchen, Brynn turns around and sets a cup of coffee on the counter before me. She's always aware of her surroundings, a skill that amazes me to no end.

"Rise and shine!" she says, too cheerful for my taste.

I grunt, taking the mug. Fresh, hot, with a dash of cream- just how I like it. Brynn always remembers the little things like that as well. The first sip melts the sand from my tongue, and I sigh contently. Brynn shakes her head at me and laughs under her breath.

"What?" I ask her between sips of coffee.

She chuckles again. "Nothing, it just reminds me of the first time Sivan brought you here." Her soul swells up in front of me, more clearly and brightly than I have ever seen before. Brynn's soul is pure, blue water, tinged black with grief, with a golden kernel in the center. Before I can react, my magic plunges me into her crystalline soul, into the memories she speaks of.

Sivan sits in his usual seat; an old wicker chair our father made when Mamma told him she was pregnant with Grigori. His leg is tucked under him, his feet bare, wearing just a set of loose pants, tied at the waist. Beside him, the pale fae woman he brought to meet me. Rhea's hair is a loose mop of curls gathered on her head, still messy from sleep. My brother has never brought a woman home, has never indicated romantic interest of any kind. She must be special, but so far, she's pretty quiet. She is definitely not a morning person, that's for sure. She sips her coffee while Sivan and I chat. A sadness emanates from her though. I can feel everyone's emotions, but hers are louder and stronger than any stranger I've met. I feel drawn to her.

"Rhea?" I ask her, and her head swivels around to look at me, her blue eyes wide and round.

"Mmm... yes?" She says, in a small voice.

I look her right in those starbright eyes and tell her, "We're going to be best friends." Her eyes widen even further, and I feel a grin spreading across my face. She stares at me for a moment, her expression unfathomable, and slowly, she begins to smile too. Mamma always said I have an energy people can't resist. Sivan says I grow on people, like a fungus.

I struggle releasing myself from the memories grip. My magic looms before me, wild and unending, an abyss of fire and shadow, threatening to consume. That magic purrs in my ear *"more, more, more."*

"No!" I gasp, as I flounder underneath the weight of my own power. Still, it wrests me for control. I cannot move, speak, or think. The world around me ceases existing.

"Rhea," Brynn says calmly through my internal haze. I didn't even notice her moving towards me, but I feel her place her hands on my shoulders, forcing back the burning shadows. Light flows from those gentle hands, cool and light as spring. Bit by bit, the light forces the shadows back, until they once again limn my skin, quiet and satiated.

Brynn's hands rise and gently grip my face. "Are you alright? I think I fixed it."

"Thanks for your help," I say, and she lets her hands fall away. "The potion Addie gave me reacted oddly to my magic. I felt it building all day yesterday, like a storm." The pressure eases a bit, but not enough.

"All due respect, future queen, that reaction had nothing to do with the potion and everything to do with you needing more training. Your powers are growing rapidly right now. I used my own magic to calm it down, but if you do not begin practicing magic on a large level then this will only be the beginning." She talks while she prepares a plate for me and slides it over. The plate is piled high with quail eggs, toast with butter, handfuls of bacon and a hearty helping of hash-browns. My mouth waters at the sight and I dig in, scarfing down the food and coffee as quickly as I can.

When I finish, I wipe my mouth and place my dishes in the sink. Only then do I turn to Brynn and say, "I hear you, okay? I will find someone, or we will find someone. Besides, I might need help after yesterday."

We haven't spoken about Brynn's foray into the library yesterday, or about my experience with Inya. Her eyes narrow, and she puts her coffee down, listening intently as I explain my bargain with the goddess and her mark on my skin.

"Her prophecy about fairies and whatnot... it doesn't make sense to me. What truth? Information from the lost years? I don't even know where to start with that type of research."

Brynn smiles at the word "research." Brynn's smile reveals nothing about her adventures yesterday. She smiles freely, and often.

"Speaking of research, the library was interesting. Faye was generous with information, and I brought back a few archaic texts." The gleam in her eye however...

"Did you flirt with the fairy so she would help you?" I ask, my own lips twitching despite my attempts to restrain them.

"She's quite easy on the eyes," Brynn says mischievously, "Oh, and she wants to meet you."

"You told the fairy about me? What did you tell her?"

"First of all, her name is Faye, not "the fairy."" Brynn says pointedly.

"You're right, I'm sorry."

"Second of all, yes, I did. Speaking as a member of your court, we need all the allies we can get. Obviously, mamma is on your side, and having the accomplished healer backing your cause helps a lot. But courts and kingdoms are made up of more than hopes and dreams. Even one person, or fairy, supporting you is one more than you had. It's important we do this correctly, that we practice diplomacy." I mull over her words for a moment and realize she's absolutely correct. I'm being way too casual about this. I'm building a court after all, and that court needs to have my back. Faye could be a potential ally.

"Plus, she is a cute little thing." Brynn adds, a wolfish gleam in her eyes. For Brynn, romance knows no bounds. She's dated dwarves, elves, other fae, of all genders, shapes, sizes, and colors. Why not add a fairy into the mix?

"Besides, what you went through was wilder than the library! And Inya *tongue-kissed* you? Lucky!" Her eyes glaze over at the mention of the voluptuous goddess.

"Pervert," I say under my breath, before adding, "It wasn't like that at all. She imbued some of her power into the bargain. It felt kind of like yours."

"Probably because the entire family is blessed by her. Our powers were all granted by Inya originally. That's why I can feel others' emotions, and my healing powers are stronger than most." I remember Sivan telling me something similar, before, but he had the ability to control water, instead of healing. Brynn can do both.

"Inya also said we should look for what we seek at the shadow market. That's on the island of Amisra, right?"

"That's correct. Have you been there before?"

"No, though my cousin, Janessa, rules over the island. It's also home to the Shadow Peak volcano, where Megara's sanctum was built."

"I'm ready to go whenever you are. I thought you might like a bath first."

"You thought correctly," I reply with a genuine smile. Brynn has an easy way about her, that makes it easier to be vocal about what I want. "Don't you need to take care of anything first?"

"No, it's already past noon. The horses will be fine at the stables, unless you want to waste your magic dust transporting them as well. My business is taken care of, and mamma can handle anything else that may come along."

"Well, alright then. I'll bathe and be out shortly." With that, I head for the bathroom. I scrub myself down quickly and efficiently, pack my things, change into some lighter traveling gear since we're going to the tropics and bound back down the hall to where Brynn sits drinking coffee and reading a book.

Her brow furrows and she sounds upset when she says, "I thought you'd take longer. I'm almost done with my book." I laugh, but I know the feeling. A love of reading is something we share. The cover looks familiar as well, then it dawns on me.

"I gave you that about a month ago, and you're still reading it?"

She scoffs at me. "Some of us are slow readers, princess. Besides this once is quite... salacious." She sighs, stands up and stretches her arms and back. "I'll put this in my pack for later. You're ready?"

"All good to go." I take out the starlight pouch and conjure up images in my mind of a place I've only seen in memories and photos.

"Once we do this, there's no going back. You realize that, right?" I ask Brynn. She reaches out and grabs my other hand.

"I'm with you all the way, sis." Her smile reassures me. All that's left to do is throw the dust. My fingers pinch what I hope is the correct amount to transport two fae, and I throw it down while saying "Take us to the Shadow Market on the Island of Amisra." The cloud of dust becomes impossibly thick for the small amount I threw. It swallows us, the whirling darkness reminiscent of my own shadows, pushing us through a void of starlight and green smoke, before spitting us out on a pristine beach, with black sand lining it as far as the eye can see.

***

Despite the blaring sun, the sand is a comfortably warm temperature when we touch it, so Brynn and I both take our sandals off. A soft, summery breeze drifts by, carrying the scent of the sea as well as the scent of citrus. The ocean stretches on for miles and miles, the most water I've ever seen in my life, the turquoise waters reflecting the sun merrily. There's not a single cloud in the sky. No wonder my parents escaped to Amisra as often as they could when I was young—this place is a veritable paradise.

Brynn looks awestruck, her gaze glued to the water. She walks forward to where the ocean meets the shore, letting the foamy water trickle over her feet. All magic users are strengthened in the presence of their element. This much water... for Brynn, it must be a miracle.

"How does it feel?" I ask as I tilt my head back and let the buttery soft sunlight warm my face.

"The ocean.... It's magnitude... the way my magic reacts to it... I've never felt anything this powerful before." Indeed, she sounds as devout as any of Inya's acolytes, maybe even as much as Addie. While she gazes out into the sea, I scan our environment.

A battered wooden sign points travelers in all different directions. One path leads down the beach towards the Shadow Market where tents and stalls of all different shapes and sizes lie waiting for tourists to come and spend their hard-earned coin. The Shadow Market is filled with the usual bits and bobbles: it is an endless array of clothing, jewels, weapons, food, and even livestock. However, it also boasts psychics and fortune tellers, goods from other realms, and of course elicit goods. It is said the market will lead you to where you need to go, not necessarily where you'd like to end up.

"Brynn, look," I say pointing in the direction of the market, "Let's go check it out!"

"Shouldn't we make some sort of plan first? Like how we're going to find what you're looking for?" She stands, and lets the sand fall off her clothes, then brushes off what remains.

"The way Inya made it sound, just by coming to the shadow market, we would find what we need."

"Maybe I can help the two of you!" A tiny voice pops out of

nowhere.

Brynn and I both stare at each other, eyebrows raised?

"Did you-?" I start to ask—

"No, I thought you-" Brynn interrupts me.

A puff of gold glitter pops into existence between us, shoving us apart as it grows and grows; when it settles, in its place stands a short, curvy woman with flowing red hair and tanned skin that shimmers in the sun. Her ocean blue eyes are light and full of joy, and her clothing.... Is unlike any I've ever seen. Her cobalt pants are tight at the waist and ankle, but the rest looks loose and comfortable. Her top looks more suited for swimming, with little gold pieces hanging from the bodice.

"Hello, hi, that was me!" The woman says, unbothered by our confusion.

"Faye!" Brynn nearly shouts, "What are you doing here?"

Faye pouts, her brow furrowing and her lip sticking out like a younglings. "I told you I wanted to meet Rhea, but then you left without talking to me! You left one of your kitchen windows open, so I heard the two of you talking about the dust and shrunk into my fairy form and hid in your bag. Then, surprise! Here I am!" She waves her fingers in the air cheerfully, as if we should celebrate her arrival.

Brynn says nothing, just blinks at Faye several times, so I take the moment to introduce myself and figure out Faye's motive. I draw upon some of my power carefully, letting Faye's aura come into view. It's sparkly and golden, through and through. No hint of deceit or pain, or anything beyond that sunshine she puts out. A little more of the pressure beneath my skin releases.

"Hey! You can read auras too? Neat trick!" Faye smiles a dazzling smile at me, and I search for any hint of her motive.

"You could feel me doing that?" I ask. Only Addie and Sivan ever noticed before.

"All fairies would." She says simply, before adding, "I wanted to meet you so badly, I figured I'd just come with you." She shrugs, her red hair a fiery crown around her, as if that explains everything.

"And what about the library?" Brynn asks her, her cheeks reddening.

"Oh, Adeline told me to follow my heart! And it led me to you," Faye says with a wink in Brynn's direction. I stifle a laugh. Brynn says nothing, blushing like mad. I've never seen Brynn get tongue tied around anyone before. She's normally upbeat, cheerful, flirty... much like Faye. Is the fairy too much for Brynn to handle?

"You might as well follow us to the market then," I tell Faye, determined to be pleasant.

"Oooh! I love shopping," she squeals in return, "What are we shopping for?"

"We're not sure," Brynn answers, "We were hoping it will find us when we get there."

"Come on, let's go before next century," I say and head off towards the market, not bothering to check and see if they're following me. As we get closer, the smell of spices and meats mingle in the air. The shops are packed into a makeshift square overrun with fae. Hidden restaurants and alcoves boast cooled sitting areas, with iced tea and bread to beat the heat in between looking for wares. We pass a cloth merchant, whose shop smells heavily of incense. When I run my hands over his fabrics, they are the softest things I've ever felt.

Donkeys and horses pull carts from all different directions underneath colored paper lanterns. Faye, Brynn, and I link arms as we walk so that we will not get separated. Underneath the market's thrumming energy, a pulse of danger spices the air. What would happen if a crowd this size were to panic? The feeling of being crushed looms over me so suddenly, I stop dead in the square. The hair on the back of my neck stands up and gooseflesh lines my arms.

"Wait," I say to Brynn and Faye, both trying to pull away and look at some shiny baubles on a jewelers table. I duck into the nearest shop, forcing the two women to come with me.

"Someone's following us," I tell them.

"Who?" Brynn asks.

"How do you know?" Faye asks.

"I don't know who and I can't explain how I know... I just know. Let's shop here for a moment. Who knows, maybe there's something interesting in here?" I say gesturing around. This shop is set up in one of the larger tents. Cages and pens line up neatly around the tent, with a few different shopkeeps roaming around if a shopper should need their help.

"Oh, cool, it's a shop of familiars!" Faye says excitedly, the gleam on her skin turning into a brilliant jewel like glittering, and points to a small wooden sign labeled "The Ninth Life: Shop of Familiars."

"Familiars?" Brynn asks. I've heard of them before, when I lived in the royal city, but my parents never let me enter one of their several shops in Darrid. They said a pet would be a distraction from my studies, not that they taught me anything outside of how to use my powers for their liking.

"Familiars are magical pets that are bound to your life force. There are some monstrous ones like minotaurs or dragons, though those are rare! You can also find normal canine or feline ones, but why wouldn't you pick a dragon over a puppy? That is, if you can afford it."

I don't bother telling Faye there is nothing in this realm I cannot afford. Despite leaving my family, my wealth wasn't tied through blood bonds, but soul ones. No one could deny the heir of a goddess her inheritance.

We roam through the aisles, seeing if anything catches our eye. Faye delights in seeing a nine-headed phoenix, taking out a journal and scribbling notes about the creature while murmuring under her breath. Brynn gets lost in the aquatic section, watching the selkies and Nixie's swim around and around their voluminous tanks.

Nothing pulls me in, and the feeling of being watched doesn't disappear. I turn around quickly, see no one there other than the handful of people looking around when we walked in, and curse myself under my breath at my paranoia. I'm just about to suggest we head to another shop when I feel the urge to check another section. My feet move at a normal pace, but without my conscious control, leading me to a poorly lit corner, cluttered with cages of varying sizes.

I stop in front of a large, metal cage, with runes and wards drawn all over it. The cage is empty, except for a tiny cat curled up and asleep in the center of the cage. The cat is black, with one white spot over its left eye. I feel drawn to her. She lifts her sleepy head, looks into my soul, and blinks at me. Just like that, I belong to her. I blink back, slowly, and she puts her head back down.

I whirl around, intending to find a shop-keep, but there's already one facing me. She appears mostly human, aside from her gently pointed ears. Her gold-brown hair is in a simple braid, and she wears the simple tropical fashion we'd seen most of the women in the shops wearing. Light, loose, and breezy to keep one cool during a full day of shopping. Her mouth is set in a stern line, however, and I wonder if I've done something wrong.

She looks more concerned than anything else when she sees me contemplating the cat and says, "You don't want that one, she's dangerous." *That's been said about me before, as well.*

I look back at the cat in question and ask, "how so? She looks like a perfectly normal cat to me."

"She's a shadow cat, lady, not normal at all. Everyone who's attempted to buy her has met with unfortunate fates. She always ends up back here within a few hours. She cannot be controlled or tamed." *Good thing I have no interest in either of those things.*

Brynn and Faye find us then, at the back of the shop, in a cramped corner. Seeing that I'm speaking with the shop keep, they stand there silently.

"Does she have a name?" There's a kinship in this world between broken things and that cat will be mine.

"Nay, my lady. She's never been owned long enough." *And none of you cared enough to give her one?* I'd seen at least four or five other shopkeepers milling about the familiar's tent.

"How much?" I ask the woman.

"Really, I'm not sure you can afford it. She's quite special."

"Give me a number," I say, the patience leaving my voice. The woman gulps but answers. Brynn and Faye's eyes widen at the number, and widen even further when I tell her, "It's a deal."

"If you're certain lady, I'll draw up the contract. As soon as you have the money in hand." The woman's tone suggest she doesn't believe I can afford it. She crosses her arms and stands there expectantly, as if waiting for an excuse or assuming I will leave and never bother coming back.

I take two coins out of the pouch I keep with me and hand it to her. Brynn and Faye watch on, eyes wide and eyebrows raised.

"I didn't even know they made coins in denominations that large!" Faye exclaims, eyes twinkling over the shining coins.

"You keep that much money on you all the time? Are you asking to get robbed?" Brynn asks, concerned lacing her voice.

"We can discuss this later. Now, as for the contract," I say turning away from Brynn and back to the shop keep.

"Yes, of course my lady—what was your name? If you'll follow me to the office, I'll have one of the hands grab that beast for you, and we can bind you two together." Of course, once you hand over the gold, people fawn all over you.

"You may call me Rhea. These are my friends, Brynn and Faye." That's all this woman really needs to know about us. I'd like to get through this quickly, and see the rest of the market, and then we'll need somewhere to sleep this evening.

"My name is Vasta. Follow me, this way please." She ushers us out of the corner and away from the cat. Each step away from the little creature feels like a step in the wrong direction.

We wind through the myriads of cages and into the office, where Vasta sits us down on thick leather chairs with tea and snacks while she heads off in search of a handler to get the cat. The office is a small room, stuffed with tea tables, several chairs, and a large wooden desk cluttered with documents and metal objects.

Honestly, the whole thing seems unnecessary. I would have taken the cat with me if I had known it would take this long. Faye and Brynn dig into the snacks right away, but my appetite has absconded. I tap my fingers impatiently as I watch the small clock in the office tick away.

Finally, endless minutes later, Vasta returns with a small box. At the sight of it, my shadows writhe around me in anger. That box is hardly larger than the cat itself. How these fae can fear such a tiny thing is beyond me.

"Take her out of that right now." My voice is full of shadows and fear, a sentence laced with violent promise.

"It's standard procedure lady, to keep them in until you're ready to sign." Vasta shrinks back from me, and a dejected sigh escapes me at the sight. As angry as the treatment of my cat makes me, what kind of ruler will I be if I accomplish my goals through fear and coercion? No, I need to do this another way.

"I will give you another gold coin, right now, if you release her from that dismal cage. Please." I say, aiming for pleasant, but the words have a hint of a hiss with them. Vasta gulps, sets the cage down, then wipes her palms on her skirt before smiling nervously at me.

I take the coin out of its bag, and put it on the wooden desk, quietly.

Vasta scoops it up and releases the clip holding the cage shut before jumping back quickly, as if terrified of whatever lies within.

That little black cat walks out the cage, looks at Vasta and....

"Mew." The tiniest noise escapes the cat, as if half-way through she forgot what a cat sounds like. Vasta screams, an unearthly blood-curdling scream that ends just as quickly when Faye slaps her hand right over Vasta's mouth.

"Pardon me but you are hurting my ears." The contrast between the screaming half-elf and the petite fairy causes Brynn and I both to giggle. Faye cracks a smile as well, and releases Vasta.

The cat ignores all of us, curls up on the rug and begins licking her paws, each dagger like claw glinting in the light as she does.

"See, she's a perfectly fine cat." I say triumphantly.

"That thing has killed at least two fae warriors, lady, so you'll forgive me if I am a little on edge." I shrug at her response, and she continues, "Anyways, I apologize for my unprofessional behavior. Shall we continue with the contract?"

Vasta doesn't bother waiting for my answer, clearly as eager to get this over with as I am. She opens a drawer hidden in the desk and pulls out several vials, a bowl, and a thick looking paint brush. From another drawer, she pulls out an ashen looking material. At our inquisitive looks, she explains.

"This is grave dust," she says gesturing to the ashy material, "And this is hell-water, nyktos essence, and death flower essence." All materials used in soul rituals, though not any I had ever been allowed to perform. She grinds the liquids into the ash, until it's an oily mass in the bowl.

"Come here," She crooks her finger at me, "And pull your shirt up."

My eyebrow raises at her demand, but I acquiesce, lifting the muslin material out of the way. Vasta takes the brush and dips into the substance, then paints it onto my stomach in thin, precise strokes. At first, I feel nothing but the cool wetness of her painting my skin, but slowly it begins tingling, then burning. Eventually, I grit my teeth against the searing burn while Vasta softly chants foreign words.

Vasta stops suddenly and asks, "What will you name her?"

Brynn's eyes narrow. "She doesn't have a name already?" Vasta rubs her temples as Brynn speaks, as if the interruption grates on her.

"No, milady. It's our procedure to allow our customers to name their chosen pets."

"Okay," I say, tempted to roll my eyes, "How about Grim?"

Brynn looks at me suspiciously. "And what would that be short for?"

"Uh, Grimalkin?" I say as seriously as I can manage. Faye begins giggling immediately. At the sound of that pealing laughter, Brynn's eyebrows furrow impossibly further, her face screwed up in a little knot. Brynn always gets angry when she's confused.

"What is a grimalkin?" she asks, irritation seeping through her voice.

"It's just another word for cat, dear." Faye steps in, her hand on the small of Brynn's back, not eager to let Brynn devolve into a fit of rage. I've known Brynn long enough to know her mood will blow through like a storm. Indeed, at Faye's quick explanation, Brynn laughs a bit as well.

"You can't name a cat, "Cat." That would be silly, and you're practically a queen already. Your familiar should reflect that, Ri."

"If being a queen means I can no longer have fun, then I don't want the crown." I say, a teasing lilt in my voice.

"Ladies, as amusing as this is, I do have other customers I need to attend to." Vasta has a tight smile pasted across her face, but she sounds patient enough. "A name, please."

A long moment of silence follows. I've never named anything before, and I would hate to give the little creature a name that doesn't suit her. Faye breaks the long silence by saying, "Look at the mark on her face. It looks like a crescent moon. Maybe Luna or Celeste?"

My eyes take in the mark, which in the light indeed looks like a moon.

"Luna," I say testing the name on my tongue. "Lu-na." It feels right, simple maybe, but right.

"Alright, Luna it is." I turn to Vasta, "Please, continue."

Vasta asks me to pick Luna up. When I do, the softness of her fur amazes me, and she nestles easily into my arms. As soon as Luna is secure, Vasta continues her incantations. As she finishes, a soft glow encompasses Luna and I, and I feel the connection in my soul.

I take a deep breath and let the strange new feeling settle over me. Checking my own aura, I can see Luna's connected to mine, a small ball of shadows. What can this little cat do, that terrorized so many?

"The connection is similar to that of a mating bond. In theory, she will fight for you if you care for her, but with that shadow cat, who knows?" Vasta looks down her nose at us and adds, "No refunds."

"I don't plan on returning her."

With that, I motion for Brynn and Faye to follow me as I leave the office, both of them cooing over the new addition to our party.

"Let's get her a bed and some bowls and some cute outfits..." Faye's excitement overrides her good sense.

"We haven't even found an inn for ourselves yet." Brynn points out.

"We can do all of that and more, if we can just leave, please."

CHAPTER EIGHT

THE air has cooled a bit when we exit the familiar's shop, the scent of rain light and lingering in the air, but the day is still bright and there are many more shops to explore. We stop at one stall near the familiar shop, and I buy a new pouch for Luna to lie in while we travel. Brynn and Faye buy kabobs from another stall, perfume from another, books from yet another. Faye, it seems, collects anything and everything that catches her eye. Brynn is slightly more discerning, looking over items for an agonizingly prolonged period of time before buying it or walking away and shaking her head as if she's disappointed.

"That last shopkeep, a wonderful dwarven fellow, told me there's an inn named The Drunken Kraken at the edge of the shops. It's also a tavern, so I understand if you'd rather rest elsewhere," Brynn tells Faye and I over dinner, as she cracked the leg of some poor crustacean open. We had found a restaurant tucked away under the stairs of another business earlier in the day and marked it for later. My companions' eyes twinkle in the twilight as we take in the incredible view.

The sun slowly slips under the sky, kissing the ocean as she begins her slumber. The three moons reflect off the unending ocean as a warm breeze sweeps through the open space. The scent of roasting meat fills the air as we wait for our food to arrive.

"I have another option if you don't mind!" Faye says, "I met another fairy at the bookshop, and she said all the fairies stay at Marble Falls. It's a magical inn and guaranteed to be far safer than one filled with sailors and adventurers." She shows us on the map, and it's equidistant to either inn.

"Do you have a preference, Brynn?" I ask her right as the waiter appears with the rest of our food. Brynn slurps down the last of her crab and then we take turns piling rice and meat on each of our plates, Then, I pour heavy glasses of the spiced mead the waiter had given us, handing one to Brynn and one to Faye. In the gentle twilight, everything ceases to matter.

"The fairy inn does sound intriguing. Once you've seen a regular tavern, you've seen them all." Indeed, the tavern conjures up images of crowded tables and drunken revelry, which while occasionally enjoyable, also means the hint of danger dances in the air. Thieves and assassins use the sounds of the night to cover their tracks. On the other hand, considering Inya's warning, heading into a den of fairies seems... foolish.

Faye turns and looks at me expectantly, her red hair shifting over her shoulders, as if the decision is mine alone. Brynn follows suit and I debate both sides for a moment.

"The fairy inn, it is. Can you lead us there after dinner?" I ask Faye, after a few sips of mead. The spice keeps me warm in the cooling night air.

"Oh yes, do not fret one bit! I'll have us there before you know it!" I find myself smiling. Faye is growing on me, I guess.

We finish the rest of our meal in silence, pay the bill, and slip out into the sultry evening. We walk along the beach on our way to the inn, Brynn and Faye ahead of me as I trail behind. While they chatter about the various purchases they made that day, I simply take in the evening. Luna sleeps in my bag and I wonder if she'll ever wake up, but she seems quite comfortable enough. I politely asked the server back at the restaurant for a bit of fish to take with us, so that when the little shadow cat wakes up, I'll be able to feed her.

Palm trees sway in the night breeze and waves glide along the shore. With the stars bearing down on us, and those three ever watchful moons, a sense of peace washes over me. How long has it been since I felt relaxed?

"We're nearly there," Faye looks over her shoulder and calls to me.

"Sounds good!" I reply.

Suddenly, that feeling of being watched creeps over me again. My eyes dart around the mostly empty beach. A few couples lie in the sand, and we've passed various faeries here and there, but other than that I see no one of interest. Well, it was a nice moment of peace.

"Brynn," I call out quietly, "Do you feel that?" I reach out into the night with my power, but not a single shadow answers my call. Not hesitant or scared like when Rhiannon appeared, but simply... absent. As if each and every shade has left this realm.

Brynn and Faye stop walking. Brynn cocks her head to the side, listening with those keen fae ears. Faye watches us, blue eyes wide, waiting for one of us to tell her what to do.

After a long moment, Brynn says "I don't hear anything that shouldn't be here."

"Are you absolutely certain?" My heart rate increases bit by bit, my nerves rattling.

"Yes, I'm sure. My powers are much stronger here by the ocean." The agitation in her voice calms me a bit, despite my annoyance. Brynn's right—I'm probably just tired after the long day.

"I'll let you know if I sense anything!" Faye says brightly, cutting through the mood like a sunbeam.

"I don't know a lot about fairy powers," I admit to Faye, "I'm not sure what you can do."

"It really depends on the fairy. I can read and speak elven, dwarven, various fae tongues, fairy, the old tongue, and I'm working on learning various languages from the human realm as well. I can touch a book and absorb all of its knowledge instantly. But all of us can sense other magical creatures." She pauses for a moment, tapping a finger against her sparkly cheek, not a sense of humility in her body.

"Oh, also I'm pretty good at archery and I once won a mead drinking competition!" She laughs, her blue eyes lit up at some memory and then adds, "I think that's about it."

"Wow," Brynn says staring at Faye unabashedly, a dreamy look entering her eyes.

"You must make an impressive librarian," I say with a grin.

With that, I relax a little more, but still, we stride down the beach a little quicker than before. I still feel like someone is watching us, or me. The awareness tickles the back of my skull begging me to listen, to look, to see. Something calls out to my very soul, yet nothing is visible. How can I see the unknown if even the shadows themselves have left me? Ignoring my instincts, I shake the thoughts off and follow Brynn and Faye.

This time of night, the air has cooled immensely, and we walk the rest of the way in a blissful silence. Faye stops in front a cave hidden at the far end of the beach. Thick green vines hang over the entrance. Tiny, iridescent lights float in the air. Other than that, the air is still. No signs of life from within the cave. I whirl away from the entrance and ask Faye, "Are you sure this is the right cave?"

Brynn snorts and points out, "Why would there be lights here if it was the wrong cave?"

"There's no one in that cave. I find it a little suspicious."

"You're paranoid," Brynn says, rolling her eyes, "What could possibly go wrong?" Her question brings up visions of murderous creatures I'd seen in fairy tales growing up. Beautiful young women entering caves only to be devoured by the lustful, angry creatures inside. It's definitely not the way I want to go out. My eyes cut towards Brynn, a biting remark on the tip of my tongue, but then Faye's bell like laughter rings out through the night. The sound stops Brynn and I from arguing further.

"You two are funny. Are all fae as funny as the two of you?" She smiles. I wonder what it is like to give smiles up so freely. To feel so fully and completely that smiles slip out unbidden.

"Watch me," Faye says. Faye places a hand on the rough stone outside of the cave. Her skin begins glowing from inside, a brilliant beaming light, soft and buttery like sunlight. She begins singing, a melodic beautiful harmony of words in a language I don't recognize. The cave begins glowing as well, pulsing with the beat of her song. When her song ends, a door materializes where the cave entrance was. The door is fat, round, and green. A heavy brass knocker is the only conspicuous part of it-—two fairies depicted entwined in an amorous exchange. The only hint of what may lie beyond.

Faye steps back and admires her handiwork. "Easy as pie!" she says. Brynn moves forward to open the door, but Faye shoves a hand in front of her to stop her.

"I have to open it. You won't like the results if you try. Only those of fairy descent may open fairy doors." With that explanation, Faye opens the door and steps inside. Brynn and I exchange a look.

"After you," I say.

"Actually, after you." She responds and at the look on my face she adds, "You're going to be a queen. I'll head up the rear. Go on ahead."

Another reminder that what I want, and what I must do, are wholly separate things. I try not to let my disappointment show as I step through the door.

CHAPTER NINE

MAGIC tingles along my skin as I pass the threshold, and the taste of strawberries zings on my tongue. The room I find myself in is almost as luxurious as Inya's sanctum. Stone walls ascend impossibly high into the heavens. A round skylight shows an endless expanse of stars whose light shines down on a hot spring in the middle of the room. Beyond the hot spring, a large wooden desk sits and behind it is…. An elf? Her ears are slightly pointed, and her white hair hangs in one long, straight sheet. However, her skin glitters as if encrusted with diamonds.

Brynn and Faye wave to me, breaking me out of my reverie. "Over here!" Faye shouts across the large room. For such a little thing, she sure is quick on her feet. They both stand near the front desk. I wind my way through clusters of fairies, murmuring apologies here and there when I bump into a few and receive dirty looks in exchange. A few other faerie's roam about the room, engaged in various activities. I suppose they had a friend bring them through as well.

When I reach the front, Brynn and Faye are in deep discussion with the woman at the front desk but stop once they see me.

"And here she is now!" Faye squeals, leaning on the top of the desk.

Brynn's face gives nothing away, but I can tell by her eyes she's far past tired. Her voice is flat when she says, "Princess Rhea this is Coralie, the manager of the inn. She and Faye were discussing rooms and then they got distracted with gossiping." *We're using my title now?* I'll have to ask Brynn about that later.

Coralie is an apt name for this lovely woman who looks as if she were dipped in stars.

"That's because I'm half-elf and half-fairy," Coralie says.

Wait—I didn't say that aloud, did I?

"No," Coralie says, and at my confused and slightly terrified face she adds, "I can hear your thoughts. Yours are quite loud in particular."

"Can all fairies read minds?" I ask her, daring a small look in Faye's direction. Inya's warning rings in my head.

"No! No! Just like different fae have different powers, so do the fairies. I've told you the extent of my powers. They may grow or change over time, but no one in my family is able to pierce the veil of the mind," Faye hurriedly explains. A small smile plays on Coralie's lips.

"If we're all done chatting, may I show you to your rooms?" she cuts in politely.

"Oh, yes, we got two rooms. It's all been taken care of." Brynn says, her eyes sliding over me. "There's even a bathing room."

The thought of bathing is nearly enough to bring me to my knees. Traveling always leaves me feeling bereft and after shopping the day away in the humid climate, a bath would go a long way towards making me feel refreshed. A good bath can cure a bad day-- An old adage my mother used to share with me in a rare moment of peace together.

Wait, just two rooms? My eyebrows raise in question when I process her sentence. Brynn notices and winks at me.

"Don't worry, my queen, Faye and I will do fine sharing a room. I know how you value your space." Her tone is light and easy, but I hear the roguish intent behind it.

Coralie leads us to our rooms, explaining how the inn works along the way. She tells us that there is a single portal from each room, and where you end up depends on your intent. Coralie opens the first portal for us out of courtesy and leads us to our rooms.

"A door connects the rooms, so you need not worry about portaling. Simply ring the bell by the door if you need anything and one of my employees shall help you immediately. Dinner will be served in the dining hall shortly, but you have plenty of time to rest up and bathe should you wish. Remember, only think of where you wish to go, and the portal will lead you there." With that, Coralie bows out of the room leaving the three of us alone.

Brynn and Faye glance at each other, a shy silence descending upon them. The air in the room becomes thick and charged between them, an invisible tether binding them together. At the sight of it, my heart stills. That unending, vast grief again looms before me and I'm content to drown in it. But Brynn and Faye are looking at me expectantly and I realize they are waiting for me to dismiss them or command them or do anything really.

"I'm going to find the bathing chambers, if you'll excuse me." I say curtly to the pair, the tension between them palpable. It's none of my business what consenting fae do, but it's simply unbearable for my heart at the moment. How I long to see Sivan look at me like that again, but he never will. I will never again see his hazel eyes darken as he drinks in my presence; never again will I see his desire for me overtake him. That unending darkness threatens to swallow me yet again, inescapable and inevitable.

I leave my bag on the bed, set out the food and water we had acquired for Luna, and leave her sleeping on a thick moss pillow.

"I'm going to bathe," I shout through the closed door leading to Brynn and Faye's room. I stride into the portal before they respond, intent on thinking of the bathing chambers but all I really desire is a drink. The moment I pass through the portal, I know I'm nowhere near the bathing chambers. I'm in a large room, just off the main chamber of the inn. Through a long tunnel I can see the front desk and moonlight, but it's far enough the light doesn't impact the darkness of the tavern room.

A large stage occupies the far end of the room, across from the bar. In the middle of the stage, a fairy sits with her iridescent wings proudly behind her back. Veins of gold run through those wings that light up like fire in the candlelight. Her hair is a dark-blue coronet upon her head, her freckles like stars on her midnight skin. A harp formed of leaves and twigs rests between her hands, but despite her heavenly visage the tune is rhythmic and thumping. A few other fairies dot the stage behind her, each with various stringed instruments in their hands. The midnight fairy opens her mouth, and her voice is like honey whiskey, thick and pouring through the room like an aphrodisiac. Her voice reaches deep within my soul and tugs on that kernel of grief within me. I do not bother wiping my tears away as they fall, as the singer on the stage sings about epic love and fierce battles resulting in loss.

"Who is that?" I say more to myself than anyone else, but an entirely drunk fairy overhears me and tells me the fairy onstage is called Tryamon, a popular singer on tour from their homeland. Slowly, the darkness coiling itself in my limbs eases itself. Here, I feel invisible amongst the various faerie folk drunk on fairy wine, entwining themselves behind sheer curtains or dancing in the center of the room. My hands comb through my hair, releasing my dark curls from their braid and I loose a sigh of relief. Walking along the edge of the throngs of fairies, I begin crossing over towards the bar. I'm halfway there when a male presence dominates my space, backing me against the stone walls of a dark corner before I realize what's happening.

"I've been looking for you," a harsh voice says as my head bangs against the stone. Stars spark in my vision at the contact.

"What the--?" I just have enough time to bark out before a hand claps over my mouth, a warm body covers mine.

To anyone passing by, we might look like any other lovers too caught up in the subtle magic being woven by the fairies to force patrons to spend more money. The few fairies near us don't even spare a glance our way. But there is nothing romantic about this strangers' rough hands pinning me in place. *Danger, Danger!* My instincts scream out.

My breathing comes out rough and ragged and I force myself to look at my assaulter. I reach out blindly with my powers, looking for any shadows to assist me but they feel... null. Quiet, like they were back on the beach. All I can do is look and observe, use my senses to serve me when I cannot access the shadows. I squirm against his grasp but it's futile.

"Get off of me," I hiss as I bite into his palm. His grip loosens just a bit, and I elbow him in the ribs as hard as I can. Surprise dots his face.

"You want to fight?" he growls, his voice low and warm, yet still sharp.

"I don't want to fight you, I simply want you to leave me alone," I retort, but he shoves me against the wall yet again.

"Then stop making this so difficult for me," he snaps, his breath hot and heavy against my neck. Shivers run down my spine at that heat. Tension crackles between us, a strange energy gathering in the air.

Ignoring it, I twist against his grip, spinning with the force of the motion until I twist out of his hands. We circle each other in the small dark space, blending into the rest of the dancing fae. Our eyes lock together as we rotate, the frustration apparent on both of our faces.

"What do you want from me?" I demand as that strange energy builds, something about him calling to my very soul. I hate it.

"Answers, as my queen insists," he spits out, the fury on his face apparent. The proximity is electric as the tension between us grows. He again pushes me towards the wall, but this time I shove back, the opposing forces locking us together. I still long enough to notice that despite his manhandling of me, he's quite handsome.

His skin looks hewn from granite, with a mess of black hair and gently curling horns rising from his temples. He's tall, so tall I shift my head back, pressing my body further into his to get a better look. His own body is hard, lean, and *male*. Stubble clings to his rough-cut jaw. And his eyes... oh his eyes look like shadows, whirls of black and green smoke electrified. My eyes look up into him, his hand still on my mouth, and the world shifts, as his smoke and cedar scent hits me, and it smells like coming home. *Impossible.*

Memories shoot past me faster than I can keep up with and nothing I can make sense of: a boy's hands holding a sword against a wolf-like creature; a woman with skin black as night and familiar-looking horns; Rhiannon seated on a throne of onyx and bone. As the memories fly past, a new tether forms beside Luna's, something dark, ancient, and heady.

"What is this?" I whisper as my body relaxes into his against my will.

The mating bond clicks into place as we gaze into each other's eyes, our hatred and fury mixing together as it does so.

"Oh, fuck," He mutters, his voice husky and low. A demon's temptation, that voice.

Oh no, Oh no, no no no.

The gorgeous stranger, my mate apparently, stumbles away from me. As he does, I notice a dagger in one of his hands. Instinctively, I shove him even further away from me, mind whirling.

"Who are you?" I demand, "Did you come here to kill me?" I don't need to ask who sent him. There's nothing Rhiannon wouldn't do to secure her crown, including sending an assassin after me. It would be simple for her, child's play in fact. I've heard stories of secret assassins from the Under-Realm. Problem being, once you kill enough people, you're no longer that secret.

"I—I don't—ugh. Fuck. Yes, yes, I was." I know little of the mating bond besides the stories I was told as a child, but those stories told me mates can neither lie to nor cause harm to one another.

"Has this bond already addled your brain?" I ask him, crossing my arms. "I asked who you are."

"My name is Sebastien." he says, putting the little dagger away, somewhere unseen. He's wearing leather pants and a loose shirt. Honestly? Leather pants in this heat? His pants are tucked into thick looking boots, with little metal spikes adorning them.

"I guess you already know who I am, since you're here. How did you even get into this place, *Sebastien*?" I spit his name out. Silence greets me. He's smarter than he looks, I'll give him credit for that. His name, so similar to Sivan's, feels like a caress on my tongue despite my harsh delivery. What a cruel joke the cosmos must be playing on me.

"Well, forget about whatever you think is going to happen between us. I have no need for a mate, and I have other things that need tending." His nostrils flare at my words, the only sign that I've discombobulated him as thoroughly as he has me. Good. I meant every word. He shifts his head and narrows his eyes at me.

"What makes you think I want a mate? This," he says, gesturing between us, "is only going to complicate my life further." I just stare at him, shaking my head, words beyond me.

His eyebrows soften and he sniffs in my direction.

"You are.... Grieving," he says simply. It has me fighting the urge to scream each time I am forced to remember Sivan, that he is gone, he is gone and the likelihood that I will fail him, that I will not recover his soul is far greater than none. How am I to be responsible for the one thing I value above all else? There is nothing I would not do for Sivan.

"My husband," I respond, looking at the ground, at the bar,

anywhere but his eyes. I grasp deep inside myself for the anger that I need to keep myself going. Sebastien being understanding and kind will only make this harder. I need to hate him. I need him to hate me.

"Ah," he murmurs, before an awkward silence once again ensues. Staring at him, this man meant to kill me, now my mate, causes my grief and fury to wrestle within me. My eyes slide past him to the bar again and I find myself stalking past him towards the bar.

"Wait," Sebastien calls out in surprise, his hand reaching out to catch me. I'm too quick for him and dance past his outstretched hand. Reaching the bar, I sit on a little three-legged stool.

A male fairy tends the bar, his skin of turquoise and gold swirling together like marble. He wears an open vest, showing off his well sculpted body. He has short dark blue hair, and a broad smile.

"I'm Ambrose," he introduces himself in an appreciative tone, his eyes roving over me in a confident, but not disgusting way. An accomplishment. I suppress a smile at his gaze. "What can I get you?" There's an underlying current to his words, and his eyes narrow as Sebastien walks up behind me. A shiver runs down my spine at his proximity. It's not from fear.

"What's the strongest liquor you have?" I ask Ambrose, ignoring Sebastien as he perches himself on the stool next to me.

"We have a delicious elderberry fairy vodka in stock, just portaled it in this morning fresh from Ela' Varen." Fairy liquor is a sought-after commodity, as its effects can be quite potent and cause all sorts of faeries to experience tremendous pleasure. I've had faerie wine but never fairy vodka, so why not?

"Great," I tell him with a tight smile, not wanting him to view it as anything other than kindness, "I'll start with two." He slides two small crystal glasses over to me, and I gulp them down as elegantly as I can manage. The effects are nearly immediate and a pleasant warmth oozes through me.

"Can you not stop at just one drink?" Sebastien says, his dark eyes filled with concern, pushing his hair back from his face. His concern is simply kindling for my ire. With the vodka making its way through my bloodstream, the desire to gaze into his eyes and know each and every nuance to them overcomes me. My hands shake from resisting the desire to touch him. *What the fuck is this?*

Pushing away the desire, I side-eye him instead. "What are you, my father?"

Pushing aside my tumultuous feelings, I stop for a moment to think about it. I truly do. I weigh and measure my life, my responsibilities, the challenges ahead. Even after thinking it all through, being rational and methodic... there is not a single part of me that does not want another drink. Irresponsible? Sure, but Brynn and Faye are safe in their room, Luna is asleep on my bed, and my heart weighs much too much for me to carry any longer.

"Another, please." I ask the barkeep, smiling a bit more freely at him, and Ambrose slides another crystal glass over. My *mate* stares at me, baring his teeth, and growls as I raise the glass in his direction and say "cheers!" I slam the vodka as fast as I can, the fiery liquid hitting the back of my throat and burning all the way down. My stomach is only upset for a moment, and then I slide a little closer to oblivion.

"What'd you do to my shadows?" I ask Sebastien, still baring his teeth at me. What does it matter anyways? I had my great love. I do not need another, especially not one working for the bitch queen.

He looks at the ceiling while he's thinking, and I wonder if it's a habit for him. As if I care about his habits.

"A question for a question," he replies grabbing a nut from a bowl on the bar counter and de-shelling it. He says it casually, but I hear the caution in his voice. He settles back onto his seat, appearing slightly more at ease as Ambrose moves away to tend other patrons. There is a gracefulness to his movements, the way the fairy lights bathe him.

"An answer for an answer," I respond, raising a brow at him and tilting my head. My fingers toy with the empty crystal glass, something to keep them occupied. He may be well versed in fae rules, but as am I. The side of his lip spasms up for a moment, but he forces his face calm. Do I amuse him? Do I care at all if I affect him? The vodka must be messing with my thoughts as well.

"Very well then. I did nothing to the shadows; they and I are simply antithetical to one another." He says it as if it were the very portrait of reason.

"What does that mean?" I ask, brows furrowing in confusion, "How can one be antithetical to the shadows?" One would think the opposite of shadows would be light, however there is nothing light about this man.

"Ah, but it is my turn to ask a question and receive an answer. When did your husband die?"

The question stuns me into silence. All the questions I've been preparing in my mind relate to his power, his relationship with Rhiannon, what he thinks he will be getting from me now that he thinks we are mates. I clear my throat before answering, "It's been a little over six months." His face remains stony, but I swear those dark eyes soften at my answer.

"Who did you lose?" My voice comes out barely above a whisper; he strains his head to hear me over the lilting music.

When he realizes what I've said, he scoffs slightly, shaking his head a little, and then says, "My sister, though it was long ago."

"Loss leaves a mark on everyone it touches," I say as I signal to Ambrose for two more.

"I know we've only just met, but certainly there is no way someone as little as you needs two more shots." Two more crystal glasses appear in front of me, and I push one towards Sebastien. He's right. I don't even need this one more shot. The last glass has only now begun creeping up on me, and I feel the urge to be nice to him.

"One's for you, actually." *Smart-ass.* A fuzzy feeling enters my head, droning on and on in the background. It is all at once, horrible and wonderful. I lean an elbow on the bar top, hoping it will keep me upright as my liquor catches up with me.

He tips his head back and I watch the muscles in his throat as he drinks the vodka; his gaze shifts to me as he finishes and I immediately glance away, suddenly preoccupied with downing my own.

"What is it you want?" He asks. The question catches me off guard. He does that a lot so far. No one has asked me that question, not a single person, since Sivan passed. Not even Brynn or Addie.

"The answer is complicated," I say hesitantly, rubbing my shoulder, "I am unsure what you want to hear." He considers that for a moment before asking me why I feel the need to conform to his desires.

"A bit strange, that," he says slowly, licking his lips and glancing back up at my eyes. My teeth catch on my bottom lip and my breathing hitches at that look. I am quite young still; it's only natural my body might feel things that my heart disavows. It does not mean I have to give in to that desire. As I wrestle with myself, his dark eyes lock onto mine and he takes a deep breath.

"So, again, what do you want?" He asks earnestly. "Take a moment, think about it if you must."

"I want to lay his soul to rest. And I want revenge. I am now on a journey to achieve both of those things at once and yet... there is a part of me that fears this journey will take something integral from me. That I will get lost betwixt the shadows and souls and no one will prevent me, too busy wrapped up in their own wants and needs." *Why am I telling him all of this?*

"Sacrifice begets sacrifice. Tell me, was your husband a good man? Did he care for you?"

"Clearly, he wasn't my mate," I say raising my brows in Sebastien's direction. Sometime during the conversation, we slid our stools closer together, and now his breath is hardly a hair away from my own. "I chose him. Every day, over and over again, I chose him above all else. And he chose me, over and over again. Some say love is madness, but love is a choice we make to keep going, to keep fighting. We did that for one another. I loved him so completely and thoroughly; I feel his absence as if that of a drug." My cheeks burn, aware that I've talked for longer than is polite, and a nervous laugh escapes me. Here I am, baring my most intimate secrets to a veritable stranger in the middle of a strange place surrounded by fairies.

"Well, Sebastien, I find I must take my leave of you, but it has been lovely not being murdered by you this evening." A clock on the wall nearby strikes the hour, and I realize we've been sitting talking with one another for nearly two hours now. Those lengthy silences in the beginning took up a lot of time. I had not even noticed how quickly it was passing. Brynn and Faye are surely wondering what has become of me, and I have yet to bathe.

His eyes shutter for a moment, and then he responds, "I know how to find you. You will be seeing me again. Soon." *I can't wait.*

"Whatever you say," I retort as I slide off the stool, not entirely steady, and focus on keeping upright. Brynn and Faye will want to hear about this as well, but that can wait til I'm less sloshed. My ass is sore from sitting for so long. The days of horseback riding, climbing the steps to the garden sanctum, little rest, portaling to this island, and now dealing with some sort of cantankerous daemon.... Ugh, that bath can't come soon enough. What was I thinking, drinking with my enemy's right hand?

Sebastien stands, and inclines his head to me, before sweeping out of the tavern room towards the portal, several women eyeing him excessively. A possessive snarl slips free of me and the delicate fairies gasp before I realize what I've done. Being a mate... will it take away all my free will and better judgment? Already, he belongs to me. The problem is that I will never belong to another man as long as I live. Even the mating bond cannot fix a broken heart, though it seems inclined to make me forget mine. The thought sobers me just enough to leave.

I hurry down the hall and portal to the bathing chamber immediately. This time of night, few are awake, but I see a few fairies bathing in the hot springs. I bathe quickly, scrubbing the dirt from my nails and face. Exhaustion, deep and true, climbs over me, and by the time I finish, I am ready to pass out. Walking through the portal yet again, finally I arrive at our rooms. Flinging open the door, I am positively intent on crawling into bed with Luna and passing out. What I see in the bed stops me short.

A naked woman curls up on the center of the bed, where I had left Luna. Her hair is the same dark shade as mine, but impossibly long, and fans out over the bed. And on top of her head, two cat-like ears.

CHAPTER TEN

"BRYNN! Faye!" I yell into the adjoining room, "Get in here... now, please!" The door between our rooms opens, and the two rush out looking flushed and excited, each of them holding a book in their hands.

"What is it?" Brynn is the first to ask, following my line of site to the bed and raising her eyebrows so high I think they might detach from her forehead and run away. "Did you bring a girl here, Rhea?"

"Yes, I brought a girl home from the bar, and the first thing I wanted to do was tell the two of you about her." The sarcasm flows out naturally, the absurdity of her insinuation a welcome break.

"No, Brynn, look at her eyes," I say, hoping to avoid an argument, but Brynn looks at the girl's eyes. Indeed, there upon the girls deathly white face, a black heart shaped mark over her left eye, as if the cat had turned itself inside out.

"Is... Is that your cat?" Faye chimes in. Faye starts muttering to herself and rushes back into the other room, frantically looking for something. Something thuds and I can hear what sounds like Faye dragging something across the floor.

"I know I've read something about this!" Faye yells from amid the cacophonous sounds, "Give me just a moment, if you please."

While she's searching, Brynn and I keep an eye on the girl. A purring sound emanates from her causing Brynn and I to exchange a look, sharing in the absurdity of the situation.

"Sounds really strange coming from a human body," Brynn says first.

"I can't believe I adopted a child," I respond. The absurdity of it all finally hits the two of us then, and we begin laughing. Every time we think we calm down, we look at each other in the eyes, the mirth and exhaustion on our faces co-mingling, and begin laughing again.

At our laughter, the girl on the bed finally moves. Her arms stretch up and out, and she stretches her body, arcing her ribs and spine up and out as well. Brynn and I politely look away as her hair shifts around her naked body. How old is this girl? How did she end up in a shop of familiars? She sits up in one fluid movement and groans, before she opens her eyes and sees us, her entire body going still. Her pupils are slits as she observes us, gauging whether we are predators or not. I start to move towards her, but a slight hiss slides out from between her teeth, revealing two small fangs on each side of her mouth. I stop immediately and debate my options in my head. Most of them are not very good, and many of those options would bring about unwanted attention to our situation, perhaps even from my mother and father. Instead, I think talking to the girl and seeing what she says might be the easiest route.

Kneeling to the ground, I look at the girl and introduce myself gently.

"Hello, I'm Rhea. With me are Brynn and Faye. We will not harm you." Her posture relaxes slightly, her breathing regulating itself with each inhale. Faye clears her throat subtly from the doorway, a thoughtful way to announce her presence, before sitting next to me on the floor. She carries a large leather tome and opens it as she sits down, flipping between the pages in search of whatever information she needs. After a moment or two, she says "ah! here it is!" and begins reading aloud from the passage.

"It says here: *'The Grimalkin were a highly secretive feline species originating from Echosia. No one knows where the Grimalkin originally settled, as only remnants of their society have been found in archaeological digs sponsored by King Devlin and Queen Vyara. From what little they've left behind, we can infer that they were feline, with some sort of magical ability, and that a great tragedy caused them to flee from the Cobalt mountains where the first set of Grimalkin remains were uncovered. Where they fled to, and what happened to them, thereafter, is a mystery.'"* Faye finishes reading, lifting her head from the page, eyes searching for our approval. The mention of my mother and father's names courses through me, but I ignore the feeling, set on dealing with the issue at hand. The girl on the bed watches silently, her dark eyes wary, still sitting in a defensive position. She raises her round face slightly, sniffing the air with her cat-like nose.

Brynn speaks up before the silence grows terse. "You think this girl could be a grimalkin? I thought it was simply an old word?" She turns to stare accusingly at me, as if somehow this were my fault for merely mentioning the word before. I shrug at her.

"What is it you'd like me to say? I do not believe in coincidences. Inya did say I would find something unexpected, though I do not believe I've heard of... a settlement of Grimalkin before." There, let that be enough on the matter. Brynn's suspicious stare burns through me, so I add, "I simply enjoy reading, is something so wrong with that?"

Faye looks between the two of us, concern shining in her ocean-like gaze. "Surely we have more pressing matters at the moment than as to how we got into this situation. I also do not believe in coincidences, so without a doubt this girl must be important." Faye shifts forward, onto her knees and palms, before extending one shimmering hand towards the girl on the bed. The girl looks at that hand for a long, long moment, before she sniffs and looks away. Faye seems easy-going, and far more accepting of anything that comes our way than I would have thought possible, especially now that she and Brynn seem to be growing closer. Brynn puts on a persona around most people, pretending to be outgoing and boisterous, but she's nearly as moody as I am.

"You bought me?" The girl says, her voice low and throaty, surprising all of us. She does not look at me, but somehow, I know she's speaking to me, the bond between us a fluid, flowing thing.

"Yes. I did." Blood rushes into my cheeks at my admission.

Mother moons above, what must she think of me? She turns to me then, a slow languid movement, no rush in it at all. She blinks at me slowly before saying, "Ah, yes, I remember you." She cocks her head at me, analyzing me through narrow eyes again and asks me, "are you worthy?" The intensity in her dark eyes paralyzes me, as if she can see right through me, as if she can see all that I am and all I will ever be.

"What?" I ask, shaking my head a little, confused by her questioning.

"Are you worthy of owning me?" Those wide dark eyes strip me of all pretenses, their solemnity louder than words. Am I *worthy? What kind of question is that?*

"Of course not!" I blurt out, the words popping out as soon as I think them. That terse silence, thick with tension and chaotic promise, fills the room once more. Brynn looks at me as if to say *are-you-out-of-your-mind?* Faye's expression darkens, but she looks inquisitively at me, like she is keen to figure out where I'm going with this. I chew on my cheek for a moment while I think before asking the girl if she has a name for herself. The girl's large dark eyes fill slightly with water as soon as I ask.

"Have you not given me a name?" She asks with a sniff of her delicate nose. She sits very prim and properly, with a stiff spine.

"I did give your, um... cat form? I apologize; I am unaware of the proper terminology. But the little you, we named Luna." My face flushes as I realize I probably sound nonsensical, and I watch for her reaction. Her nose and lips spasm, like she's holding back a smile, so maybe I didn't sound as odd as I felt.

"It is acceptable," she says. My eyebrows knit together as she does so, and I share a glance with Faye and Brynn. It's beginning to frustrate me a bit, their casual expectation of me to lead them through all things. If this is what it is like to be queen, then exhaustion shall be my new companion. The past few days have been overloaded with information, and I know not what to do with all of it. "No one's ever given me a name before. They simply called me 'the cat.'"

I swallow hard, ignoring the sudden stinging in my eyes. Living your whole life without a name, with no one who knows you, or cares for you... what a lonely existence she must have led.

"How old are you?" I ask Luna.

"Seven-and-twenty," she tells me, easily. A sigh of relief goes through Faye and Brynn. At least we haven't bought a grimalkin child. I know what needs to be done, however.

"Luna, I have no right to own you. You're not a pet. Is there anywhere we can take you? Anyone who may be searching for you?" Luna's face falls at my words, and she cast her eyes down towards the bed.

"I don't think there's anyone left... it has been years since I arrived on this island. Others have bought me. They were not as kind as the three of you have been," she smiles viciously at some memory, the points of her delicate teeth shining lightly as she does.

Brynn walks over and sits on the bed, on the edge so she doesn't startle Luna. "You mean, you don't have any family?" Brynn asks, concern and sadness shining in her eyes. For someone like Brynn, who grew up surrounded by family and adored by them, being alone is the worst kind of pain imaginable. At least in death there are no worries. My thoughts drift away to Sivan, grief stabbing me in the heart.

"Not anymore," Luna answers and lets out a little yawn, "Except for you, the one to whom I am bound." She thuds back on the bed lightly, her hair covering her body again. Well, I don't see any reason we must act this evening. Faye pulls a chain by the door that alerts the front desk we need their help, and one of Coralie's employees rushes in to help us. We explain to the fairy our need for clothing and additional food, and he heads off to fill our request, not even blinking an eye at our new guest count. I had almost forgotten anyone could be a spy in these halls; the fairies are too good at their jobs, slipping in and out before we even know they were there.

The same fairy returns within fifteen minutes, with a set of soft-looking golden clothing, and some fresh seafood from the kitchen. Luna puts the clothing on, surprised to see the fairy made sure to find clothing with space for her tail in it. I watch her observe her appearance in the half mirror over the dresser and groan in frustration over the tangles in her long hair. As I watch, her aura begins to glow before me, unlike any other I've seen. Strange purple and gold marks swirl around her, whispering and interacting with one another almost as if they are sentient. From the mirror, she catches my eye and shakes her head slightly. A plea, not to question it. She can tell that I can see her aura, yet she wants me not to mention it to the others. I dip my chin at her in acknowledgment.

"Can I braid your hair?" I ask her, coming up and standing behind her, raising my hands in askance. She nods. The two of us shall get along easily, whether that's the bond or just our personalities though... time will tell. I often sit in silence for hours, especially now that Sivan is gone. Maybe she will be content with that. Or maybe she will want to leave as well. I'm not sure, but it won't hurt to be nice to her in the meantime. I ask her to sit on the floor, and I sit behind her, carefully plaiting her hair in two, thick sections. Her smile grows wider and wider, as she watches my fingers transform her hair from a pile of knots into the simple, but efficient braids I place it into. Her memories wash over me before I realize what's happening-- the bond between us must amplify the effects of my magic as well-- and I find myself inside a young Luna's memories.

Mama looks pretty in her wedding gown, a dress of cobalt blue with white accents like stars on the skirt. It's got a corseted top. I stared at it so long that Mama promised me I could have it when I get married. It's been a long time since I've seen her look this happy-- when papa died, I think she wanted to go with him. But she didn't and now. here she is! Marrying for the second time in her life, finding love for the second time in her life. It's so romantic, almost like a story book! Mama braids my big sister's hair, and then she will braid mine, two matching coronets on the tops of our head, complicated braids perfected for centuries and passed from mother to daughter. Mama will teach me one day, and then I will teach my daughter, and so on for centuries. A chill on the wind makes its way through the bridal tent, where all the women in our litter gather, readying themselves for the ceremony. Meows and mewls result as of the sudden cold, but a chill cuts down my spine. I find myself looking away from Mama, away from big sister, and then suddenly-- the screams ring out from outside.

Luna's memory cuts off abruptly. Her eyes are closed, as if warding against the bad memory, and her petite chest rises and falls unnaturally quickly. Her long tail twitches uncontrollably. I debate what I should do for a moment, but before I can do anything, Luna opens her eyes and thanks me, in a small voice. The pain is clear on her face, but the love is clear there too. She turns to face me, eyes watery.

"What happened?" I ask, the horror in my voice apparent. Luna's fangs press lightly into her bottom lip while she thinks, before slowly responding.

"The Shadow Queen. She... unleashed something on my people. Something too horrible to speak of." The fear in Luna's eyes washes away all the happiness there only a few minutes ago. She and I are alike, in that we have both experienced something no one should ever have to go through. Maybe she will tell me about it when she gets more comfortable with me.

I nod slowly, like I understand, but far from it. If no one else has heard of the Grimalkin in years, and they've supposedly gone away somewhere, how did Rhiannon pull this off? And for what purpose? I don't see a single thing she has to gain by destroying an entire species. Certainly, it's not for sport. There will be plenty of time to worry about it all later, however, as right now Luna needs a distraction from the grip of her painful past.

"Would you like to know a secret?" I ask her. She nods, eyes locked on mine, her chest still heaving erratically with each of her shallow breaths.

"I am the next shadow queen," I whisper to her and her eyes go wide, "And if you stay, then you are officially apart of my court. I will give you the choice whether you wish to travel with us or not. If not, I am sure the fairies would welcome you, or we can take you wherever you wish." The fairies protect many endangered species, from a wide variety of planets and planes and times, in their home realm.

I'm still determining exactly how many people to let into this court of mine, as well as how many people to tell of it. Brynn of course, but Faye certainly seems to have motives of her own, that are indiscernible at present. Sure, she seems happy and brilliant, but she's far too intelligent for her to be as silly as she's been pretending. She needs something, I just don't know what yet. Brynn and I have yet to even discuss what she found in her research as we were too absorbed into the drama with Luna. We should discuss how much we want to tell Faye as well. She could be useful in teaching me more about ruling. My parents taught me much before I left Darrid, but it's been almost an entire year since any of my lessons.

Then there's Sebastien, whom I had nearly forgotten about in the aftermath of the cat turning into a woman. The others would want to hear about our encounter, but I have had enough weirdness for one day, so it can wait until the morning.

"It's gotten quite late, and no one needs to be making rash

decisions at this hour, so let's all reconvene in the morning. We can go to breakfast and discuss our plans for the day then." In other words, please get out of my room so I can get some semblance of sleep. Faye is the first to move, rising to her feet in one quick movement. She grabs Brynn's hand easily, and they say goodnight as they walk into their room, shutting the door behind them. Brynn and I will definitely be having a conversation about that in the morning. With the two of them gone, Luna and I find ourselves alone. She tugs her feet underneath her, tucking her tail in neatly alongside them. She opens her mouth a few times as if to speak, but shuts it each time, whatever words apparently dying on her tongue.

It's only when I turn away that she speaks, the words soft and low.

"If I stay with you, will you promise me something?" Soft, dangerous words, depending on what she wants.

"If it's within my reach to do so, then yes." Luna smiles a genuine smile then.

"You're smarter than you look," she says with a flick of her eyes in my direction. She's cunning, but I should expect no less from a woman who survived the massacre of her people and then survived years in hiding in our country. She presses her lips into a thin line and then asks me, "If I stay with you, will you avenge my people? And help me find whatever remnants of them there may be?" Her face hardens at the end of her question, a mixture of anger and sadness warring on it. I tell her I will become the queen of death, and she asks me for such a small favor? And one I'm already planning on accomplishing as is. I recognize the favor for what it is-- a plea for help, a yearning for connection. It must be tiring, running away year after year, being enslaved to unkind fae males.

"Tell me one thing first: did you really slaughter all of those men?"

An altogether feline grin crosses her face, those sharp fangs once again peeking out. The look washes away everything else, and I know the answer before she tells me.

"They wanted things that were not theirs to take. I ended them for it." A memory tugs at me, one bathed in blood and fear, but not her own. I ignore it, willing away the magic in my veins so that I can stay in the here and now. Black spots tinge my vision with the effort, but slowly the magic recedes. The magic demands use, but the part of me that loved my magic died with my husband. Hearing her own pain makes me decide that I will wait for her to share those memories with me, rather than peeking in on them without permission. Especially considering her odd aura.

"Then yes, I promise to avenge your family and find your people. In exchange, I want you to teach me all those skills you used to kill those men." She laughs at that but stops when she sees my face.

"You're serious? You want me to teach a death queen how to kill?" She looks doubtful.

"I should like to stay alive if I am to take the throne. I have not trained in years, and you've certainly picked up the skills not only to kill what I assume were men much larger than you, given your small stature, but also stay alive in the years since your city fell. A smart queen knows when to ask for help. So, I am asking for your help. Will you be a part of my court? And teach me other ways to be lethal?"

Her answer reverberates down the bond, but she confirms it out loud anyways. Luna still looks miffed, but perhaps this is a new pathway forward together. Exhaustion slams into me, now that the current situation has been dealt with. There are still so many things to do, but they will have to wait until the morning. Luna opens her mouth as if to speak again, but I wave her off. By the time my head hits the pillow, I'm already asleep.

CHAPTER ELEVEN

THE next morning, Brynn wakes Luna and me up for breakfast, ignoring our groans and complaints. I throw my pillow at her and she catches it, chuckling slightly. Cracking my eyes open, I'm pleasantly surprised to find the bedchamber swathed in the same warm lighting as the night before. Luna is curled delicately against my side, her breathing even and peaceful, her two dark braids still intact. Relief rushes through me at yet another small sign of trust. A small smile tugs at my lips, and I give in to the urge. The grief from Sivan's passing still holds my heart in its grip, but the past few days of traveling have been joyous at least. A dark spot on Brynn's neck stands out even on her brown skin, and I know hers has been joyous as well.

"Looks like someone enjoyed their evening," I tease her as I burrow even further into the soft blankets.

Brynn blushes, surprise lighting up her eyes, but shrugs, "I did, a lot."

All I can do is smile in return. She deserves happiness in whatever form behooves her.

Brynn clears her throat and uses her best authoritative voice. "Alright, get up!" she practically yells as she begins pushing me, trying to get me out of my cocoon.

A sigh escapes me at the thought of leaving the warm bed, but after another five minutes of endless complaining, I finally drag myself from the soft, warm blankets. Luna cracks one eye open then rouses without any input from Brynn or I, stretching her spine out in one big arc, then turns to stare at us.

"I'm ready," Luna purrs as she sits up and begins licking her claws.

Faye glides through the adjoining door not a moment later. Today, her red hair is piled high on her head in an artfully messy arrangement that would make me look unkempt. She's wearing the same style of loose flowing pants and a top that bares her mid-drift, but in a deep cobalt color that shimmers iridescently, similarly to the shimmer on her skin. She offers Luna and I a morning greeting, before smiling shyly at Brynn and looking away.

"How did everybody sleep?" I ask, while changing into a fresh set of my own clothing. My mind wanders to that gray bastard from last night. I wonder if he will like the red top and skirt I've chosen today. I know it will highlight the redness of my lips and the darkness of my hair. The thought stops me cold like a bucket of water. Why does it matter what Sebastien likes? This mating bond shouldn't even exist. Blood rushes into my cheeks at the thought, enough that Brynn raises her eyebrows at me questioningly. Might as well have this conversation now. If I put this off until we head down for breakfast, then the others might think I'm hiding things from them.

"Before we head out to breakfast, there's something you should know." As I turn to face the three of them, I note Brynn's expression especially. She might think I'm replacing her brother if I handle this poorly, but my love for him will never be replaced. I don't even

133

know if I accept this mating bond. Not even if Rhiannon throws a hundred soul bonded mates at me. The thought tickles something in my memory, but Faye, Brynn and Luna are waiting for me to speak, the weight of their eyes weighing me down.

"Last night, when I went to bathe, I ended up at the tavern. The reasons why are unimportant, but while I was there, I met someone." Brynn's eyes widen and her brow furrows as she tries to work out the connotations of what I am saying. Luna seems uninterested, or maybe she's already aware of what I know through our own bond. Can she feel Sebastien's bond with me as well? Faye raises one eyebrow, peering down her nose at me. Impressive feat for one so small. Taking a deep breath, I let the words wash over me as readily as my grief.

"This gray bastard pulled a knife on me and was going to either torture me or kill me. Maybe both. He was sent by Rhiannon, but then... the mating bond slipped into place." Again, that little doubtful voice in my head tells me to look, to see past the veil, but I ignore it.

At that, I take in Brynn's expression. Her expression has soured a bit, the shock and confusion turning into something resembling contempt, or disgust maybe. It's hard to tell with Brynn, but she's certainly not pleased. Despite my reservations about Luna's aura, I call on my power to see Brynn's. Grief, pain, disappointment on the surface... but underneath it all, a hint of worry and relief. Memories of Sivan swim underneath her aura, each of them too painful for me to watch.

Faye says nothing, merely observing Brynn with one shimmering hand placed over Brynn's arm. A comforting touch in her time of need. Jealousy pangs through me, almost as fearsome as the grief, but I squash it down. The action takes nearly as much effort as calming my dark magic does, but down it goes. I calm myself, taking another deep breath. I'm doing a lot of deep breathing these days. Sivan used to remind me to breathe when my worries became too troublesome to bear, and now his voice guides me in my mind.

Brynn twists her lips, contorting her face oddly for a moment, but then she gives an odd grin and says, "Alright, when do we meet this soul mate of yours? He better have balls the size of the Cobalt mountains if he's going to be stuck with our family for the rest of his life." I nearly burst into tears at her words. My throat grows uncomfortably tight. She so casually accepts the appearance of another male in my life, after the epic love I had for her brother.

"Hopefully not soon," I say, looking to Faye.

Faye seems to make up her mind based on Brynn's.

"I'm here to help however I can. Making judgments of the future queen wouldn't be very good for me now, would it?" Faye says. Her tone gives nothing away. It could be a joke, or she could simply have her own interests in mind. Only time will tell.

Luna's stomach audibly growls then, and we all share a chuckle before exiting the room and portaling to the breakfast hall, which is really just the tavern in the daylight. Patrons mill about the room, and my eyes search frantically, searching for his face amongst the many. A sudden anxiety pops up that maybe he left, reporting back to Rhiannon.

Or maybe he decided that he'd rather not be a pawn in these games between two death queens. He said he worked for Rhiannon, he never said he enjoyed doing so. My heart hums in my chest when I hear a short, curt greeting uttered behind me. I whirl around and find Sebastien standing in the room.

"Good morning asshole," I practically growl at the sight of him. Half of me is pissed off, the other half.... Well, I won't even attempt to name the bubbly feeling growing in my chest.

He smiles in return, as if my greeting were honey pouring from my lips.

"Good morning, little raven," he says, voice low and sensual. His friendly demeanor takes me by surprise. I can't even think of a response.

Seeing that he has stunned me into silence, he turns, introducing himself to first Brynn, then Faye, then Luna. When he gets to Luna, he takes her delicate hands between his own and offers her a formal gesture of greeting. My eyes narrow. Is he doing that because he can feel my bond with her?

"Well met, ancient one." Sebastien says to Luna, his voice raspier this morning than it was last night. I'd hardly call her ancient, at twenty-seven, but I have no idea how old Sebastien is. What must those dark eyes have seen over the years? It is entirely possible Sebastien encountered the Grimalkin before they disappeared.

Faye chuckles nervously. "Milady," she begins turning to me, "You never mentioned this man of yours was a daemon." Her glare turns slightly accusing, but part of the reason I did not tell her was because of this reaction. Not much is known about the daemon species, other than they originate from the Under-Realm and that fae parents warn their children of them in fairy tales.

In response, Sebastien bows a horned head in Faye's direction, a toothy grin pasted across his grey face. His hair is slightly damp, as if he visited the bathing chambers before he arrived here. His clothes are fresh, and in the modern loose style of the island, though the colors are too dark for a day in the sun. His nails are trimmed and clean. I only notice because his clean-cut image is at odds with the gritty demon I met in the tavern just last evening.

"It's not exactly first date conversation," Sebastien responds jovially, casually. The whole group turns and stares at me at his words, a slight shock running through each of my companions. Sebastien notices, of course, and his expression falls immensely.

"Date?" Brynn spits out, her face equal parts enraged and confused. Faye wisely says nothing, deferring to Brynn. Luna steps closer to Faye, pressing against the fairy as if sensing a brewing storm. A deep sigh escapes me as I think of where to begin, but Sebastien saves me from explaining.

"I apologize ladies. Date would be a stretch of the term. Your queen and I met here last evening, and I decided to see if she would return for breakfast."

"Cease speaking. This instance," I implore Sebastien and then turn to Brynn, "You see? He's practically stalking me at this point." Faye, sensing the tension in the room, steps in and prevents any more animosity by asking Sebastien if he's hungry. When he confirms that yes, he is indeed hungry, she leads the group of us to a small table in the corner of the room. We each take a turn in the small buffet line and return with plates piled high with the overindulgent pastries the fairies are so fond of and several questionable-looking breakfast meats. A mostly comfortable silence stretches over us while we eat. Maybe this is why I always look forward to mealtimes-- little expectation of conversation. Meals bring the fae together. Once we've had our fill though, it's time to discuss our plans.

"Now that you can't kill me, what are you going to do?" I ask Sebastien while playing with a hand towel, keeping my hands busy while awaiting his response.

"I am sworn to my queen," he says, staring into my eyes for a long moment, "What can I do?" I cock my head to the side in one fluid movement, capturing him in my own predatory gaze.

"What of your future queen?" The question slices the air between us. He brings out a bit of that darkness in me. My shadows shiver around me in excitement.

Sebastien debates my words for a moment.

"What would you do as queen?" His question is weighted, and my powers stir in response, soft shadows creeping over my skin and reaching out towards his imperceptible aura. An ancient chill descends from Sebastien, echoes of powers emanating from him. The shadows pause before him, unsure, and he glares down at them. I snap the shadows back to my skin.

Faye and Luna appear unruffled, watching the two of us with merriment in their eyes. Brynn, however, seems interested in my response. A few days ago, she chastised me for not taking my responsibilities seriously. Maybe she's testing me or maybe she simply wants to know the answer herself. Whatever the case maybe, I find myself considering his words for a long moment. What would I do as queen? I haven't truly taken a second and thought past my plans for revenge. During our ride to Nisaba, there were long stretches where Brynn and I spoke not a single word to one another. We rode swiftly enough that the wind ripped away any chance of words, lest we slow down and lose precious time on our journey. Instead, my imagination gorged itself on various images of Rhiannon as I delivered her death blow. Eventually, the blood thirst receded, and I was left feeling empty. Again.

I had not spared a moment's thought of what ruling the Under Realm would actually entail. What type of people live there? Are there people or only the daemon? The land of shadows and death, of time unyielding.

"Honestly? I am unsure. I've never been to the Under Realm, and what little I know of it has been watered down by my lack of studying." A slow smile breaks out over Sebastien's face, like my non-answer was somehow a perfect answer.

"Why are you looking at me like that?" I ask him, confusion surely dotting my features. The expressions on his face change ever so slightly and with the light hitting his face in that way.... That insurmountable grief again courses through me. For just a moment, he looked just like Sivan. Are the stars playing a cruel joke on me? A light shake of my head clears the painful thoughts. Besides, Sebastien and Sivan are nothing alike. Sivan's skin was a rich golden brown; Sebastien's skin is impossibly grey. It's silly of me to compare the two.

"I have been alive for a very, very long time little one. For most of that time, I have lived under Rhiannon's rule. I have seen her admonish advisors for the smallest of infractions. I have seen her flay the flesh from daemons for the mere crime of questioning her. But I have most certainly never heard her admit to not knowing something." An understanding shine breaks through his dark gaze. I know what I want to do now, but Brynn's opinion is of the highest importance to me.

"Sebastien, would you mind stepping away for a moment?" I ask him bluntly. His eyes dart to the side, the most surprise he'll show, but he stands up, bows slightly to the rest of us before striding across the room on his long, long legs. Not that I was watching. Faye watches the daemon's backside unabashedly, while Brynn watches Faye with an annoyed look on her face. Luna heads off on her third trip to the buffet line, blissfully unaware of our impending conversation.

"Well?" I ask Brynn and Faye lowly, glancing over to where Sebastien stands. Brynn cracks her knuckles absentmindedly, her face pinching up the way it usually does when she's mulling something over. Faye bounces her knee impatiently. The effect is nearly comical.

"Brynn, the man is hot. Dangerous. Old as the Under Realm. And he's mated to our queen." I try not to look surprised at her casual use of the term "our queen" though I admit her quick loyalty surprises me. My lip catches between my teeth at the force of holding back from speaking. Putting my opinions on my friends is the last thing I want to do. Faye continues, "He could be an extraordinary ally in the challenges lying ahead." Brynn nods her head a few times, her brown eyes like honey in the light.

"I agree he *might* be a useful ally, but that does not mean we should fully trust him yet. He is still sworn to our enemy; we've yet to understand his true motives. I'll trust each of you know not all soul bonded mates treat each other honorably. There are still many unknowns. But, if he is willing to help us with a few things, then I think we can trust him well enough for now." Wise words, but I expect nothing less from my closest friend turned advisor.

"What do you want his help for? And what if he wants something in return, or refuses to give us the information we need?" I ask, intrigued. Brynn shifts forward in her chair, the beads in her hair clacking together gently.

"If he's really that old, and dangerous, then maybe he will train you to be more adept at combat. I know your dagger is usually enough, but it will not be in the days to come. He was sent to kill you, and when he does not return, I am betting that the bitch queen will send more of his kind after you. How many warriors might she have at her disposal? She has kept a tight leash on much of the information coming from even your shadows. He can give us that information, and much more." Her analytical look turns nearly pleading, sad.

"I am not asking you to love him. I know that even with a soul bond, you are not past the grief of Sivan. But we will avenge him." She pauses, letting her words sink in for a moment, "We will. I have not a single doubt. You will heal, eventually, and maybe Sebastien will be a part of that healing. In whatever form you allow him to be." My head begins to ache as she finishes her sentence. Too much information all at once. And here I thought I would be the one convincing her that Sebastien would be beneficial. I should give Brynn more credit in the future; after all, she's always supported me before. Brynn smiles, her freckles stretching across her face like stars in the sky, and I smile gently at her in return. A smile is worth a thousand words.

Faye cuts in. "Something's wrong. Look." She says, jerking her head in the direction Sebastien trailed off to. He stalks toward us, worry etched into his stony features.

"Apologies, ladies, but it appears the fairies may have sold information to the queen about your party. And they let it slip that my allegiances may be in question." He looks nearly apologetic, as if the thought of putting us in danger pains him. How quickly things change. The shadows on my skin link themselves even tighter together. They have been acting weird since we got here, but now they're gone silent as if with fear. What do the shadows have to fear?

"Faye," I say turning to address her, "What's the easiest way out of here?" She picks at the skin around her fingernails, examining them while she thinks.

"Our group is too large for your dust. I think it best if we split up and rendezvous later. You, Luna, and Sebastien make your way to the front entrance. Brynn and I can sneak out the back and meet up with the rest of you at the beach." Worry shines in her ocean eyes, and I start to protest but she waves me off.

"Brynn and I can take care of ourselves. We do not have the time to argue about this, and your role in this is far greater than you realize." She looks at me, expectation filling her gaze and filling me with unease. Suddenly, I get the feeling that I've been left in the dark about a few things.

Sebastien steps in front of me. "We need to leave. Now. If we're going to do this, we need to do it now." He shares a look with Brynn, and she narrows her eyes at him.

"If anything happens to Rhea.... you will answer for it with a price far greater than your life." The intensity in her voice does not surprise me. She's always been loyal, unyielding when it comes to protecting her family. While she has great magical prowess, it was always expected that Sivan would lead his people when Addie passes. The question of inheritance is now up in the air, but Brynn was trained as a guardian, with the expectation that she would guard her families' secrets and treasures with her life.

I step past Sebastien, briefly squeezing Brynn's hands between my own.

"Be careful, sister." I urge and then step away. Faye brought her bag with her to breakfast, and she pulls out two cloaks from within it. She and Brynn don them, then turn away and exit the room. Luna's tail twitches back and forth as she watches them leave, the expression in her wide eyes unreadable. Sebastien casually slips his hand into mine, then the other into Luna's. He murmurs a few words under his breath and at my questioning look, he explains he's placing a glamour charm over us.

"See there, by the door?" He asks me so quietly I have to strain my head up towards him to hear. I nod imperceptibly, my face a calm mask of tranquility. The shadows have gone still again, like they did when Sebastien was intent on killing me yesterday, before the bond snapped into place. By the door, what can only be described as a warrior strides into the room. Another daemon man, this one impossibly pale as if he was created and carved from ice, much like the crown upon his brow. His hair rests in odd blue spikes on his head. He wears clothing of all white, and fur that must be uncomfortably warm in the tropical air. The only weapon on the man that I can see is a bow on his back, white and glittering in the soft light.

Sebastien whispers again, bending down and pressing his lips directly against the shell of my ear. "Victorum." Fear takes hold of my heart just then. Sebastien looks uncomfortable as well. However, none of the patrons milling about the room seem to take notice of the man. His odd looks and imposing demeanor are impossible to miss, so either he's using magic to hide like we are, or the fairies themselves helped him find his way here, like Sebastien suggested.

Luna grips my hand tightly, her nails digging into my skin. The pain does not bother me, in fact it helps me focus, helps me remember all that I have to lose. If I stop at this first obstacle, this first sign of danger, then I will never accomplish my goal. Megara's sanctum is but a few miles from here. All we have to do is make it to the front entrance. I look up at Sebastien, and he looks down at me.

We nod at each other, then slowly, inch by inch we make our way across the room. We do not speak as we make our way, instead tracking Victorum's movements around the room and communicating using our eyes. We're nearly at the threshold when Victorum ceases moving, his nostrils flaring wide. Sebastien's eyes go wide and a primal chill stalks down my spine.

"My scent." His voice grows frantic, urgency lacing every word. The mingling of our scents, an unholy bond, hangs in the air like a noose. Victorum's head swivels, eyes scanning the room with predatory precision. When they lock onto us, we maintain our glamour, feigning casual conversation, but my heart races. I look away from him, into Sebastien's eyes.

Victorum's grin spreads, lips peeling back to reveal razor-sharp teeth. I realize my mistake too late. He angles his body toward us, lethal intent shimmering in those crystalline depths. "Run!" I shout, shoving Luna into motion. She bolts, a sleek shadow darting from the room, and I grab Sebastien's arm.

"Go!" I yell, and we sprint after her, but the tavern erupts into chaos. Shadows whirl around me, violent and frenzied, as I summon them like a dark siren's call. Dishes and patrons collide in a frenzied scramble, but there's no time to look back. I can feel Victorum's gaze searing into our backs, his presence a suffocating weight.

We weave through the throng of fairies, dodging tables and the remnants of the breakfast buffet flying in every direction. A hefty dwarf yelps as I shove him aside, and I can hear Sebastien's heavy breaths beside me, the fatigue evident in every stride.

"Faster!" he rasps, glancing back. I dare a look over my shoulder and see Victorum closing in, his movements fluid and predatory, clearing a path through the chaos as if it were nothing.

I pull Sebastien into a side corridor, the narrow space offering momentary respite. "We can't stop! We need to—" But before I finish, the sound of shattering glass echoes behind us. Victorum is relentless, and the sound spurs us on. Sebastien grabs my hand and pulls me along faster.

We burst out the other side of the corridor, back into the main hall, but it's packed with scrambling patrons. Panic surges through me as I spot a staircase ahead. "Up!" I shout, and we surge toward it, pushing past the crowd, adrenaline coursing through our veins.

As we ascend, I can feel the ground tremble with the force of his pursuit. The shadows around me churn, ready to be called upon. I glance back once more, and Victorum is right there, his icy eyes fixed on us, lips curled in a chilling smile.

"Whatever you're going to do, do it now!" Sebastien urges. I fumble for the traveling dust Inya gave me, my fingers trembling as I retrieve it. We reach the top landing, but there's nowhere to go.

Victorum is almost upon us, his hand reaching out, desperate. "Now!" Sebastien roars.

With a final breath, I unleash the dust in a brilliant puff of green smoke. The world warps and blurs around us, the chaos fading into echoes as we scatter between realms, leaving the tavern and its horrors behind.

CHAPTER TWELVE

MY insides twist violently this time as we are transported, which I attribute to the lack of clarity in my thoughts. All I could think of when I threw the dust down was getting away from Victorum, finding Brynn, Faye, and Luna, and not dying. Maybe not in that precise order.

The dust spits us out angrily onto a beach, the two of us thrashing together in a tangle of limbs and sand. My head spins as my body tries to make sense of its surroundings. My hands are pressed into Sebastien's hard lined chest, the top of my head nestled into the base of his throat. When I open my eyes, the world is still spinning so I shut them tightly while I wait for the effects to subside. A roaring sound drones on in my ears, then dulls. The spinning ceases and I open my eyes to find Sebastien staring up at me. I hadn't taken notice of our positioning with all the spinning. Indeed, I landed directly on top of him.

He says nothing while I untangle myself from his body. He simply lies there, neither helping nor preventing me from doing so. Despite his demeanor, my cheeks burn. My eyes fall to the sand, no longer feeling confident enough to make eye contact. Pristine white sand greets my view and my heart falters.

"What is it?" Sebastien asks, his tone indiscernible. He stands and dusts off his leathers, as if he can sense my emotions without even needing to see me. My emotions bounce back and forth, and I can only assume it's due to the bond. Or maybe it's the constant change in my life lately.

"The sand. It's white. The sand on the island is black." I run my hands through my hair as my worries build inside me. Worry and frustration. Anger lances through me white and hot, and I kick the sand in frustration, sending a slew of white scattering on the wind. Sebastien raises his eyebrows at me, as if questioning my actions.

"Little raven, the sand on the south side of the island is black. The sand on the north-side is white." He says it calmly, as if to soothe my anger. I turn away from him so he can't see me rolling my eyes. This anger, this annoyance, isn't fair to him. It has nothing to do with him, and everything has to do with the constant ache in my soul. Each setback I encounter only further proves to me that I am not good enough, that I cannot accomplish my goals, and that trying to endure all the pain ahead will be worthless. The anger shifts into something dark and heavy. A heavy sigh escapes me as the weariness once again consumes me. My thoughts, negative and positive, all cease. My fingers rub at a knot in my neck. I need to focus.

"Don't call me your little raven. I'm not your little anything."

"Yet," he teases in return. I press my lips together to avoid smiling, though I want to.

"Are you trying to cheer me up, or is that an accident?" I ask.

"Why? Is it working?"

The audacity of this daemon.

"Not even a little," I say as I stare up into the sky, one hand shielding my eyes from the harsh sunlight.

The sun is centered in the sky indicating it's midday. The section of beach we landed on is a thinner strip than the other side of Amisra, with far sparser greenery. The tree line will provide little shade, and with the sun glaring down at us like an island goat, we'll dehydrate quickly. It frustrates me not having a plan.

"What did you come to this island for?" Sebastien asks me, pulling me out of my observations. I might as well tell him. He faces me, crossing his arms across his chest, the muscles underneath flexing with the movement. Not that I'm looking.

"I've come to seek an audience with Megara. Goddess Inya told me that Megara has a way to help with the struggles to come." I also summarize Inya's prophecy as quickly as I can, not wanting to linger on it any longer than necessary. Thinking back over it, the two souls' reference could have been referring to the mate bond. If we regroup with Brynn and Faye, Faye and I can start on some of that research we've been putting off.

Despite my quick summary, shock registers on Sebastien's face. His entire body goes still, as if danger is near. He opens his mouth and shuts it several times, whatever words dying on his tongue. Finally, he swallows hard before saying, "Victorum is one of the riders. The Four Death Riders of Rhiannon's court. Victorum, Bellum, Esuries, and Infernus." My eyes narrow at him as I process the information.

"You'd dare speak their true names?" I ask, but the words have no venom behind them.

"No, their true names are a carefully kept secret." His dark eyes pierce mine, almost as if willing me to understand. I know why. I suspected it the moment we saw Victorum enter that room.

My next question comes out as barely more than a whisper.

"Which one are you?" A ghost of a smile plays on his lips then, and appreciation flows down the bond between us. The feeling warms me in a surprisingly pleasant way.

"Inferus." My spine nearly threatens to buckle at the word, as if some ancient part of me recognizes the name. I ignore my fear; it may not be irrational, but it's certainly unhelpful.

"What do each of you... do for her?" I ask the question slowly, unsure of what the proper wording is or if he'll even be willing to tell me.

"We control the immortal plagues. We lead her majesties armies. Each of us has our own set of skills, utilized in a variety of ways. Whatever pleases her at the time." He says the words bitterly, as if he's not quite thrilled with that fact. Absorbing the information, I'm careful not to make any faces or movements that give away my thoughts. Bad enough that we can apparently feel each other's emotions. He's also not being very specific.

"Do those plagues include an illness that causes a person to waste away before your very eyes?" I ask, my voice nearly a whisper, shadows swirling violently up and down my arms.

Wariness flashes in his eyes, and he looks around for a moment as if wishing he could escape. But he doesn't. He again makes eye contact with me and nods his head. Palming one of my knives, I bite my lip hard, focusing myself, forcing myself not to cry. Tears and grief are wasted on my enemies. The only path forward is revenge. My spine stiffens, taller, stronger. None of the past matters if I am unsure where the future lies.

"And what happens when I become queen? Will the riders follow me then?"

"Yes, they are sworn to follow the queen, regardless of who she may be."

"What about you? Does your loyalty change so easily?" He laughs, as if my question is ridiculous in nature. The heat of the sun begins burning my face and I shift uncomfortably.

"Have I not shown that I am loyal to you already, by betraying one of my brothers? You are my soul bonded mate. I have dreamt of meeting you for a lifetime, though I did not expect you to be fae, or a queen. In the short time I have known you, you have shown yourself to be a loyal friend, a protector of those in her care, as well as being fairly kind to me, of all people." Sebastien closes the gap between us, blocking the sun from my skin and peering down at me.

"I have spent years watching Rhiannon destroy those around her, destroy the Under Realm bit by bit, and savor every moment of it. I thank the sun above that I am lucky enough to be mated to someone like you. I feel your grief, as if it were my own." Pain shines in his eyes, and I know his words are true. He tilts his head, his hair shifting around those gently curling horns, and my breath is drawn away by the sheer beauty of him. For a moment, my grief disappears. For a moment, I wonder where that touch of grief reflecting back at me from his eyes originates from.

Sebastien's voice becomes intimately low, though he remains still, and bends his head lower until our foreheads nearly touch. The world slows, centers to the two of us. The breeze shifts his hair around his horns, shadowing his gaze from my view.

"I have spent lifetimes waiting for you, my queen, and I will continue to wait until the moment you are ready." The confidence he voices, the belief he has in me... my eyes sting with the threat of tears. This man understands the depths of my grief and yet still believes I can come back from it. Maybe having a mate isn't the worst thing that could happen to me. I am a widow, after all. The suspicion still lingers among that scant swirling of desire.

"It's not that I want to insult you or hurt you in any way. But you'll forgive me if I find it extremely difficult to believe that you would fall in love with me so quickly. Bond or no bond. Certainly, we get a choice in the matter."

He nods at me, as if this is a possibility he has already considered; an answer he has already prepared, "I have lost everything because of Rhiannon. Then she shoves you in front of me as if you are a gift. And while I do cherish you due to the bond, yes, I agree there is a degree of choice."

He runs a hand through his dark hair but doesn't elaborate. He simply tilts a horn.

"You've brought us to the edge of Megara's Sanctum," he says casually and continues surveying. He points towards a grouping of odd-looking rocks. "See, there? Those are volcanic rocks. That's the beginning of the pathway up to the volcano." I nod, sweat beading down my back as the sun continues blazing overhead. It will only get hotter, as Megara lives in an active volcano, but there are more trees on the pathway from what I can see. Sebastien glances down at me.

"Are you ready to face her?" He asks. I lift a brow in his direction. I thought I was asking for her help, not "facing" her.

"Each of the goddesses have their own trials and reasonings for providing a gift or boon. Megara requires that you face her challenge," Sebastien explains further.

"How do you know all of this?" I ask him, confused.

"I have been alive for a very long time. I have met each of the goddesses personally, but the riders are not allowed to enter their sanctums without their express permission," he tells me while wiping the sweat off of his dark skin, "Let's continue this conversation while we walk. The sun here burns far hotter than the ones in the Under Realm."

It does help to know he's not invincible, and I smile at the two of us sharing a dislike of the heat. We begin walking up the pathway, and soon we notice more of those volcanic rocks acting as markers along the path. When I inquire about the length of the journey, he tells me "Half an hour at most, then we arrive at the gates," and refuses to elaborate further. At first, I pass the time by observing the various flora and fauna in the area. Delicate orange flowers float in the air, following an unseen current. The trees grow thicker as we walk, providing more shade, reminding me of his comment about the sun. I spot a purple lizard sunning itself on a large rock, but he skitters away when we get too close.

"What's the Under Realm like?" I ask him when I grow used to the beauty around us. I want to learn more about the place I am meant to rule.

"The sky there always looks as if a storm is about to break, and we have two suns instead of one. We have cities and towns and mountains and lakes just like here in the fae realm. But the shadows are everywhere there." Sebastien pauses and moves a tree branch off the path for us before he continues. I simply listen, content to let him do most of the speaking.

"Fear permeates the air, everywhere you go. Rhiannon has begun enforcing rules and laws so outdated, even the few people she allows in government do not remember them. Her fear of losing her crown has made her paranoid; she banished all but the riders from her sanctum. The priestesses had to build their own, adjacent to the palace, using magic. It exhausted them for months after." The picture he paints is a dark one, but what else can one expect from the realm of shadows and death?

Sebastien senses my apathy and tells me that the Under Realm was not always this way. "When I was a boy, we had another queen. Ravenna. She ruled with kindness and fairness, seeing the darkness as only one facet of our society. It was her view that death is not something to fear. We all come from the source, and we will all return to it. That is a thing to be celebrated and not mourned."

"That sounds a lot like what the dark fae believe," I admit to Sebastien.

"That makes sense, considering Ravenna was the first dark fae and the daughter of the first queen. The dark fae were born of daemon and the fae. Long ago, years before my family existed, the Under Realm was ruled by a dark and vicious king, King Madrid. It is said that he met his match in a beautiful fae woman, and the result of that union was Ravenna." I know a bit about Ravenna, enough to know she's an ancestor on my mother's side. But I thought she was the first to be blessed by a death goddess. I had no idea she was a death queen, and the daughter of the original one as well... I knew my family kept much from me in order to control my progression, but I had no idea their deceit went so deeply as to keep me ignorant about our history, our culture.

"Who was the woman?" I ask, wanting to know more about her. It doesn't matter now that my family didn't teach me-- Sebastien is willing to teach me, and so are Brynn and Faye. Together, we'll uncover more of the history that's been hidden.

"Unfortunately, the name of Ravenna's mother has been lost to history. We only recently began keeping physical records of citizens. The daemon used to pass on traditions and history via stories and spoken word." His eyes shutter a bit, as if the thought pains him. My hand reaches out towards him, as if to soothe him, but I halt it midair. I'm not quite ready to accept this relationship and touching him feels like a line I am not ready to cross.

I opt for another question to brush past the awkwardness burbling within me.

"Are there different types of daemons?" I ask as we enter a thicker copse of trees, still following those rocky markers.

"Yes," he says stepping over a large branch blocking part of the pathway. He offers a hand to me, as if to help me step over the branch, but I brush past his hand, giving him a polite smile as I do so. Sebastien looks unaffected by my decision, continuing on without hesitation.

"Like there are many kinds of faeries, daemon is just a catch-all term for the denizens of the Under Realm," he halts, "as much as I am enjoying giving you a history lesson, we've arrived." I stop short at his words, noting the large gates that have seemingly appeared out of thin air. The conversation did hold my interest, but surely, I would have noticed... these.

The gates are made of the same volcanic rock we've been seeing for the past several miles. Impossibly black, slick stone spirals into the air, twisting together into sharply glinting spikes at the top. Sebastien inspects the ground for a moment before picking up an errant pebble and tossing it at the gate. It hits the gate with a sizzling sound and inflames before our eyes, leaving nothing but ash in its wake.

"Wards-- to keep out any unwanted visitors." Sebastien explains.

"And are we unwanted visitors?" I ask bluntly.

"Have you ever met Megara before?" Sebastien turns to me, avoiding my question.

"No," I admit somewhat reluctantly.

"It's simple," he says in a way that makes me think the opposite, "You simply touch a hand to the gate, and it will decide if you are worthy."

I snort in response. Of course, it's so simple. All I have to do is touch the wall that just vaporized a rock. Sebastien gestures towards the gate, his dark eyes unreadable. I step forward, noting the holes forming in my boots. I'll need to replace this pair soon if we're to be traveling this often or find a craftsman to repair them with magic. Sivan used to do that for me, often times taking care of it before I even noticed my shoes needed tending. Sadness shoots through me at the thought, but I push it away. There will be time for grieving when I accomplish my goals.

There are two circular disks on each side of the gates, each appropriately palm sized, each bearing a sigil of a volcano. When I press my palm against one of the disks, I can feel the magic coating it. Ancient, oily magic. It feels similar to my own, yet far deeper and more powerful. The sensation crawls uncomfortably up my spine.

The air is pulled from me in one long arc as a melodic but cruel voice fills my head. This is death magic in its rawest form.

Well, well, well, hello little queen. What brings you to my mistresses' domain? Do you seek glory and fame? Do you crave power the likes of which you have never known? Tell us what secrets lie in your heart.

The strangest feeling overcomes me, as if using my magic in reverse. Power courses through me, flowing out and into the gates. The gates drink it all greedily, as memories echo around me. Memories of Sivan and our love, memories of my parents and horrible dark rooms, memories of late nights with Brynn. All the most minor and obscure details of my life, all sucked up and into the gates. Every horrible thought I've ever had, every kind one, is pulled from me. Just when I begin to worry about the amount being taken from me, the feeling slows and tapers.

You may enter.

My eyes meet Sebastien's, a bit worried, but he looks unconcerned. He smiles at me as if to reassure me and it's enough for me to relax a bit. The gates begin opening slowly, metal and stone grinding together in a cacophonous melody. They grind to a halt and Sebastien gestures for me to walk ahead of him.

We cross the thresh hold, that same oily magic sliding over us, and then we are out on the other side in a large courtyard. Large, gnarled trees with dark leaves in square planters line the courtyard all the way down, blocking out the sun above, casting the courtyard into shadows. Beyond it, the monstrous volcano Emberpeak looms, soft plumes of smoke spiraling out of it. Megara's Sanctum was carved into the volcano itself, and legends say that it is her power that prevents the sleeping giant from erupting once again. Megara saved the continent from an eruption hundreds of years ago, and her followers developed the surrounding island into an oceanic paradise. Her sanctum was built soon after and she has lived here for as long as anyone can remember.

We walk for a while along the stone pathway between the planters when I see dark red smears on the path ahead. I hold out a hand, signaling Sebastien to stop. I should have been more perceptive of the intense silence when we entered. The sanctum should be teeming with priestesses and visitors, just like Inya's. Even the hushed tones and quiet steps of the priestesses provided a comfortable sort of silence. The waterfalls roared continuously as well. In the absence of waterfalls, the volcano's soft smoke seems dangerously quiet.

Sebastien pulls me down with him into a crouch, his nostrils flaring, his pupils narrowing to slits.

"Do you smell that?" he whispers to me, directly along the shell of my ear. I lift my own nose to the air and the unmistakable tang of blood burns through my nose.

"Blood. A lot of it."

CHAPTER THIRTEEN

"WHERE'S your dagger?" Sebastien asks me, concern lacing that gravelly tone of his. I pull out my dagger, the slim handle slipping into my palm with ease. A familiar action, an old friend my dagger.

"How adept are you with it?" he asks me and raise a brow at him in return.

"I can take care of myself well enough with a dagger. Thank the goddesses that I chose to wear pants today," I jest, my attempt at humor getting lost in the seriousness of the situation. I lower my voice an octave, "I also have my shadows." They writhe around me, silent snakes waiting, protecting me.

Sebastien nods at me, his eyes lightening a bit.

"I apologize," he says, "This bond between us has me feeling a bit protective. Moon's Grace, I will control myself."

I bit my lip, holding back a soft smile. As odd as it sounds, he and I are a lot alike.

"Do you have a weapon?" I ask him. We're still halted in the middle of the courtyard, assessing our situation before moving forward, but the trees provide little in the way of cover. We need to start moving.

"I am a weapon," he jokes with a toothy grin, but reaches a fist out into the air and squeezes. Black and green smoke billows from his fist, warping in on itself until a sword appears. A really wicked looking sword. It's black from hilt to tip, the metal gleaming with a rainbow of color. Symbols I don't recognize line the mid-length blade. An interesting choice for a warrior.

"Beautiful, " I whisper appreciatively, "Now, can we get moving?" He inclines his head again, but glides in front of me.

I'll take point this time.

It only shocks me slightly to hear his low timber inside my mind. I've heard that mates can share their thoughts if so inclined. It never seemed useful to me before; Sivan and I were so in sync with each other, it was as if we could hear the other's thoughts anyways. I never envisioned I'd find myself in the middle of a blood bath with my mate, though. Lack of creativity on my part, I suppose.

I follow behind him as we slowly advance through the courtyard. The sunlight twists down through the branches, glinting off of something near one of the planter boxes ahead. I angle my head, unable to understand what I am seeing, when the pieces click into places and bile claws up my throat.

What is it?

Sebastien follows my gaze, to where a dark head of hair peaks out from behind the planter box, the suns above glinting off a metal circlet lying near the head. Sebastien and I share a look of concern, before getting closer. A slain priestess lies face down on the stone, an impossible amount of blood matted in her blonde hair. Tattoos line her arms, markings of her goddess, and her red and orange robes are stained dark with blood. The way she lies suggests she was running away, as does the blood smears along an intersecting pathway.

What was she running from?

I push the thought from my mind to Sebastien's, following that thread running from soul to soul. He shakes his head in return and responds, *"one of my brothers."*

Anger courses through me, replacing my disgust with burning hot rage. My shadows writhe around me, pulling more shadows from the area, feeding my powers.

Which one?

I practically throw the thought into his head, and he winces but moves closer to examine the priestess's body in more detail. He shakes his head, sadness plain on his granite skin.

"This looks like Bellum's handiwork. He's known for being... messy, " Sebastien says almost apologetically, "but then again, everything I know about my brothers comes from Rhiannon. She enjoys keeping us ignorant."

I kneel by the priestess and turn her body over with care. Her eyes are wide open, gaze milky and unseeing. A tear traces a pathway down my cheek, and I wipe it away quickly. I close her eyes with a gentle hand, intent on saying a prayer for her.

"May the embers embrace you; may the shadows guide you; may the eternal waters lead you home. From darkness we come, to darkness we'll go, but in this lifetime and the next, you are never alone. Walk into your ancestors' arms, friend, and know you are at peace." A breeze shifts through the courtyard, and the priestesses body begins glowing. At least for me it does. For a death queen with the ability to see souls.

Sebastien's eyes reveal nothing as he watches me in a curious manner.

"Can you see it?" I ask him. He purses his lips.

"Not really. Not the way you can."

Not really an answer.

The priestess' soul does not fight; she ascends from her body lightly. An aura of peace surrounds her, as if even in death she felt safe in her mistresses sanctum. The strength of this priestess's soul pulls me in, showing me her final memories.

My name was Egan, and I was Megara's most trusted High Priestess.

Her soul speaks to me, a sign of great power in her life. And then I am thrust into her memory.

"Egan, are you ready to break your fast?" another high priestess, Amalina, asked Egan earlier that morning. She had just finished her morning chores. All the priestesses did their share of chores, regardless of rank, in Megara's sanctum.

"Yes quite," Egan replied, her stomach growling in echo to her response. The two priestesses shared a laugh. Egan appreciated Amalina's laugh-- a hearty, robust laugh. One that made others want to share in the joy and laughter as well. Amalina was one of the oldest priestesses in the sanctum, the lines on her face a testament to her strength and wisdom. Megara was-- is -- a wonderful goddess to all in her sanctum.

A part of me sighs in relief at Egan's confirmation that Megara lives. For a goddess to die... it is a great and terrible tragedy. The ramifications would be like none our realm has ever seen before. Egan's soul pushes at me impatiently, eager to impart her memories on me so she can depart this realm. I envy her ease in death.

Bells began ringing from the east wing, heavy ancient warning bells used in war time to warn the others of an impending attack. Those bells had not been rung in centuries, and yet there it was in the early hours of the morning, an omen to all that danger had arrived.

Amalina's spine stiffened impossibly. She was always in perfect posture, but that stillness.... Amalina had the power of precognition. Whatever her brown eyes were seeing, it was enough to send fear coursing through Egan's veins. Amalina shook off her vision, gripped her fiery robes in one hand, and ushered Egan back into the closet where they had just stored their linens after finishing the laundry.

"Do not use a magelight or faelight. There is a darkness coming, something none of us could possibly hope to outrun. A rider of death, the war-monger, is coming. His minions have already breached the Northern and Eastern towers. I will run out of here in a moment, towards the western tower and you will run towards the Northern. It is imperative you make it to the courtyard. Do not run after me, do not look for any of your sisters. Can you do this for me, High Priestess Egan?" Amalina said in a hushed tone. All Egan could do was nod, sweat soaking her robes from the fear. Egan was young for a High Priestess. She'd never seen war before. Amalina looked at Egan one last time, before slipping out the door into the hallway. Egan's ears strained trying to hear in the silence. Every little sound made her skin crawl, but she stayed quiet. Finally, she felt the screams had quieted enough she could slip out unnoticed. Egan slid out the closet door, despite her better judgment. Egan didn't have powers. She was the only high priestess who joined the sanctum out of her own resolve, her own love of the goddess's deeds. For a long time, she felt she could not

offer anything in comparison to the other priestesses. What was she worth, against precognition or the ability to tender a fire without tools?

But, she was a worthy friend. She was a compassionate, kind woman who always lent an ear to anyone in need. She wasn't afraid of hard work or doing the things that went unappreciated by her friends and family. And she did not resent them for it. For through her sacrifice, she saw that other people were desperately trying to connect with one another. Trying and trying and sometimes failing but always trying. It was beautiful to watch. Egan's great power came from her ability to love, to forgive, to understand others through a smile or a kind gesture.

It did not save her life.

Egan was nearly to the courtyard when she felt his presence.

Bellum.

She felt the madness take over her. She dropped to the floor, writhing in pain, unable to conceal herself any longer. Then, he stepped out of the shadows. His armor was bulbous, pompous, gaudy. Large, rounded sheets of metal covered his arms and legs, highly impractical. His hair was blood-red and his smile moon white. She hated him immediately. Not for what he was doing to her, but for the condescending look on his face as he stalked over to her, placed one large foot over her leg and stomped. Hard. Milky white eyes watched hers with eagerness, as if he were ready to drink in her pain.

Blinding white pain arced through her, her teeth locking together in a macabre grin. Bellum smiled, his blood red lips pealing back to reveal those deadly teeth, like he would rip the throats of his enemies out if given the chance.

"Hello, weakling," Bellum chuckled at Egan. She refused to make a sound, refused to move a muscle. She would not give him the satisfaction. She could feel the bone sticking out of her lower leg, but she ignored it. She had burned herself on coals in Megara's inner sanctum more times than she could count. She could endure pain. She could endure this. Bellum's grin turned sour when he realized his prey refused to die a dishonorable death. A dangerous glint shone in his eyes as he took out a small dagger, the blade coated with a paralytic to enhance his victim's pain.

Egan's soul swore she had no powers, and yet her soul was impossibly perceptive in death. Egan is granting me a gift greater than any other: the gift of knowledge.

Egan knew she needed to get to Megara's inner sanctum, the secret entrance and phrase to enter known only to the high priestesses who would never give up that secret even if cost them their lives. As it had this very morning. Bellum drew closer, taunting Egan, but she ignored his taunts. Egan remembered Amalina's instructions in times like these. She waited as he drew nearer to the middle of the corridor, she was running down... Egan turned, pressing a button hidden in the side of a doorway, and sent a flurry of fire shooting towards Bellum. She needed only one moment's worth of distraction. The fire hit Bellum across the cheek, and he roared, falling backwards and holding his face in pain. Pride flared in her chest at being valuable, at doing something to fight back.

Egan turned and ran. She was in the courtyard, by the trees when she felt something lodge itself in her spine. The pain was a brief flare, and she was falling towards the ground. She felt him walk up behind her, but by the time he began cutting into her still warm flesh, her soul had already separated from her body.

Tear after tear runs down my face, a testament to Egan's sacrifice. Her soul stays silent until my tears dry.

"Thank you for bearing witness." Egan's souls says to me softly, before she dissipates into that gray yonder. The brevity of her sacrifice weighs on my chest but lightens with the knowledge that she is at peace. Sebastien gives my shoulder a light squeeze in a silent show of support before he lets his hand fall back to his side. When I turn to look at him, his face is solemn but tear-free.

"Egan showed me more than just her death. I know where Megara is," my voice slides softly from my mind to his. Each time I speak into his mind, I find it easier to do so, as if his mind is becoming familiar to me. Sebastien's voice returns down the bond only a moment later.

"I saw everything through the bond, but I did not see the goddess. How do you know where she is?"

"Because High Priestess Amalina knew I was coming and sent Egan here so that I would know the way. There is a hidden pathway into the volcano from this courtyard, that can only be revealed by those who know the answer to the doors riddle. Egan's soul showed it to me."

"But I did not se--" I cut Sebastien off mid-sentence with a raise of a brow. We finally rise from our crouched positions, seeing no immediate danger. The shadows rest calmly along my skin.

Out loud, I ask him, "Do you think me so green that I cannot control the flow of information from my powers to our bond?" Sebastien bites his lips as if yes, he really did believe that. I'm not sure exactly how old he is, but he certainly does not seem to know how to work well with others. He chooses changing the subject rather than forging ahead with that line of thought.

"Look, there-- "he says, pointing to a pool of blood a few feet away from Egan's body. Footprints lead from the blood pool, back the way they came. How much time has passed since Egan died? It cannot have been more than half-an-hour to an hour at most. Bellum is likely still around, and if he brought any helping hands to finish his task. Which is what exactly?

I turn to Sebastien, my brow furrowing in confusion.

"Why would Bellum attack Megara's sanctum? Doesn't this mean the bitch queen is basically declaring war on the other goddesses? What is her plan here?" I ask him as my arms fold over my chest. This whole situation feels wrong, like we're missing a bit of key information. Or maybe I am. How exactly did I end up separated from the only people I could trust on this damn island only to end up traversing the island with Rhiannon's top warrior?

Sebastien can see the wariness in my eyes, the mistrust. Something shutters in his eyes as he watches me close myself off.

"I do not agree with what she is doing here. This is wrong, all of it," he spits out, shaking his head. He closes the gap between us, looks down at me and locks eyes with me. "I understand your reasons for not trusting me. But I swear to you that I had no knowledge of Rhiannon's plans here. This is a tragedy. One I would have done anything to prevent. As it was, I nearly refused the mission to kill you for the same reasons. In the end, I weighed each choice carefully and decided that killing you to prevent a larger war would be something I am willing to do." Sebastien gestures to the carnage around us and lays a hand over his heart.

"I was wrong. I should have known she would stop at nothing to achieve her goals. Now, I am yours. Command me as you see fit so that I may redeem myself in your eyes." A heavy sigh escapes me, and I roll my eyes. He's being overly dramatic.

"You don't need to do all of... that," I say, unsure how to proceed, but willing to trust him. For now. What choice do I have when he's guaranteed not to hurt me, and the other rider is somewhere in this sanctum with us still? At least Brynn and the others are safely away from here. It's bad enough that I have witnessed these events; I do not wish my companions to suffer the same way. A thought keeps popping up in my mind, and I decide I cannot mull it over anymore without knowing the answer.

"How does she control the riders? What makes them completely loyal to her, so much so that the only thing stronger is a predestined bond?"

Sebastien tilts his head. The look on his face tells me he expected me to ask this eventually.

"I can only tell you what I know," he says, "which isn't much. There is a contract in place. One older than the goddesses, that allows her to use us anyway she sees fit."

"For how long?"

He sighs, a loud and exaggerated sound. "Well, that's part of the issue. None of us know and she refuses to tell us. Esuries is her favorite and even he doesn't know. Bellum and I have discussed it several times, and the both of us have come up with a few things in common from our experiences being... activated."

"And? What are they?"

"We lose our memories of the entire event. Our magic is spent after being activated and we need down time to recover, almost as if a magical exhaustion overtakes us. The lack of memories is what really bothers us, as it seems orchestrated."

He stares at me for a long moment. He does that a lot.

"Follow me," I say with a jerk of my head in the right direction. I don't wish to speak on this topic anymore. Not until I've thought it over.

Turning away from him, I trace the pathway I'd seen in Egan's memories in my mind. Then, I set off without bothering to see if Sebastien follows me. I can feel his presence behind me well enough anyways.

Each unfamiliar shadow sends fear racing through my veins, but I ignore it, and focus on counting the patterns in the stone pathway. Every few steps, a different image repeats: first, the sun, then, a flame, then a volcano. Recalling Egan's memories, I count the flames and volcanoes separately and ignore the suns entirely. Finally, after nearly fifteen minutes of following the pathway as it twists and winds through the menacing trees of the silent courtyard, we find ourselves in a short corridor, ending in a large, circular door.

My mouth opens to tell Sebastien the secret for gaining entrance into the inner sanctum when a low chuckle sounds behind us, sending a wave of fear through me. Sebastien and I whirl around together, eyes wide to see Bellum, gaudy armor and all, standing in the mouth of the corridor, blocking out any means of escape.

CHAPTER FOURTEEN

"HELLO, brother," Bellum intones dramatically, bowing at the waist in Sebastien's direction. At this distance, I can see the whites of his eyes and his irises... milky white like they were in Egan's memories. His skin is a softer shade of red, an uncomfortable pink like the humans with their sunburns. His armor is every bit the over decorated, jumbled mess Egan thought it to be but is coated in blood unlike in Egan's memory. It seems impractical to me, but what do I know of daemon war customs? The sword at his back drips blood down onto the floor, and it slowly pools on the floor as we take each other in.

"And you--" he says, pointing in my direction with a dagger filled hand, "Must be Rhea." That predatory gaze falls on me, and I get the feeling he's testing me.

"A pretty girl shows up, and you forget all about your brothers. You forget about your queen. All for this child?" Bellum raises a blood red brow, the challenge in his voice clear. Sebastien puts one foot in front of me, angling his body to cover mine.

"Rhea is my mate," he barks, "And the future queen of the Under-Realm." I look between the two daemon, unsure of where to place myself in all of this. Shadows coil on my skin, and I band them around my wrists in case I need to summon my power quickly.

Bellum observes us for a moment, before addressing me.

His voice sounds odd. Something's not right.

Sebastien's voice eases into my head. I don't need to respond to keep that in mind, so I just shift my chin ever so slightly.

"Are you so weak my brother must speak for you?" Another challenge laced question. Surely, he could kill me without all the foreplay. Or at least try to. If I am going to face my death, I'm not going to do so calmly. Sebastien's right about Bellum's voice. I don't know him like Sebastien does, but his voice has a sort of echo to it. He sounds scratchy and warbly at moments.

"No, I simply choose only to speak when I feel like it. Besides, a queen does not need to rely on words." My eyes scan over Bellum as we begin slowly circling each other.

Information, I need more information. My focusing orb is in my bag with Brynn and Faye. All I have is a dagger, my natural powers, and.... a vial of poison around my neck. I'd really like to save that for later. Bellum laughs, the sound like glass breaking, children crying, the world ending. A wince nearly forces itself at the sound, but I ignore it. If my parents taught me anything, it's to never show an enemy your weakness.

"You are not a queen. Not yet," he states. A contemplative look crosses his face. He raises his palms in the air and says, "look, I would like to make a bargain with you, potential queen. Help me out and I'll make it worth your while."

I scoff at his words, annoyance plain in the sound.

"What's the bargain?" I ask with a shake of my head, "I agree to do your bidding, and you agree not to murder me in cold blood?" Bellum shrugs, a smug grin on his pink face.

"I see why you like this one, brother," Bellum laughs again, "But, essentially, yes. That is the bargain. I need to get into the inner sanctum. You need to not die. I think it's a rather charitable deal on my part." My eyes practically roll themselves out of my head at that statement. Still, Bellum remains still, not moving to attack or anything shifty that I can see.

Sebastien tugs on the bond between us, and I open up my mind to hear him out.

Obviously, we're not doing that. But, we need to proceed carefully.

Can't we just kill him?

Sebastien's midnight laugh fills my head, and I feel a sense of appreciation flow down the bond.

"Speak out loud!" Bellum practically screams at the two of us, rushing forward a few feet as he does so. A quick temper, that one.

"I think not," I hum as I dart back.

His eyes are usually red.

Bellum's milky white eyes stare out at me as his skin turns a deeper shade of red.

"Tell me: does Rhiannon need you to do her dirty work? Is she so above the rest of us that she cannot dirty her hands with her misdeeds?"

Bellum growls, the sound unearthly as it echoes off the columns lining the hall. He begins sliding a weapon out from his back and stalks towards me, arcing his sword down in stiffy, jerking movements.

I jump back a few steps, then jump to the side as he slices my way again.

Darkness explodes around the room, silence swallows Bellum's scream. My shadows vibrate on my skin, telling me *to wait, to see.* When the light returns, Sebastien is gone from my side. He has one grey hand wrapped around Bellum's pink throat, his nails slicing slightly into that sickly looking skin. The casual, relaxed energy Sebastien had previously has been replaced with the darkness incarnate. Green shadows flow from within him, an unnatural energy whispering out. The darkness of the Under Realm. The fear I originally felt when Sebastien backed me against that wall in the tavern room... I wonder if that's what Bellum is feeling now.

"You will respect my queen."

A giddy sort of happiness blooms in my chest at Sebastien's passionate words, curling through me like ivy reaching for the sun. He stands before me, a living shadow wrapped in silver moonlight, his sword gleaming with the promise of violence. His stance is effortless, the kind only years of battle can forge—relaxed, yet coiled with lethal intent.

The air hums with the sharp, electric taste of magic, and Sebastien wears his fury like a crown. His voice, dark and edged like a dagger, rings through the clearing as he makes his threat. Not just a promise of death—no, it's deeper than that. It's devotion, sharp and unwavering. A claim, an oath spoken in blood and steel.

I should focus. Truly. This is neither the time nor place to be thinking about how utterly intoxicating it is to see Sebastien threaten to kill for me. But damn if it isn't tempting. I shove the thought aside—reluctantly—and tighten my grip on my own weapon.

Because while Sebastien may be willing to kill for me, I'm more than capable of finishing this myself.

Sebastien digs his nails into Bellum's throat, "Or else, I shall rip your throat out and feed it to you." Bellum struggles in Sebastien's grasp. I stay where I am. Sebastien seems to have this handled, and I doubt I could hold my own against a daemon death rider... yet.

Darkness explodes again, but this time the room erupts with those green shadows. The room lightens enough for me to see those shadows holding Bellum suspended in the air, as more shadows pour in and out of Bellum from every direction. His eyes, his mouth, his ears, all drowning in those sinister green shadows. After a moment, most of Bellum's armor has been stripped from his body, revealing simple leathers underneath. His sword flies out of the shadows, landing behind me with a loud clang.

"You'll find, brother," Sebastien growls, cold anger lacing his voice, "That you are outmatched, outclassed, and under trained to take on the leader of the riders, though I know your ambitions have always aimed high."

The color drains from Bellum's face as he is forced to his knees before Sebastien. And I didn't have to lift a finger. That was possibly the most attractive thing I've seen a man do since I watched Sivan carve furniture for the first time. Moons above, I'm no better than a blushing youngling.

Sebastien shackles Bellum with those thick green shadows that look like they would pair nicely with mine. Every so often, Bellum flexes, as if he's testing for weak points. Sebastien turns away from him, satisfied that Bellum is secure.

"I'd personally like to kill the bastard," Sebastien drawls, "But it also seems inhumane. Something isn't right about his eyes or his voice."

I parse through Sebastien's previous memories of Bellum. In every memory, Bellum's eyes are a deep ruby. He laughs gregariously and often, telling stories for his brothers with great whimsy. He's the one they could all go to for a quick laugh, the one who left them all feeling a bit better. Nothing like this rabid vampyr before us.

The thing that worries me the most are the gaps in Sebastien's memories. None of the memories feature Bellum's white eyes, and the ones that would.... Feel as if they are locked in shadows and magic.

I cross the few feet between Bellum and I slowly, deliberately, keeping my eyes on Bellum the entire time. Fear and failure color his aura with putrid colors. This man murdered Egan, but does he even remember it? I wonder how many others have died by his hand—by Sebastien's—and he doesn't even remember

"Why did the queen send you here? What could she possibly want from Megara that she is willing to kill her for it?" I ask Bellum as I stand in front of him, looking down upon him. Bellum struggles against the shadows before spitting out, "I cannot tell you."

"Tsk-tsk, that won't do." If he's unwilling, or unable, to help me then I will simply take the information I need from him.

"Sebastien, would you please draw your shadows back a bit? Just holding his wrists and ankles?" Sebastien nods and does as I ask. Sebastien watches with a curious look on his face. I understand-- I would want to see the powers of the queen I intend to pledge myself to as well.

"If you won't tell me why, then you can show me." I tell Bellum as I grip my hands on both sides of his head. With a thought, my shadows bathe us in darkness, before I force them into Bellum's head. Under my guidance, they search his memories, looking for when he was given the orders to come to the sanctum, but also for any blockages of memory that feel similar to Sebastien's. My head falls back but I remain standing, as my power courses through the two of us. The shadows whisper to me, *come look, come see,* and I plunge into Bellum's memory, but confusion nearly stops me when the first thing I see is my own face... no, a mirror image of my face. Rhiannon.

Rhiannon was laid back on silken red, sheets, naked from head to toe, her pale skin flushed from the afternoon delights. Bellum was lying next to her, the sheets covering only his penis. He felt satisfied from the several hours long love making they had done. At least, Bellum hoped it was love. He feared his mistress only gave into his cravings due to the lack of attention from some of his brothers. He'd thought about grabbing Rhiannon's dark curls and forcing her to kiss him again, forcing her to submit to him. But, his queen was always in control. Always on top, always the one dominating. She would trust no one with power over her, not even her riders. Rhiannon looked at him then, erasing all thoughts of violence and jealousy from his head.

"Darling?" Rhiannon purred, as she reached across the sheets to place a possessive hand over Bellum's thigh. Bellum stilled, fear replacing the lust. He remembered the last time she had called him darling in that tone, that same coy touch of a hand. She'd ordered Victorum to whip him, for supposedly lusting after one of her maids. She could not tolerate her lover betraying her in such a manner.

Bellum still had scars on his back and thighs from that whipping. She had not allowed him to be healed, instead forcing the wounds to scar so that everyone would know who he belonged to. So that

Bellum would know who he belonged to.

"Yes, my queen?" He answered after a moment, his voice clear and sure. Rhiannon smiled, blinking slowly in his direction, savoring in the game she made him play, the rope she made him walk. She ran her nails through his long red hair, arranging it around his down-turned horns. Playing with him as if he were no more than a pet to amuse her.

"I have a mission for you." Rhiannon stated, suddenly sitting up right, capturing Bellum in her gaze. He started to get up as well, but she forced him back down to the bed with a firm palm. Her long nails were artfully manicured into dangerous points, the dark paint on them reminiscent of poison. She looked down at him as she removed the blanket covering his manhood, removing his only protection from his queen's dark desires. He couldn't help the painful stiffening of his dick under her gaze; she was his queen. She knew what he needed. Rhiannon climbed on top of him, her wetness smearing across him as she did so. Nothing turned her on more than exploiting her power over her men. Lust clouded her gaze as she rubbed herself over him. He shifted, trying to hold onto her, but she pinned his arms above him, a dark glint in her eyes.

"Ah, ah, darling. You know better. Be still. That is a command." Bellum stilled as the dark magic flooded through him, the blood promise he made as a rider of the Under Realm, to obey his queen and serve her in all things.

"Now, where were we?" Rhiannon murmured as she positioned herself over him.

"Ah, yes," she said as she slid down his hard length, filling herself with him. Bellum could only be still, even as the pleasure coursed through him.

"Do not cum," she commanded, a queen wild and unbound.

He could not move, nor could he cum, nor did he want to. He simply let his queen take her fill of him, loving and hating every moment of it.

"I command you," she moaned out, working herself up and down his erect cock, watching as his eyes rolled back into his head. Bellum's thoughts were scattered, on the verge of passing out with pleasure. Rhiannon released his arms, secure in the knowledge he could not disobey her, to grip his chin in her delicate grasp. She continued after a few moments, "To go to Megara's sanctum on the island of Amisra. I command you, through whatever means necessary, to murder every single priestess and visitor to her sanctum."

Bellum's eyes flew open, as the pleasure abated just enough for him to understand what she was commanding him to do. Rhiannon's moans turned into screams, and his dick became so hard it hurt. He was torn between being horrified and needing to cum so badly he could die.

Rhiannon looked him right in the eye then, the grip on his chin growing painfully tight as she lowered her face to his. She continued riding him, as if it were no effort on her part to do so, as if it got her off even more.

"And when you have killed every priestess, you will locate Megara's inner sanctum and kill her. Then, you will take the small box locked inside her chest and bring it back here to me immediately." The dark magic coursed through him, the carnal energy strengthening Rhiannon's commands, as each command was issued. Rhiannon kissed Bellum savagely then, spitting into his mouth and commanding him to cum. He tried to fight against her *command, but darkness overtook him. His eyes clouded, his mind went blank. Little more than a servant to her whims.*

Fighting my way out of his memory proves harder than forcing my way in was. My heart races, my skin flushes from the memory. My mind spins from Rhiannon's words. I stumble back from Bellum, my shadows receding into me more slowly than usual, and Sebastien grabs me before I fall. Exhaustion slams into me and it takes everything in me to remain upright. Revulsion rolls through me at the implications of Bellum's memory.

"Did you see that?" I ask Sebastien, in between panting breaths. He nods gravely, looking back at where Bellum hangs, ashamed. The milky white glaze over his eyes is gone, the ruby tones in his iris shining in the light.

"He's an incubus," Sebastien murmurs to me, "A type of daemon that thrives on sexual pleasure and gratification but dies when it is withheld from them." Disgust courses through me at the thought. How could Rhiannon claim to love her riders if this is how she treats them?

"Did she ever--?" I can't even finish the entire thought, but Sebastien shakes his head.

"I am more powerful than her, and I am not an incubus." Sebastien states pointedly, and a tremor of relief goes through me. "You are more powerful than her as well, Rhea," Sebastien adds before I can formulate a helpful sentence.

"I appreciate the vote of confidence, at least." I use my eyes to gesture towards Bellum without words, in a silent question to Sebastien.

"What do you want to do with him?" Sebastien asks me, through

the bond. Examining Sebastien's demeanor, I wonder if there is any part of him that cares for his brothers in arms.

"Bellum is an asshole. But, he is not evil. Every horrible deed I have witnessed him commit, has been on Rhiannon's direct orders. He never voluntarily hurts anyone-- it is antithetical to his powers as an incubus. He would keep to himself, were it not for his mother selling him to the court. He was chosen as a teen to become one of the Death Riders. Rhiannon decided she need a core group of warriors, loyal only to her, to protect her come what may. She invoked the ancient blood marriage pact with each of her riders, except for me, which forces them to obey all of her commands," he explains further. My head starts to ache with the constant flow of information between us. I doubt I will ever get used to that.

"What is a blood marriage pact? The dark fae in my area do not have that." Dark fae marriage contracts are celebrated over a three-day period of time, where friends and family gather around the betrothed couple and shower them with gifts for two days straight. On the third night, the couple marries under the moonlight. We even have astrologers who will tell couples what moon phase will provide them with the most harmonious marriage. Sivan's family are very traditional Autumn Fae, and their marriage ceremony involved the two of us sitting in a small pool of water for several hours as we said our vows in the light of the sister suns. We ended up doing both ceremonies to appease our families. That old familiar grief aches in my chest, and I know I cannot push my mourning off forever. But maybe just until I can see his soul to rest?

"A blood marriage pact is an old daemon ritual, usually binding a knight to his monarch, but anyone can do it. The two slice their palms enough to bleed and then hold those palms together while reciting the ritual vows so that their blood mingles. The spell is

enacted immediately and is binding until death."

"So, there is no hope for Bellum?" Sebastien raises a brow at my question, as if he wants to know why I even care.

"I didn't say that." Sebastien looks over at the man in question, still shackled in shadows. Bellum remains silent. I wonder what he's thinking.

"What if he were offered another blood pact?" My question takes Sebastien by surprise, if his quiet contemplation and stillness are any indication. The man looks like he's carved from stone and has the demeanor of it too. Daemons.

"That is unheard of," Sebastien says out loud, "But it could work. If he's willing." Bellum lifts up his head at that.

"If I'm willing to do *what?"* Bellum asks, voice raw. Turning away from Sebastien, I kneel down to sit face to face with Bellum.

"I am willing to offer you a chance. One chance to live. Would you like that chance?" I ask Bellum in return. He shifts his head to the side, his unbound hair flowing over him like a curtain of blood, the jeweled tips of his ears catching the light. The look in his eyes is that of a broken man, not that of a killer. I've seen that look in my own eyes one too many times. How many lives has he been forced to take in the name of his queen? Not only that but forced by magic so ancient that I doubt Rhiannon knows the full extent of its power. There is no light in his red eyes, only pain.

Bellum nods and I kneel down in front of him.

"You may live if you make a blood pact with me."

My words are soft, quietly spoken, but Bellum closes his eyes as if I've delivered a most painful blow. He looks softer now himself, all resistance wrung from his body.

His eyes are still closed when he asks, "What would the terms of our pact be?"

I look to Sivan for reassurance. When he nods, I take a steadying breath. I can do this. I can be the queen the daemon's need me to be.

"You will honor and protect my court and I. You will never again butcher an innocent soul. You will atone for the death's dealt here today in a way of my choosing. If your actions cause harm to another at any point in time, you will answer to me. If you agree to these terms, then I shall welcome you and yours as my own family." That feels as binding as possible, and it also feels right. Sebastien's eyebrows raise and his mouth drops open slightly. Bellum looks as if I have backhanded him.

"That's... it?" Bellum asks, unsure. Sebastien looks as if he echoes the sentiment, though he doesn't voice it.

"Is that not more than sufficient?" I ask, becoming perplexed myself.

"Rhiannon draws up several hundred pages long contracts for each of her blood pacts consisting of lists of what her riders can and cannot do, where they can go, who they can speak with, and when and what they eat. It is quite extensive, and usually takes several months with the ceremonies," Sebastien explains. Ceremonies? Do we need to have a ceremony?

"You do not have to have a ceremony," Sebastien answers my unspoken question, "It is simply Rhiannon's tradition."

"What do we absolutely need to do for a blood pact then?" I ask, tilting my head to look up at Sebastien. A ghost of a smile traces his lips before he extends a hand to me. I look at that hand for a long moment, and then accept it, sliding my palm against his and rising slowly from the floor.

He tips his head slowly to me before his posture stiffens and he takes a dagger out from one of the sheathes on his thigh. He clears his throat. Bellum watches, his ruby eyes shining with curiosity.

"Stand up," Sebastien orders Bellum, and then Sebastien loosens his shadows a smidge to allow Bellum to do so. Bellum remains silent but rises to his feet in one graceful movement. Sebastien then positions Bellum and I so that the three of us are standing in a triangle. He cuts both my and Bellum's palms and I grit my teeth against the pain.

"Do you, Bellum, offer this oath of your own free will?" Sebastien asks.

Bellum holds his hand up to mine. "Aye," he says. Sebastien then turns to me, looking fierce and protective. My roll my lips as if I can suppress the feeling as soon as it begins. I'll need to examine that one later.

"Now," Sebastien says, "Offer your oath to Bellum and then cut your palm with my blade. It's made from a stone only found in the Under Realm and is considered holy and binding. Then, he will accept and cut his palm. The two of you will mingle your blood and it shall be done."

"Is there anything else?" I ask demurely. The thought of touching Bellum isn't my favorite, but I suppose it's the path of the least resistance.

Sebastien shakes his head. "No, that's it. I am here as witness. All the requirements are met."

If this were an Autumn fae ritual, or even a Dark Fae one, this would take a fortnight. Situation being what it is, it will help in the fight ahead to have two of the death riders bound to me. My list of enemies seems to grow ever longer, as do my reasons for hating Rhiannon. Sivan would understand, and possibly even encourage, the decisions I must make in his absence. Suddenly, my throat goes dry. Is this what a good ruler must do?

"I, Rhea, the Promised-Queen of the Under-Realm, the Soul Savior and Shadow Wielder of the High Court of the Dark Fae, offer this blood pact to you..." I trail off when I realize I don't know Bellum's true name. I look to Sebastien for guidance, but he turns his gaze on Bellum, as if the knowledge is not his to share. True names are closely kept secrets, for those whose power does not guarantee them safety.

Bellum clears his throat, "Bellamy, Rider of War and Beast-Keeper." *Bellamy?*

"The other riders were chosen before their births to one day serve the queen. Their parents named them with the intent that they should grow into their positions. We use our given names in front of outsiders," Sebastien quickly explains through the bond, before motioning for me to continue with the ritual.

A lovely name, a name of a man I could potentially trust, one day. I clear my throat and continue from where I left off.

"I offer this blood-pact to you, Bellamy, Rider of War and Beast-Keeper: you will honor and protect me, my court, and all innocent persons. You shall never again harm an innocent in cold blood. To atone for today's tragedy, you will find each and every person slain here today and bury them according to their goddesses' customs. If you agree to these terms, then I shall honor and protect you as a member of my court forevermore."

Bellamy's ruby eyes go wide, and a crinkle appears between his brows, apparently awestruck.

"That... that is very generous of you to offer me protection in return," Bellamy says, swallowing hard. I lift the dagger out to him, so that he must meet my hand halfway to take it. He does, and cuts into his palm without so much as a wince.

"I, Bellamy, the Rider of War and Keeper of Beasts, solemnly swear to abide by the terms of this blood pact."

He extends his bleeding palm to me. I reach my own out and grip his in return. The moment our palms meet, the blood touches, lightning soars through my body. It settles as quickly as it came, into a pleasant buzz all over my skin, similar to the way my shadows feel when they become my armor.

Sebastien releases his shadows from Bellamy completely and Bellamy rubs the skin around his wrists and ankles. Maybe the shadows feel as uncomfortable as real shackles do. Bellamy turns and stares at me. It takes a long moment before I realize he is awaiting orders.

"Go, bury them. When you are done, meet us down on the beach," I command Bellamy. Sebastien and I watch as he skulks towards the courtyard. The moment he's gone, I breathe a heavy sigh of relief. Sebastien looks at me with a hint of concern.

"Are you... alright?" His question is tentative, as if he's afraid of offending me. I think we're far past that point.

"It's uncomfortable making these decisions without Brynn. Since Sivan died, she's been the one person holding me together," I explain, briefly glancing up into Sebastien's eyes. We haven't moved from our triangle since Bellamy left, and I hadn't realized how close we are to one another. Close enough that I can see each gentle rise and fall of his chest. If I close my eyes and focus, I can hear each calm thrum of his heart. Close enough that I can see the myriads of colors in his dark eyes. His eyes are like the moon, a soft grey with hints of lavender. Realizing I've been staring into his eyes; I take a step back.

"I am going to be a queen. I know that. I've always known that eventually, whether it's her crown or my parents, I would be a queen. I should have prepared myself better for this. To make these kinds of decisions without overanalyzing each one. I am no good to anyone if I cannot choose a path." My voice ends on a choked whisper. Tears threaten to fall, but I blink them back furiously. Stupid, stupid emotions.

"Hey," Sebastien says lowly and grips my chin in one large, grey hand, forcing me to look into his eyes.

"That type of thinking will lead you to ruin. You are doing everything that you can, including trusting veritable strangers with what could mean your life or death. Rhiannon trusts no one and therefore she has no one at her side, protecting her. We can discuss the other riders later, but for now, remember this: you will be queen because you are the type of queen the Under-Realm *needs,* and we will show everyone that through our actions."

We stay standing like that, close together, only connected where he grips my chin, eyes unblinking. In those moments, I feel a new understanding dawn between us. We're a long way off from romance, but maybe... friendship can be enough. He releases me slowly, as if reluctant to do so. He resumes his professional posture and takes a step away from me.

"What can this lowly servant offer his queen?" he asks with a polite smile, and I nearly chuckle at the attempt at humor.

"I am going to enter Megara's inner sanctum. I need you to find Brynn, Faye, and Luna and inform them about everything that's happened, as well as bring them to the beach down there. Let's say... two hours?"

"As you command, my queen." Sebastien bows with a slight flourish, before he winks at me and vanishes into thin air. I swear a dark chuckle follows him on the wind.

Left alone in the corridor, I turn and face the door to Megara's inner sanctum. On each side of the door, a similar mechanism to the one at the gates leading up to the volcano. Steeling myself, I place each of my hands on the corresponding disks on the door.

That ancient, delicious magic flows through me yet again, pulling my magic from that deep resting place within me, tasting my magic,

Hello again, sister. My mistress is in need of your aid.

The voice of the darkness, the voice of death.

"Hello... door. I would love to aid your mistress, if you would open up, please." It's hard to sound cheery when my magic is slowly being siphoned off, but I try my best.

Without my goddesses blessing, you must answer the riddle.

"Ask and I shall answer honestly," I reply. Egan's memories prepared me for this part of the door. The door was spelled by the most powerful mage in all of Amisra's history, Aza the Valiant. Aza was there when Megara saved the island and devoted himself to the goddess immediately. He spelled her entire sanctum and oversaw to the construction of her defenses and armory using rare materials from the volcano itself. This door in particular asks every person attempting entry a question and uses their answer to measure if they are worthy of entering. Having the goddesses blessing overrides the enchantment, but when the sanctum's defenses are activated, the riddle is required each time.

What must the death queen do to awaken her power?

I stare at the door, brows furling in consternation. Does this mean Rhiannon's powers are not awakened? Or this is simply meant to help me develop my own? My thoughts feel heavy, my head begins to ache. A good queen gives everything up for her people, but that is not what the door asked. What must the death queen do? There's only one thing that separates a death queen from the others. The one thing that has kept me company my whole life. The one thing we all must do, when our time comes.

"Die, a death queen must die." I answer solemnly. My mind spins with the possibilities.

A long silence follows, before that ancient voice again intones.

You may enter, sister.

And the doors to Megara's inner sanctum begin to creak open.

CHAPTER FIFTEEN

HEAT blasts me in the face as I enter Megara's inner sanctum. It's nestled into the heart of the volcano, a feat of magic and engineering. When I was a little girl, I would trace maps of the island and wonder what the inside of each great sanctum looked like. I'd imagine the day my future sisters and I would meet, how they would treat me. I never imagined the path that led me here today.

My steps echo softly on the stone as I walk, my gaze stuck on the volcano walls. Magma, trapped behind glass, flows in beautiful spiraling pathways along the walls, leading towards an arched entryway. The magma provides a warm glow, that's passable as light with my fae eyesight.

And then-- there it is again: the tang of blood, sharp and salty floating in the air. The dark, warmth of the hallway suddenly seems to swallow me. My heart flutters in my chest. The door did say Megara needed my aid, but what hope can I provide if the goddess is truly injured? Injuring a goddess isn't a simple task.

When I pass under the archway, the ceiling opens up, revealing the midday suns. A few hours have passed since Sebastien and I first arrived on that white sandy beach, and I worry he might have trouble finding the others. A large grate dominates the center of the floor. Plumes of smoke rise languidly from below, ascending towards the suns in greeting. On the far end of the cavern from me, a large bed sits pushed haphazardly against the wall, a mess of sheets and blankets atop it. A few other pieces of furniture are arranged in a semi-circle around the bed. There's no blood identifiable on any of the furniture or on the plush, fur rugs dotting the floor.

As I rotate around the room, I notice a study area along the other wall. A desk carved from the very rock upon which it rests upon, cluttered with papers and boxes and brightly colored rocks. Books are stacked on side tables, the floor, the desk, the sagging shelf to the side. So many books, I want to run my fingers along their spines just to see what memories they might hold.

Snakelike shadows slither down my body, guiding me towards a small room. A cauldron rests in the center, burbling away with a purple foam that threatens to spill over and out. My eyes continue to scan the room, but nothing stands out as extraordinary. A scrying table, another bookshelf. And sitting in a delicate looking chair: a woman.

Her olive skin looks pale and ashen. Sweat beads down her perfectly shaped brows, down her gorgeously hooked nose. Her upswept eyes and long lashes are shuttered with pain. Down her arms, swirling bands of tattoos, moving along her skin for reasons I can't pretend to understand. She has one hand pressed to her abdomen, where blood coats her golden dress. In her other limp hand, a crossbow.

"Megara?" I ask with some hesitance. She awakens, her brown eyes opening wide as her body heaves with each breath as if it hurts to do so. I stay where I am, holding up my hands to show her I mean no harm. Her eyes narrow at me.

"Rhea," she says simply, forcing herself to sit up taller, her long ponytail sweeping over the chair. Her voice is smooth and clear, despite her injury. In fact, the way she says my name reminds me a bit of Addie, soothing an ache in my heart.

"You were expecting me," my voice comes out thin and weak. The woman in front of me is a goddess--- a true one. Based in Emberpeak, she is known for being intuitive and fair, if a bit.... Casual.

She waves me off with the crossbow, a gentle smile on her pale lips.

"There's really not time for pleasantries, now is there?" Megara retorts. There's fire in her eyes, an ember I know will not go out easily. I kneel down by her side and ask if I can look at her wound. She nods her acquiescence and drops her hand. Carefully, I peel back the gauzy material of her gown and cut away some of the material to see the wound better. What I see nearly forces a gasp from me, but I bite my lip to hold it back.

"How does it look deary?" Megara asks, tone scarily cheerful. Her breathing is even, calm.

The wound is small, and jagged. The marks look like ones I've seen in the Hollow Forest, on deer that had wandered too far from safety. A wolf? Did Bellamy bring wolves with him to attack the sanctum? Blood continually oozes from the wound. A bad sign if I've ever seen one.

"I've seen worse," I say honestly. I do not tell her that healing isn't my gift. Of course, like most goddess blessed fae, I have some aptitude for it, but healing was the bottom of my list of priorities. Using shadows effectively and learning how to control my memory powers took precedence when I was child. A royal child running around spying on court members would have put an end to my parents' reign rather quickly.

"I am a goddess. It will heal," she says between ragged breaths sending another roar of fire to burn through me. Worry and anger compete. Some acts are too grievous to forgive, to atone for.

My eyes roam around the small room searching for items that I could use to heal the goddess but find little. I rush out of the room, back into the cavern, and look at the various tables dotting the area. Some contain vials and jars of herbs. Nothing is familiar. Dejected, I return to Megara. Her bleeding has slowed, and some of the color returns to her cheeks. A patient smile rests on her lips.

"How kind of you to care for me," she tells me, "But I believe we have more important things to discuss, yes?"

"Help me to the other room," Megara commands me. I glance at her but obey wordlessly. She hands me the crossbow, it's unexpected weight nearly causing me to fall, and then braces her weight on me as we shuffle to the other room in small steps. She points out a small settee by the bed, and I help her rest on it. She tucks her feet up under her thighs, snaps her fingers together, and a tea service appears from the air. Cups fill themselves with brown liquid, steam rising out of them like the volcanic vents nearby.

My shadows hum contentedly on my skin, indicating no immediate danger. Megara's sanctum feels cozier than Inya's, despite the contrasts in lighting, and I can see her living a quiet life here. Until now.

Sadness etches itself into Megara's features as we sip our tea. She seems withdrawn into herself, quiet. The silence stretches on. When nearly half an hour passes, she looks into my eyes and asks, in a small voice, "are they all dead?"

"Yes."

Her eyes close again, as if protecting herself from the blow of the word. When she opens them again, that fire once again burns bright and hot behind her gaze.

"I will offer you information," she states. I cock my head at her.

"In exchange for what?"

"In exchange, for nothing. This is not a bargain. I offer you this information out of both our best interests. I know who you are, and I know what you need. These are events that were set in motion long before you were born."

I found Brynn and Faye. They are both fine. Searching for Luna now.

Sebastien's voice entering my head is a welcome distraction from the conversation at hand.

Thank you.

I send an echo of appreciation back down the bond.

Returning my attention to Megara, I indicate for her to continue. One of her eyebrows raises at me, but she voices no question about my momentary mental absence.

"Do you see that desk over there? The one with the large, black chest on it," she asks instead, pointing to the desk I saw earlier. I nod, and she tells me to open the chest.

"That's it?" I ask.

"Open the chest," she says.

"Do I need a key?" I ask.

"Open the chest." The room rumbles around us as Emberpeak

roars with in unison with the flare in Megara's temper.

Her sudden seriousness sparks my nerves. I wipe my palms on my pants, then stand and stride over to the desk. The chest sits on top of it, all black with no adornments, just a small lock with no keyhole. The moment I touch it, my shadows react. Violently. They scream out of my body, and dive into the chest, popping it open with ease before it settles on the surface with a thud. A small black box sits inside the chest, my shadows pushing it up for me to take. My heart thuds at the sight of the box, as if a part of me recognizes it.

Oh, joyous day, another box.

"Bring the box over here," Megara calls from across the room. One of my eyes twitches as I suppress the urge to roll my eyes. She's just lost every priestess she knows and cares for, ones who died to save her out of returned adoration. The very least I can do is take my role in my own destiny seriously.

When I return, sitting next to her this time, she turns to me and holds out her palm. I place the box into her outstretched hand. A shudder goes through her when the box contacts her skin. Her brown eyes flick to mine, expression indiscernable.

"I will give you a choice," she says gravely, "This box is called The Veil of Shadows. Inside this veil lies the key to all of your problems. You will learn the history of predecessors, you will learn and master your powers, and you will gain the key to defeating Rhiannon."

"But?" I ask. There is always balance in the world. What must I lose to gain all that I seek?
Megara nods approvingly, her hair bouncing over her back like a great chestnut wave.

"For you to gain all that you seek, you must die. Inside of this box is a poison: it will grant you immortality. You will lose your life as you ascend to true godhood. If you fail... well then, you die."

My mind screams. My body does not move, though it isn't without great effort. Despite everything, and my supposed comfort with death, the thought of dying burns my arms and legs until my entire body succumbs to flame. I am powerless to stop it. Megara understands. She waits, staring at me, but offers no comfort. There can be none in a time like this, though I long for Sebastien's sarcastic remarks on the situation.

"There's a test?" I ask, when I swallow the grief and panic of my own demise.

She nods. "Isn't there always?"

My eyes inspect the ground for long moments. I feel Megara's eyes on me as I cast my own downward, trying to center myself. This choice is easy. This choice is impossible.

"Have others been offered this choice?" I ask her, still not meeting her gaze.

"Yes," she says plainly and takes a sip of her tea. She relishes the warmth for a moment, before continuing: "Every single death queen has been offered this bargain, same as you, as will those who follow you."

She does not elaborate further, forcing me to ask, "Did any accept it?"

"No," she replies, "They decided the risk was far too great. They let their fear dominate them, rule their choices." She sips her tea again, and I get the feeling she's doing it on purpose, for dramatic effect. I remain silent. I was an only child, raised in the shadows; I can wait out the silent treatment, Sensing I won't say much more without more information, she sets down her cup and sighs.

"When you drink the potion, there is no guarantee you shall ascend. You will be tested. I do not know what or whom you may see, so do not ask me, but I know that this challenge is older than this realm. It is shaped by who you are, what your unique fears are. If you choose to drink it, if you are not worthy, you will not wake up."

That doesn't seem like that bad of a choice to me. What worse can I endure than the loss of my love? Since my husband's failed funeral, I have been repeatedly forced into situations I did not want. He was taken too young, and it was all because of me, because of my potential. What is death in the face of failing the ones you loved? And then, to be granted my soul bonded mate in the midst of the deepest grief I've ever known? The fates must be laughing at me from the heavens.

Dying has always been the only certainty in my life. When I was young and my parents locked me in a dark closet for so long at a time, I knew eventually they would retrieve me again. When I declared my love for Sivan, leaving the capital city to settle in a cursed forest, I knew my life would not be easy. But through it all, I knew that one day I would die. I would die and so I needed to make my life worth living, whether that was by giving love or being kind or helping another in need. Either way, the end result has always been the same. None of us knows what happens then, not even me. Not truly.

"I will drink the potion and prove my worth," I blurt out.

What other choice is there? If I stop at this first, real challenge, it will all have been for nothing. The priestesses' deaths... a tragedy, but death is an old friend. Overcoming it may be no small feat, but it is one I am capable of, nonetheless.

Megara's brown eyes blaze approvingly, a curve beginning on her lower lip.

"Very well then," she says, and helps me lie back on the settee, my head in her lap. Her thighs are soft, comforting, like what I imagine most mothers to be. Maybe her presence will ground me while.... I endure whatever is about to occur.

"Dream easy. Be brave," Megara chirps and then takes the potion out of the box, holding it above my head for me to view. The vial is shockingly plain and small aside from the small etchings in the glass. The liquid inside is black and thick. It reminds me of Sierra and Orla. I wonder if they've ever heard of such a poison.

Megara removes the seal from the glass while I finger my own vial of poison still resting in my pocket. She brushes her hand over my hair soothingly while she offers the liquid to me. It's such a small amount; it trickles down softly and easily. I expect it to taste poorly, but the flavor is light, almost honey-like. Deceptive. My eyelids flutter closed.

After a few moments, a languid buzzing flows through my limbs, images of volcanic eruptions dancing behind my eyelids.

"Isss nah workinnnnggg...." I attempt a sentence but find my ability to speak gone. My limbs are limp and useless, my ability to control my muscles obliterated. I feel wonderful and safe. My eyes remain closed, and I drift off into a dream world.

CHAPTER SIXTEEN

WHITE swirling mists encompass me. My body feels lighter here, freer. When I glance down at my hands, I find them devoid of shadows, but the thought does not panic me like it should. Instead, it feels as if all is right in the realm. Balanced. When I look up at the sky, I see an endless expanse of stars. No sister moons.

My warm-weather clothing is gone, replaced by a simple white shift. It bears no design or markings but feels like it's made from the softest silk. Peace and ease float over me. A tugging sensation pulls from within me, guiding me away from the mists towards a tree in the distance. The pathway appears only as I step on it, feeling like soft green grass on my bare feet. At first, I walk towards that tree, but after a moment, joy surges within me and I begin jogging. Wherever this path leads, I know that I am safe. That I am home. That I am loved. Something annoying whispers in my ear, and I swat my hands at my ears to be rid of it. Darkness has no belonging in this place of holy light.

The pathway seems far longer than it looks. As I jog, I let my hands spread out in the air around me, basking in the elements. My hair is wild, unbound, a mess of curls cascading around me. Just how Sivan likes it. My body hums with an unusual power. I feel strong, healthy, and at peace. Is this what my powers could be? Isn't that why I'm here? Those worries seem so far away, especially when the love radiating from ahead is healing me, making me whole, repairing the damage of grief and time. I can't imagine such love could ever be a bad thing.

Flowers spring upon the path as I near the tree, gently curling white bells on white stems. They chime as I pass them. From the distance, the tree seemed small, but now, standing below it, it looms over me, white branches reaching to the sky, white leaves and flowers blooming before my very eyes. A small bridge separates the tree from the path, and I intend to step over it, to cross the bridge and investigate the tree but stop when I see a man. He's standing on the other side of the bridge from me. Every part of him is as familiar to me as my own body: the curve of his shoulders, the bridge of his nose, his warm brown skin. Sivan. My love, my heart, my chosen mate.

A choked gasp escapes me and then I am running, scrambling, to him. Our bodies collide, his arms folding around me just as they used to before he wasted away to nothing, before Rhiannon stole him from me. He feels solid and real. Tears stream down my face, joy and relief overtaking me completely. I do not bother trying to wipe them away. He understands, as he always did.

"My love," he says, over my sobs, "Everything is alright. You made it here. You did everything perfectly. Breathe."

The kindness that permeated his life remains in death. When my sobs quiet down, I'm calm enough to ask him a question.

"Am I alive?" I ask, my forehead resting on his chest. His grip on me tightens for a moment, before he says, "we should talk over here" and leads me over to a small bench made of white stone under the tree. A small brook runs below a bridge nearby, burbling softly away in the night.

"You are.... in-between," he says, gripping my hand lightly. We sit, knees together, hands held and stare into each other's eyes for a moment.

"Can I go back?" I ask. I'm not sure if I want to... not if it means leaving him.

He smiles, and another part of me heals.

"The choice has always been yours. From this side, I can see everything much more clearly. The other queens came to this place as well. They each saw someone they loved that had passed. They each had their choices," he says seriously. The smile fades from his face, looking at me with worry... worry much like Sebastien's.

"How did they survive if they didn't pass the test?" Again, a feeling niggles in the back of my head, like a memory trying to come loose.

"That's not for me to say," he tells me and smiles, "But you will know soon enough."

The warmth and sunshine he had in life has persisted through his afterlife. Something tugs in my chest, right where my bond with Sebastien would be. I gulp as I realize I need to tell Sivan.

"I--I've met someone. My soul bonded mate. His name is Sebastien," my voice comes out in a hoarse whisper, tears clouding my vision. Sivan lifts one hand to my face, brushing away my tears, before using a gentle hand to lift my eyes to his.

"I already know, my love. Did you think I would want you to grieve me for the rest of your life? That I would not put your happiness above all else? I am not there to hold you each day or carry your burdens like I vowed to. I have always known you would be a queen one day-- you were already the queen of my heart. I cherish the time we spent together. I loved you more than life itself," he pauses, sadness reflecting in his hazel eyes, "I had always hoped to outlive you, so that I could spare you from dealing with my soul in death. Placing a burden like that upon you... was unfair. You gave up everything for me, for our life together. I would not trade that time for anything in the world."

We knock our foreheads together in a small gesture of affection, before sitting in the silence a moment longer. Something else dawns on me.

"Wait, but Rhiannon, she had leashed you! Chained your soul to her. She told me that she would find you in the soul stream and destroy you." Sivan laughs at the expression on my face. At first, I find it annoying, but before long, I join in on his laughter. The sound peals out of me, free and light. I haven't laughed this much in months.

"What you saw was a shadow, love. A shade of my soul, but not my real soul. Rhiannon is not strong enough to survive in the soul stream. Haven't you realized yet?" he asks, raising a dark brow at me. I shake my head "no." He snorts a bit at me before continuing.

"Rhiannon is not a true death queen," he tells me.

"What does that mean exactly? The goddesses speak in riddles and prophecies, or in half-truths. I still do not understand," I say, frustration leaking into my voice. A light breeze floats through the tree branches then, and I take a calming breath. Anger is not needed here.

"I have a choice to offer you: you can accept the last true death goddesses blessing and maybe return to Halcyon, or you can return now and live once more, knowing only a fraction of your potential power. This is how the others survived—they feared their unworthiness more than anything else."

"Who was the last true death goddess?"

"Thania, great-grandmother of Ravenna. She is the one who dominated the Under-Realm, during the forgotten years. For better or worse, she is the one who started all of this. She will tell you a story and offer you her blessing. If the blessing accepts you as a true death goddess, then you will be reborn a goddess and ascend to the death throne by right."

"And if it does not accept me?" I ask. Sivan gives me a long look.

"While I believe you will be accepted, if you must know: if you are found unworthy, then you will die the true death and ascend to the after realm." A long silence.

"Will you be there?" I ask, turning my head and looking up at him. The brook babbles away in the background, providing a soft silence during our long glances. There's no choice, not really. Our hands stay intertwined, and I soak in the feel of him, the sight of him. I will never be ready to let go.

"When your time comes, my love, I will be waiting for you. Waiting to hear of all the adventures you've had without me." He smiles again, tears shining in his eyes. He understands too, as he always had. Sivan always made decisions for me-- not because I was incapable, but because I did not want to make decisions. In the first month after leaving my family, a storm overtook my mind. I had little knowledge of running a household, even one with just two members, and found my parents sheltered me to an incorrigible degree. I knew little of the world outside Darrid, besides the information my parents allowed my tutors to tell me and became overwhelmed at how much I needed to learn. Sivan was patient, and kind, and a wonderful husband. I will never forget him, nor will I ever stop loving him.

But in his death, I was forced to care for myself. He was no longer there to make sure I ate a decent meal when strong memories pulled me into my shadows grasp for days without end, or to care for the horses, or chop firewood, or help me keep the house tidy. Immediately after his death, his family came by often, offering meals and words of support, but after a few months, even they had lives to return to. Brynn and Addie checked in on me when they could; Sienna and Orla wrote letters and sent gifts.

None of it eased the ache in my chest. Until that day Brynn and I set out on horseback, an adventure in our veins, the promise of vengeance on our lips. Until I met a sunny fairy with bright red hair, who offered to help out of friendship. Until I met a little cat with a sharp tongue and claws to match. Until I met a grey-skinned daemon that promised to honor me, whether I ever choose to pursue a romantic relationship with him or not.

"Sivan," I begin, "I will speak with Thania, and ask for her blessing. I will ascend and become a goddess. I will do this because I have to, because the Under-Realm deserves better than a queen that would rule by lies and deceit, rather than by her own strength and favor of her people. One day, I will be back here with you, and I will share all of my stories, and you will know that I lived my life well."

The brevity of my decision hits me squarely in the chest. I do not want to say goodbye, not again. But it's not a goodbye forever, it's a goodbye for now. The cycle must end here.

"I know," he says, full of understanding even in death, "I also know that you did not fail me. You told me once that not everyone truly wants to know what happens in death and beyond. I think you should remember that customs in death are just our way of dealing with the fear and unknown. My soul is safe, even without your guidance. You did everything perfectly right. Do not let your enemies use fear to warp what you know to be true."

He stands up from the bench then and holds out a hand to help me up. I place my hand in his, and rise, feeling lighter than air. He kisses my forehead and wraps his arms around me. The finality of this meeting stokes the ache of grief within me.

"Can we have one last kiss?" I ask him, not ready for this moment to end.

"Anything for you," he says and bends down until our lips meet. It's a soft and gentle kiss, one full of love and promise. The warmth of the kiss makes it way down into my toes and I softly sigh.

"Well, let's get going then," I say with fake cheer as the kiss ends and we step away from each other. Sivan pulls my hand into his again, unwilling to let go until the last moment, and we walk to the base of the large tree.

"The tree of life and death," he says as he gestures up to the tree's large branches. He drops my hand, kisses my forehead then backs up a step.

"Where you are going, no other may roam. Do not fear the tests to come-- I will always be with you," he says, hand over his heart. This time, I do not fear our goodbye. This time, we said everything needed. What else is there, but delaying the inevitable end result? His body shimmers, becoming less corporeal and fading into mist.

I stand watching him dissipate, the change in time marked only by my own heartbeats. The star filled night remains, each star shining brightly, their positions unchanged. A breeze sweeps through again, my dress ruffling around me. All that's left is the path forward. I turn towards the tree, and as I do, a doorway reveals itself. The door is small, and simple, the coloring the same as the great tree above it. I've already made my choice. I knock on the door-- it seems the polite thing to do. No one answers from within, and so I turn the wooden knob, open the door, and step into the world within.

CHAPTER SEVENTEEN

THE new area I find myself within contains the same mist as the one before but feels.... balanced in a way the other one did not. The scenery remains the same: in the distance looms another great tree, this one evergreen and radiant amongst the darkness around it. The stars above are seemingly endless, but a moon sits proud in the sky, shining down her radiant light on the trees and water below. Forest surrounds the large green tree, an abundant green wave rolling over hills of impossible heights. The edges of this world seem hazy, blurry, and when I look down at my hands, my shadows cover my skin once again. A smile radiates across my face at the familiar sight. A sense of accomplishment spreads its way through my limbs. The shadows curl closer to me, content to be with me yet again. I get the feeling I've passed at least one test.

Another figure stands in the distance, this one unfamiliar. My pace is still light and carefree, but determination overtakes me as I stride forward. It must be Thania who waits for me ahead, who waits to test me. Consequences be damned, I will succeed here. There is no other option. The others before me cowered when faced with their own mortality. What is a leader if not willing to sacrifice everything in order to accomplish her goals? There may be much I have yet to learn, but I know one thing: if I am not willing to risk it all for that which I love, that which I ache for, then what is the point in ever having lived at all? I will die, everyone will die. Death is the one connecter between all living things, from the lowest mushroom to the highest beings. Even goddesses may come to find a time where their powers are futile in the wake of a higher power. Never can we be prepared for life's great tragedies.

What do we accomplish when all else has been stripped away? When there is no glory in forgiveness nor honor in winning? Surely, being a ruler calls for knowing when a problem is too great for you alone to solve. The others on my journey, the friends and family who helped me rise up from ashes after I thought my world destroyed... I would dishonor them to stop now.

Each step towards that hazy figure in the distance sends a rush of sureness buzzing through my limbs. My pace remains sure, unhurried. My shoulders are straight, my posture perfect. The long white shift flows around me as I stride forward, ready to meet my future, ready to meet my destiny. Each step strengthens my resolve, strengthens my vision, and soon I can see raven hair on a pale figure. As I near, her curls bounce in the nighttime breeze, her smile draws me in. She feels like all the love and light in my life clustered into one being and created... her.

Another bridge and burbling brook. Everything is familiar and yet changed. As I near, the figure straightens and turns her head towards me. Her black hair, her pale face, each of her features as familiar to me as my own.

"Thania," I sing, "Hello!"

I bow deeply as I approach her, the joy sapping from my limbs, being replaced by decorum.

"Hello, youngling," she speaks, her voice carrying over to me like a breeze, her voice like the bright note of a songbird. When I cross the bridge, a strong breeze blows across. The gentle night turns ominous. Dark clouds gather over the verdant tree as thunder grumbles along with it.

She turns towards the bench below the tree, and sits, patting her palm against the spot next to her.

"Come, sit next to me. You must be tired after your journey."

The commanding tone in her voice has me rushing over and sitting down quickly.

"You must rest," she says, "You have endured so much. Let me tell you a story while the storm passes." Her voice is comforting, a kind mother to a mischievous child. I get the feeling that many versions of me have rested here in this same place. Her approval means life or death, yet I feel not an ounce of worry. The outcome will be what it will be. If the outcome is a beneficial one, then I will thank the mothers above for their compassion. If it is not, then I suppose worry will be the least of my problems.

The wind howls around us, the brook in the distance angrily splashing over its boundaries. Despite the weather growing angry, calm still radiates through the glen. Worry does not build as it did at my husband's funeral.

"In the beginning," Thania states. Her body begins to glow as she recites her tale.

"The three goddesses, the three sisters, descended upon this world when it was still in it's infancy, arriving on these lands during a time of great war. Each sister boasted gifts of varying strength. The youngest, the sister with fire in her veins and war in her heart, wooed the warriors from the volcanic islands of Amisra."

On distant shores, my mind floats away from my control. Thania continues, and I am so very sleepy. I must rest. She must continue.

"The middle sister, who controlled even the mightiest of seas and oceans but whose touch healed the gravest of injuries, settled in mountains shrouded in mist and waterfalls and taught her followers the ways of healing. The oldest and most powerful sister was not content to stay in this world, where her sisters had claimed such power and acclaim for themselves. Darkness filled her blood and corrupted her soul. Shadows seized her mind, turning her already deadly night-kissed powers into something otherworldly."

Thania sings rather than recites her tale. Her voice rings out, a siren in the night, "Her obsession with power and old magic lead her to yet another world, one that was not ready for her. This world was filled with lost, ambling creatures, who thirsted for violence. Their barren lands yielded no crops and suffered no fools, but this was of little consequence to what would become the dark queen. For she had stumbled upon the realm of death and souls, and it called to her magic like a candle in the dark. Brimming with her new power, she claimed that other world for herself, casting those who already lay claim to the land aside...."

As she speaks, the shadows vibrate and swirl together. Memories whisper to me, and in my tired state, pull me into their thrall with little resistance.

War, war rages on all around me. Unsightly green fires burn in the night. Bodies lie slain on the ground, dirt and blood becoming undistinguishable from one another. The cries of pain and anguish reverberate through the night, reminding me of why we came here. One of my warriors, Declan, steps forward. Lacerations pepper his skin, but nothing that looks fatal. He can continue on.

We're so close to our goal, we must continue on.

"Your grace," he greets me, bowing slightly, ever the formal one, even in the midst of war.

"Report." My command is brisk, but there is little time left. My eyes pour over the battlefield, looking to see where we stand but the brutality is unending, the chaos thick. In the haze from the fires, I can barely make out more than a few yards ahead of me. We could be winning; we could be losing. We need an edge, and we need it now.

"The invaders have overtaken the eastern battlefield. Reinforcements are due to arrive from the north in the next half hour. We have a sure grip on the southern front, but the western is losing ground. They need support." Declan's hand rests on his sword at his hip, a sure sign he has more to say.

"What else?" I ask.

"The King wishes to meet with you."

I knew he did not mean the Under-King. The Realm Walker, the Banished King, Lucifer. He has made many an attempt to reach me, no doubt to offer his aid in exchange for a price that no wise immortal would ever agree to.

"Tell him no."

Declan raises a soot covered brow in my direction, his dark eyes flickering with an emotion I am too tired to name. I wave him off.

"If you decline, your majesty, then I am sure he will rush to offer the same deal to Ravenna, " Declan says patiently, ever the devoted warrior.

"If she's smart, she'll decline as well." It's not as if she needs

assistance, but she's arrogant enough that she may accept simply to rub it in my face.

Green smoke swirls around me and dissipates as the memory's pull weakens.

"Now, child, do you understand?" Thania asks, her eyes a perfect mirror of my own, of Rhiannon's. Are we all forced to play out this vicious cycle, time and time again? To what end?

"Not everything," I say slowly, still trying to work the pieces out, "What was that memory?"

Thania stares at me for a long moment. "I made a grave error, an astronomical miscalculation," she admits to me, "I thought that any true immortal could never be so misguided as to accept a deal with Lucifer. But, I was correct in a way. It was a mortal queen's ambition that let Lucifer in. Rhiannon saw the power her immortal sisters held, and all she had to show for it was her unnaturally long lifespan. She stole into my realm, made a deal with a forgotten devil, and cemented her place in history."

"Is there no way to defeat her, then? Is this all for naught?" I ask Thania. She tilts her head to the side, the motion full of weighty thoughts.

"She made a deal with the devil, and the devil is soon coming for his pound of flesh," she muses.

"What was the deal? Please, please tell me."

"I can tell you one thing child: the deal she made, not a single one of her ancestors has paid the price for. If you accept the immortal powers, then you agree to pay the price, lest you be driven mad over time and lead to your own demise. Then, another shall be born to fulfill the bargain." Her eyes fall on me then. Great.

"Do you accept?" Thania intones. It's hard to agree to a bargain when one doesn't know the cost. But, I said I would do whatever it takes to avenge Sivan. To avenge those priestesses, and all who came before them. If I refuse, as so many of the goddesses before me clearly have, then am I any better than them?

"Yes, I accept," I answer, and then the world explodes in a flash of light.

CHAPTER EIGHTEEN

DARKNESS and shadow swallow me whole, devouring any traces of light. Thania, the tree, the beautiful brook... they are all torn away by the storm of death. I float in an endless abyss thrumming with shadows as we rise up and up and up until I am suffocating. I claw at my throat to no avail. The shadows overwhelm me so completely, I do not even feel panic.

The shadows are a song in my blood, filling me, ringing like Thania's voice as shadows pour into my throat, my limbs, every fiber of my being. They feed me, strengthen me, taking my fae body and honing it, strengthening it. The amount of power flowing through me is all at once amazing and horrifying, but the storm gives me no reprieve, no time for thought nor breath nor need. Shadows tear at my hair, my clothes, my nails.

Beams of moonlight burst from my soul. My nails lengthen and grow, honing themselves into lethal looking points. The curls in my hair feel lighter, springier, less a weight on my head. Every inch of me feels healthy, strong, eternal. Slowly, the roaring ends; the shadows calm and rest peacefully on my skin. They feel smoother, somehow, as if we are now made of the same substance.

Slowly, I return to the physical world. My eyes refuse to open. A droning sound fills my ears as a strange sensation squeezes my ribs, as if being forced into a corset two sizes too small. And then suddenly, painfully, my lungs fill with air for what feels like the first time.

"Rhea, come back to me," Sebastien's pained moan comes from the shell of my ear. His hands hold my slumped body up as life returns slowly to each and every limb. Despite my newfound immortal grace, I feel heavy, fuzzy, like I lingered on the other side for slightly too long. Every muscle in my body tremors as I fight my way back into this world.

"Please wake up." A small voice carries over to me. Luna? My senses finally return to me enough to feel relief at the sound of her voice. My eyelids flutter open, holding back the light for as long as possible. Through my hazy vision, I can see Brynn and Faye sitting on the rug below me. Sebastien still holds my body in his large, grey hands, his eyes shining with sadness. Luna curls up on the end of the sofa, her body warming my legs.

"Oh wow, everybody's here. What a party," I say, weakly. I thought becoming a goddess would hurt less. In truth, it warms my chest knowing my friends are safe. I can't wait to hear from Sebastien how he found everyone. Megara still sits beside me as well; her healing much further along than it was before I went to the other realm. She rises from the sofa with an easy grace and announces to the room that she will be back with refreshments in a few moments.

A few poorly disguised coughs about needing assistance later, and the rest of the group rises to leave. Brynn cups my face softly with a delicate hand as she passes by, the look in her eyes saying more than words ever could. Luna gives me a tight smile that gives me the inkling that maybe she understands what I went through today. I'll have to ask her about that later. A quick flash of light and Luna returns to her grimalkin body, following closely behind Brynn and Faye as they exit the room, leaving me alone with Sebastien.

"Rhea... The bond went dark, I was terrified," Sebastien says in a hoarse voice. He holds me even closer to his chest, and I return his hug with all the grace of a newborn colt. We haven't touched each other much up until now, but after all I have just experienced.... what's the harm? I feel unsure in my body now. It feels almost exactly the same, but altogether different. Like putting a shoe on the wrong foot. Hopefully, the feeling will ease with time. When I first came into my powers, I often felt this same discomfort but much of that was attributed to growing into womanhood.

Sebastien's shoulders tighten at the first contact of my fingers on his shirt, but after a few moments, that tension within him uncoils itself. A few hot, wet drops splash down onto me. The realization that he would cry for me... an intimate act among the dark fae.

"Sebastien, I am fine. I promise. It was... enlightening, and anything but easy, but I promise to you-- I am alive." And likely will be for a very long time, I think but do not add. Thinking about it however.... the pace of my heart is slow, much slower than I am used to.

"What was it like?" That easily he accepts my answer, accepts my boundaries.

"I saw Sivan," I whisper to Sebastien. His eyes widen a bit before he asks, "your husband?"

I nod, mind still whirling at all I have learned today.

"He told me that his soul would be fine, no matter what path I took. It was never Rhiannon's choice. She has never accepted the full power of a death queen. She would not accept the cost," I explain.

"What was the cost?" A wariness enters Sebastien's eyes. After decades of working for that bitch-queen, how much has he given up? Paid for with his own soul? I am sure he will understand that in order for me to become the queen that the Under-Realm needs, there is much I will need to sacrifice. My mortal life is only the first piece of the puzzle. There is still so much for me to learn.

Before I can answer, the rest of the group returns. Megara enters first, followed by Brynn and Faye. Luna trails after them, back in her cat form. Luna strolls over, and hops up onto the chaise with me, settling against my side with a small "mew."

"I understand much more than I did before, but I do not know everything. I passed the test, I think," I say and look to Megara for confirmation. Her eyes hold a knowing glint as she nods, the look on her face grave still.

"If you did not, you would not be here," she points out. She snaps her fingers and the refreshments she spoke of appear on the table before us: a heaping assortment of cakes and cookies, tea and coffee. A little something for everyone, even a bit of fish for Luna to have.

"Welcome, sister," Megara tells me as she walks over to a bookshelf near our cozy sitting area. Faye's eyes trail Megara as the goddess appears to be searching for something important. I'm unsure if I am imagining the worry within them. Faye's specialty is research after all. She would know if any information is baneful or useful.

"Where is it?" Megara murmurs before one of her hand's lands on a book and she sighs. A deep sigh that tells me she wishes she hadn't found it. The sound of her sigh triggers a flurry of activity in the cavernous room. My companions surround me then, fussing over me as if I were a newborn babe, but I wave them off. We can all have a nice chat about my experience later. Megara returns, the black leather tome in her hands.

"Only the sister of the shadows may read this tome. For all others it will appear blank. You have earned it." Her voice is solemn and low, thick with ancient magic. At her words, a title appears in silver filigree across the tomes black surface. In swirling letters, it reads "Shadows and Souls: The Death Queen's Promise." Faye's mouth pops open, her eyes wide with surprise.

"Have you heard of it?" I ask her. She nods, apparently speechless. Megara hands the book to me before finding a seat in a nearby chair. The moment my fingers make contact with the leather, a zing like lightning courses through me. I taste chocolate and strawberries on my tongue; I smell amber and cedar floating in on a phantom wind. All at once, the power is delicious and too much. I let the tome fall into my lap, hesitant to see what secrets it may contain.

"Faye? Do you know what's inside this book?" I ask the fairy, turning to meet her ocean eyes. Her gaze is wide and full of awe. She blinks at me for a moment, apparently at a loss for words, before clearing her throat.

"It is rumored that the first death queen put all of her knowledge into a journal, bound by death magic, so that all who followed would understand the burden of becoming the Queen of the Under-Realm. It contains records of the missing years, as well as personal records of the queens. It was thought to be lost to time. No one knows much more than that I'm afraid," she says, her eyes glazing over with desire.

"I... I shall read it when I am alone then."

The weight of everyone's eyes suddenly feels like a burden on its own. What little energy I had dissipates. My body feels heavy, tired, and a thousand thoughts flitter across my mind when Sebastien speaks.

"It has been a long and tedious day. Let's find rooms and retire for the night," he says, gesturing to Megara. She arches a brow at him, her brown eyes full of grief still.

"There's a set of rooms nearby that I suppose are now unoccupied. You may use them. This will guide you," she says, voice hoarse as she waves a hand. From her fingertips, a small ball of light bursts into existence.

"Do not lay a hand upon the orb. It burns," she adds before rising to her feet. Even with the glow of a goddess upon her, Megara looks fatigued. A bone deep weariness overcomes me at the realization that I must appear similar. The events of the past few months, days, hours.... even the shadows coiling tightly around me have lost their vibrancy. While it is comforting to know Sivan's soul rests easily, there is still so much unknown. There are still secrets to unravel.

"You good there?" Brynn asks and I realize everyone is once again staring at me.

"Just tired. Thank you, Goddess, for your kindness," I tell Megara politely and she responds with a light nod. As I stand and turn to leave, she stops us with a frown.

"What do I do with all the bodies?" The Goddess Megara asks us, in a small broken voice. The sound nearly cleaves my heart in two. It's been a long while since this sanctum had seen battle. Much of the landscape of the islands has changed in the several hundred years

Megara has reigned peacefully. Normally, her priestesses would handle tomb services and rituals for the dead. Maybe Egan would have done so, as a trusted high priestess.

Faye perks up from the chair she's claimed.

"If I may, Goddess," she says bobbing her red hair in Megara's direction, "I have studied all of the three sister's death rituals. I would be honored to perform them for the brave souls that lost their lives today." Faye walks over to Megara, and bows gracefully, formally, holding her position until Megara taps her on the shoulder in return. Megara's brown eyes shine with tears as a deep shuddering sigh goes through her.

"Yes, I accept. You may," she responds, voice strong and clear. The voice of a kind goddess to a worthy priestess.

Faye smiles in thanks before she says, "Thank you, Goddess. I will conduct the ceremony at sunrise, as is customary for Daughters of Megara." Megara dips her head slightly at Faye in response, before turning to me.

"Their souls are at peace, and we have taken care of their bodies," I tell Megara, knowing she will understand my gentle words. Her eyes close briefly, before she mouths "thank you" to me, then turns and disappears through a hidden doorway. The rest of us gather up our meager belongings. We will have to add new supplies to the ever-growing list of tasks we need to accomplish, in addition to finding time to discuss all that's happened.

True to Megara's word, that magically burning orb leads us out of the inner sanctum, down a few series of hallways, before stopping abruptly in the middle of one and blinking out of existence as easily as it came.

"I guess we're here," Faye jokes with a light tone. She and Brynn claim a room on the left while Luna chooses one on the opposite side, leaving Sebastien and I alone in the hallway together. A flush creeps over my skin, and I rub the back of my neck uncomfortably. That moment between us earlier was beyond intimate-- I'll admit I didn't hate it. That does not mean I am ready for more. What Sivan told me, changes nothing of my feelings. The silence lingers as we both try and think of what to say.

"What happened with Victorum earlier?" I blurt out around the flurry of my thoughts.

"He stalked them through town, thought he had them cornered. He wasn't expecting the fairy to disappear before his very eyes," Sebastien tells me with a chuckle, "It's a bit anticlimactic I'm afraid. I met up with Brynn and Faye at another tavern nearby, and they gave me a rundown on what happened. That fairy has a few hidden talents that helped them escape, and then I led them here. We were almost back to the sanctum when I felt the bond disappear. As did Luna."

Words die on my tongue, get caught in my throat. Anything I could say feels wanting. Sebastien stares down at me patiently, his onyx eyes unfathomable.

"I'm not very good at speaking, " I say, "The right words always seem to elude me."

"I'm not expecting anything from you, you know," Sebastien responds, cocking his head to the side as he debates my words, "You never have to be anyone other than yourself." A snort is my only response while I think of how to respond.

"That's part of the problem. My life has been entirely upended over the past year. I'm not even sure who I am anymore," I admit.

The indecision, the quiet moments, all of it... entirely foreign to me. Before Sivan died, no one would have said that I'm quiet and hard to understand.

"Then I will wait, as you figure out who you would like to be. I've got time," Sebastien says quietly. Mother moons above. Can I really be this lucky? I stare up at him for a moment, again at a loss for words. Then, I surge forward, placing my hands around his waist and hugging him.

"Thank you. I'll see you in the morning..." I say, my words muffled against his shirt. Then I turn and stride down the hallway, entering the room Luna had chosen a few minutes ago. I tug the door shut behind me then turn to lean against it, sliding to the floor with a hand over my heart. My cheeks burn.

"Are you alright?" Luna asks from the large bed dominating the room. I debate my answer a moment before responding.

"Not yet," I tell her, "But I think I will be."

CHAPTER NINETEEN

AFTER a long night of peaceful, unbroken dreams, I find myself in a good mood the next morning. The priestesses room Luna and I slept in is a cozy size, not too large or too small. The walls are largely unadorned and painted a soft white sand color. One window takes up the entire wall opposite the door. Luna opens up the window while I get ready, seating herself on a bench below it and facing out. I watch her for a moment: the peaceful rise and fall of her chest, the contemplative look in her eyes as she gazes out at the landscape in the distance, and the twitch of her tail on the ground behind her. Her hair is long and unbound down her back, still tangled from sleep. A small smile settles on my lips at the sight. After all Luna's been through, she deserves the gentle peace of a sunrise. Sunrise. At the thought, my good mood nearly evaporates.

"Luna, the soul ceremony should be starting soon." I tell her softly, hating myself for ruining her moment of peace. She will have many days of peace ahead, if I can succeed in the trials to come. Another quick braid and my own hair slips down my back, out of the way. The only clothing I have is the same red skirt and top combo I wore yesterday. The color seems garish considering I'm attending a soul ceremony, but I'll make do. A quick blast of my power vanishes the wrinkles from the light material instantly, as shadows flow over me in one quick movement. There's a small standing mirror in the corner that I use to check my appearance over. For a moment, I'm thrust back home, back to the cabin, my own memories rushing at me and pulling me down.

I stared at the dirty mirror in our bedroom, unseeing, eyes glazed over. I looked through my eyes but felt as if I was a passenger within my own body, as if I were not fully in control. The shadows did not move on my skin, every bit of them as cold and unfeeling as I was. Even grief could not reach me. My reflection stared back, her hollow eyes revealing nothing.

"Rhea," Addie said from behind me. I did not move. I did not speak. I could not. "Rhea, they've taken him. He's gone," she said. The words were meaningless. I knew. I had known since the moment he stopped breathing. That unending ceaseless grief threatened, building from somewhere deep within me, accumulating in my throat and burning, burning, burning, burning. Addie grabbed me by my arms then and spun me around to face her.

"Can you hear me, child?" she asked, worry in her eyes for me, even as her own grief tangled with her. Slowly, with as little movement as possible, I nodded.

It's Luna, frantically calling my name over and over again, that pulls me back to the present.

"We have to go," she breathes, "The others are waiting for us." I rub my temples and notice there's a thinner, more flexible layer of shadows on my skin. They feel different, stronger. I'll need to find time to read the Goddesses journal, as well as talk with Brynn and Faye and Sebastien and the ever-growing list of things to do. I need to control my newly strengthened powers. The shadows writhe on my skin in irritation and I shove my magic down, imagining it as snake I am trapping. A shudder runs through me as I wrest control from that ancient darkness. Luna stares at me, her eyes round with concern.

"Okay, everything's alright, we can go," I tell her, and she rolls her eyes at me. She appears ready, however, and the pounding at the door suggests the others are as well. Faye and Brynn have found new clothing: flowy, light colored shirts and tan pants, with soft looking boots. Brynn hands me my leather satchel with a small yawn. The lines forming on her face worry me. She's pulled her hair up into a tight bun with small braids and beads scattered throughout. She only puts her hair in a bun when something bothers her. The stress she's putting herself through... all for me. I'm not sure if I deserve this kind of dedication. I take the satchel from her, then pull her into a quick hug.

"Thank you," I murmur into Brynn. I feel her face lift into a smile, and she hugs me a little tighter, understanding my thanks is not meant for saving my bag alone. She releases me, then turns to Faye and begins discussing the ritual for that morning. Faye's hair does not reflect the same stress. Her long red hair is unbound today, flowing softly over her petite body like a wave of blood. Her hair reminds me of Bellum. I'll need to find him and see if he's finished the task I gave him.

Sebastien stands behind the others, his horns gleaming softly in the light filtering through the arched hallway, wearing the same black outfit as before. His hair is an inky black mess around his horns that has me aching to touch it. My eyes meet his. I open my mouth to speak, but as usual, the right words refuse to come. My teeth tear into my bottom lip as I opt to say nothing at all. A small smile plays on Sebastien's dark lips, as if he can read my internal struggle. He tilts a horn towards me but does not force a conversation. Luna slips her hand into mine, and we walk together, following behind Faye and Brynn as Faye leads us all to Megara's altar at the top of the volcano.

"It's amazing how quickly you've memorized the layout of the sanctum," I call towards Faye. She smiles back at me before her voice rings out at me, "I have an eidetic memory. It's a fairy gift from our first queen, Saphielle." Interesting. The place seems rather confusing to me, but if I can memorize the layout of the forest back home, then I'm sure after a day or two this will be familiar enough as well.

Some of the hallways are decorated with religious relics and offerings to the Goddess Megara. When we pass the notes of love and adoration towards the goddess, my throat burns. All those people, murdered. Megara is devastated despite her reserved demeanor yesterday. Did Rhiannon do this not only torment me, but also to weaken Megara?

Sebastien lingers by my side as we walk through the eerily silent halls of the sanctum, before we ascend a series of stairs and find ourselves at the peak of the sanctum where an altar has been built into the edge of the volcano's lip. The altar is built around a large sculpture of Megara made of that sleek black rock. The floor has been carved from the stone itself, depicting the sister moons and prayers written in the old language.

Megara stands expectantly in the center of the moons, waiting for us. Today, she wears flowing orange robes that sparkle in the growing sunlight. A crown that looks like flames extending toward the sky sits on her brow. Grief limns her being, the expression on her face echoes my own. Her memories swirl around her but interestingly enough, when I try to examine them, they slip from my gasp. Then, Faye leads us into the altar space, dipping her head towards the goddess, and I have no time to think about it.

Megara looks at me. My spine tingles with the force of her gaze, the hair on my scalp prickling with it. This is not the same injured goddess I found in a closet yesterday-- this is The Goddess Megara, the full glow of eternal fae upon her. Unease builds within me under her gaze, under the realization that this might be how others see me now, as well.

"Sister," she says, her voice formal and commanding, "The grace of immortality suits you." She turns to Faye and tells her, "I hope you know what you are doing fairy. My priestesses deserve nothing less than an eternity of honor and rest." She waves a golden hand, bidding us to continue. Faye directs the group, positioning us at various points around the etchings in the stone flooring. She tells us that each point represents something specific related to the volcano and the suns' positioning. Much of what she tells us is unfamiliar, but her tinkling voice keeps me interested as she leads us through the ceremony. At the halfway point, Faye directs Megara to kneel in the center of the altar and release a few prayers for her priestesses. Megara gives Faye a long look, and I think she's about to argue with the fairy, but Megara quietly kneels down and begins murmuring to herself. Her hands rest peacefully on her strong thighs, but that sadness still lines her, as I suspect it will for many days to come.

The ceremony lasts for far longer than either the dark fae or the autumn fae's traditions dictate. Much of it involves quiet contemplation, resting in place and thinking of memories of the deceased. The darkness of my friends and companions' memories swirl around me, pulling at me tantalizingly. It's much simpler to resist their thrall with the new power flowing through me. It's difficult to describe. I feel wholly different yet altogether unchanged at my core. Though I have much to conquer, being able to resist the grief around me has me feeling a bit more confident.

Luna's memories earlier felt.... different. Stronger, thrumming with an unidentifiable magic source. Maybe when she trusts me more, she will tell me about the Grimalkin and what happened to her.

The peace I feel is immeasurable, as if my thoughts are completely my own for once. Tension leaves my shoulders; my posture straightens. Even the knot in my jaw feels the lightest it has in months. As if he senses the change within me, Sebastien's eye catches mine and the corners of his lips curl up into a slight smile. I look away quickly, but his smile plays in my mind over and over again.

Faye brings the ceremony to its end, right as the suns reach the highest point in the sky. A sense of finality sweeps through the veranda. The waves crash loudly off the rocks behind the volcano. I feel a ghostly caress against my cheek. The sensation is here and then gone, as if a passing soul came to say goodbye. The feeling of loss is replaced with contentment. These priestesses lost their life defending something they cherished, and I cannot find fault with that, though the senseless violence makes me ill. I take the hand on my cheek as a sign that all is well, the priestesses are moving on.

We all stand there for a moment after the ceremony ends, the silence between us echoing loudly. Megara seems slumped in on herself, as if whatever force roused her from bed has suddenly left her. Sebastien stands casually, observing everything from the waves crashing far below, to the expressions on our companions faces, and every now and then he glances at me as if looking for an answer. Brynn and Luna are holding hands and standing together, a bit away from the rest of us.

Faye is the first to speak, breaking through the odd air around us.

"I'm famished. We should see about lunch," she says, sunlight beaming off her red hair, fairy skin sparkling faintly.

Megara retreats even further into herself.

"The priestesses normally handle the large meals. I can use my magic to do it, as I did yesterday, but it is a great effort for little reward, as it's not what I'm made for"

The look of exhaustion on her face reminds me of my own grief and pain after Sivan died. It never truly leaves you, that pain and loss, but you do get better at carrying it with you.

"Don't worry about that, Rhea is a wonderful cook," Brynn interjects with a beaming smile, "As am I. We'll have something whipped up in no time. Just point us to the kitchen."

Brynn's ability to remain positive in any situation always astounds me. She always seems to know exactly what combination of words will keep people calm. Megara looks at me quizzically.

"Cooking has always been one of my favorite activities. I can whip up a mean stew," I tell her, "And you haven't lived until you've tried Brynn's sour dough." Brynn blushes at my praise, but it's only the truth. Addie installed a love of cooking and baking into all of her children. She always says, "everyone has to eat, so everyone should know how to feed themselves."

Megara leads us down the stairs we came from, through the courtyard Sebastien and I first arrived in, and down another series of hallways until we arrive at a large set of wooden doors. Sebastien opens them for us, and when we enter the combined kitchen and dining room all of us collectively gasp while Megara watches amused. The ceiling domes out like Megara's inner sanctum, with a circular sunroof in the center.

A fully modern kitchen lines one wall, with a gorgeous stone island in front of it. Everything is a sleek onyx color, with pops of gold that catch the sunlight. Some strange metal machines sit on the counter, that I've never seen before in my life. What strange concoctions must they create?

Brynn breezes into the cooking space, never doubtful for a moment. If she doesn't understand how something works, she'll tinker with it until she does.

I trail after her, and together we begin cooking up a meal worthy of the goddesses. We work in tandem, shuffling around each other with an ease that time spent together brings.

"The quality of this meat is amazing. Almost as fresh as the deer we brought down in the Hollow Forest," Brynn exclaims, hazel eyes alight with wonder, as she observes the ingredients, we have available. She chops the meat, while I find a variety of vegetables and begin working on them. I work silently; Brynn makes a few comments here and there keeping up a comfortable chatter. As we work, Sebastien, Faye, Luna, and Megara settle into chairs and chat quietly about things of no consequence.

As I begin kneading dough, Megara and Sebastien's conversation catches my attention. They speak lowly but my fae ears easily hear each word.

"It's been a while, princeling," Megara says. Her words cause the flesh on my neck to prickle, as if I should listen carefully. My shadows buzz lowly around my skin.

"Yes, Goddess, much has happened in the centuries since we last met," Sebastien responds respectfully. His tone makes me think he wishes he could avoid this conversation for another few.

"Have things gone as expected?"

Though my back is turned to them as Brynn and I dance around each other while cooking, a flooding sense of foreboding fills my limbs. I can feel Sebastien's eyes on my back as he responds, perhaps a bit more coolly than before.

"No," he says tightly. Megara's only response is a slight, "hmmph."

Suddenly, I get the feeling of walking into a situation wholly unprepared. Sebastien and Megara are keeping secrets from me, and I intend to find out what. Through any means necessary.

Brynn bumps her hip into mine, tearing my thoughts away from the cryptic conversation.

"Appetizers and meat are almost ready, how are things on your end?"

Looking down, I realize I've been so focused on spying that I've barely accomplished my task. I set about chopping, dicing, then frying the vegetables before me and put any thoughts of secrets out of my mind. Before long, the scent of garlic and spices drifts through the air. Luna's stomach rumbles loudly as the fragrance wafts over to the rest of the group.

Faye laughs at the sound.

"Will stew satisfy you, little one?" She asks Luna, rousing a laugh from everyone. Even Megara in her endless grief gives a slight chuckle.

Luna responds in a tight voice, "I am as much a person as I am a feline. I can eat stew."

Faye blushes wildly, her sparkly skin turning nearly as red as her vibrant hair.

Luna's comment cuts off the laughter as everyone realizes how bigoted Faye's comment sounds. We don't know much about the Grimalkin, but that does not mean we should treat Luna any differently because of that. She's not a true cat, but an adult woman. I can see why she'd be annoyed by Faye's comment. Faye apologizes quickly and we move on.

All is quiet as Brynn and I serve the rest of the group. When I place a bowl in front of Sebastien, he grabs my wrist gently and thanks me. Then he says something that surprises me.

"Make sure you get enough to eat as well," he says, voice stern. I hear a hint of worry in his voice, as if he cares enough to make sure I take care of myself. My throat tightens uncomfortably-- Sivan used to take care of me in the same way. I shake my head a little, warding off memories. Instead of giving in to that bit of grief, I smile lightly.

"I will, thank you," I tell him quietly. My smile catches him off guard and he doesn't respond. Frowning internally, I find my own seat and we all dig into the fresh meal. Have I really been unpleasant enough that a smile shocks him? All things considered, I feel like I'm quite generous with my smiles. Always making sure those around me do not fret about my health, mental or physical.

We settle into the meal, making conversation in between bites. My meal disappears quickly, my hunger surprising me. I tap a finger on the table while everyone else is eating. Sebastien's throat muscles capture my attention, my eyes unable to peel away from that delicate bit of grey flesh. He notices me staring, his eyebrow raising at me in question.

In my embarrassment, I blurt the first sentence I can think of.

"Sebastien, what is your favorite color?"

The question catches him off guard and he chokes a bit on a mouthful of food. He stares at me for a moment as he swallows hard.

"No one has ever asked me that before," he says quietly, the look in his eyes unfathomable. As if he is partially amused and partially haunted.

His answer fills me with immense sadness, but I push it aside.

"I am asking now, and I would like to know the answer."

I would like to know you.

His eyes darken, but he answers my question.

"Sea glass.," he answers resolutely, and I feel a smile rise across my face.

"Like my eyes?" I ask. He purses his lips in return, hiding his own smile.

"Maybe," he tells me, a flirty hint to his voice.

Something blossoms within me at the sound. As if the ice around my heart has begun thawing, just a little, and maybe one day spring will bloom again. The feeling sinks into me soft and slow, and I hold onto it.

After a long moment, I look away blushing and resume eating. Faye launches into a story about one of her adventures in the great library while Luna pops back into her cat form and curls up on Faye's lap for a nap. All is forgiven, apparently.

Megara finishes her portion and excuses herself to her chambers.

Before she leaves, she tells us we can explore wherever we like, have whatever we like, for she has no need for material goods the way the rest of us do. When she is gone, the rest of us sit in companionable silence for a while, but eventually my friends begin side eyeing me. I can see them looking to me for approval, looking for what I think the next right move is. Thinking over all that has happened to our group in the past few weeks and what may happen in the future, I begin compiling a list in my head of what we should do first. Self-defense seems top of the list.

Sebastien nods as if reading my mind.

"I am trained in various types of combat. I can aid you in your quest to strengthen," he says, grey face solemn and serious. I wonder what drives him, what motivates him. Is it genuine care for me, or something else?

"I know a bit. Not enough to truly defend myself. If Rhiannon had wanted me dead, she could have killed me by now," I tell him, and his dark eyes flash with knowing. At this point, I am certain he's hiding something from me, but I cannot tell how serious or monumental it is yet. "Then we will start with strengthening exercises, then hand to hand combat, and then weapons. If that's alright with you," he adds looking over me to ensure it is. At my nod, he continues on, "It may take a while. We should find a room here for training and gather supplies as we can. Plus, you will need to explore the new limitations of your powers."

Gulping, I nod and then direct my attention to Brynn and Faye.

"You are welcome to join as well, of course."

Brynn snorts in a way that tells me she would join whether I welcome her or not. Faye says she would rather not, but that she would watch. Luna simply perks her head up at me, blinks slowly, then very deliberately turns away from me and resumes her slumber. My throat burns with a feeling that suggests a turning point in my life. If I accept Sebastien's help, then I accept that my life shall never return to normal. I accept that one day I will rule over the Under Realm and all that entails.

Sebastien catches my gaze as I drown in my own thoughts, pulling me out of my sadistic reverie. His gaze is deep and penetrating. I have very little left to lose except for my friends, and if the goddesses dare take them from me then I will destroy this world in order to bring them back again.

Brynn knows this and calculates everything around my foolishness. Without her, I would be a ship lost to stormy seas. Ignoring my tumultuous feelings, I turn towards Sebastien-- his eyes are calculating and cool.

"When do we start?" I ask.

"Tomorrow, at dawn," comes his fanged response.

CHAPTER TWENTY

I find myself in a small circular room, tucked away in a maze of forgotten hallways. The domed glass ceiling above catches the twin lights of the sister moons, scattering delicate rainbows onto the walls. The patterns shift with the faintest movement, an ethereal dance of color that feels both tranquil and otherworldly.

The bookshelves are built directly into the walls, each one overflowing with volumes that seem to have waited lifetimes for someone to notice them again. My fingers brush against the spines as I wander, the leather soft and worn, their titles whispering promises of stories long untold. Despite the sense of abandonment, the room is immaculate, untouched by dust or decay.

A large love seat sits at the center, paired with a few armchairs that look as though they were designed for stolen hours of reading and quiet contemplation. Everything about the space feels intentional, crafted for comfort. It's so unlike the rest of the sanctum, with its grandeur and divine detachment. Here, there is only warmth, as if the room itself remembers what it means to be human.

The stillness here is a sharp contrast to the rest of the day. Faye and Brynn spent hours laughing and flirting in the kitchen, their voices bright as they roasted birds and decorated cakes. I'd stayed with them for a time, but their frosting-smeared kisses sent me fleeing, seeking a reprieve from their intimacy. Luna had been no better company, lost in a world of romance novels with Megara. Sebastien, distant as always, was off hunting for Bellum.

And so, I wandered.

Now, standing in this forgotten sanctuary, the storm in my chest finally quiets. The weight of the day slips away as I sink into the love seat, its cushions embracing me like an old friend. Above me, the moonlight continues its gentle play, and for the first time in hours, I feel... at peace.

The cozy little room is all centered around a fire pit. The sight is familiar, though I have never been here before, the comfort it proves me like that of my shadows, my oldest friends. As I gaze at the pit, a fire jumps to life in its center, warming the slight chill in the room.

"Hello," I say in response to the fire, then curse myself for being so silly. Of course no one responds and so I curl up in a chair and pull out the journal, ready to dive back into the world of the last true death goddess.

War of the Queens, Day 478:

The Under-King has offered me a deal. He wants one thing from me, and then he will assist me in destroying the invaders as well as their dark queen. I hesitate to take it, given his history, but... the war has gone on for over a year now. My citizens are tired. The land has turned dark with blood and ash. Davos, Kiernan, Gnash and Emerson have all been slain, within days of each other. My heart grew weary long ago. I have no one and nothing. No advantage. And that bitch has taken everything from me with only the help of a few traitors. The shadows whisper to me, telling me everything they can think of to help me win, but I fear it's no use.

I rub my fingers over the text, the brevity of her words reading like a memory. Speaking to the shadows sounds useful. I doubt they speak the language of the fae, so I wonder how they speak? Perhaps through memory. The rest of the page is filled mostly with details of the queen's anxiety. My patience thins, and I flip a few pages forward.

War of the Queens, Day 485:

The Under-King came to see me this morning. He inquired as to my decision. I still had not made up my mind, but I looked into his dark eyes and what I saw there had me agreeing to his proposal. We outlined a contract together. He'll be back later this evening to fulfill the contract and seal it with our blood. The shadows are oddly silent. They have not commented on my decision. In fact, it's been two days since I felt much of anything from them at all. Worry, worry, worry. It's all I seem to do these days, yet my intuition tells me something is wrong. I feel that I will not live to see another day, despite the Under-Kings offer of assistance. I have lost too many souls; I have had to release more to the afterworld than I can count. Yet, that bitch keeps coming. Her armies advance further and further each day. My territory has been reduced to the castle.

That queen's memories end there, as her words have been smudged, but it looks like it was done intentionally. It's abrupt, the ink having encompassed too much of the dry leathery paper, and most likely recently done. The shadows on my skin writhe, their smoky tendrils reaching towards the tome in my lap. Their presence soothes me, centers me so I can continue reading.

The next entries are a few blank pages later, tucked away in the book. When I observe them more closely, they have been ripped from the tome, presumably earlier entries, and they are written in a smaller and neater font than the one before.

Rituals and Spells:

-Herbs and Ingredients

-Aspects of Marriage

-Spells for protection

-Rituals for protection and safety

-Summoning dark creatures (3 of the known ancients)

-Raising the dead

-Necromancy & Ethical Acquisition

-Blood Magic

-Soul Binding (USE AT OWN RISK)

-Poetry

I chuckle a bit, some of the entries very odd to me. I flip to the poems section just for a bit of rest from the intensity of the rest of the journal, as well as because that seems the most interesting to me.

The shadows sing

If you dare to listen

Listen with your heart

And your worst intentions.

My spine straightens as I realize these are no poems. These are spells she didn't want to share with anyone but the true soul queen.

Maybe she was afraid someone could bypass her magical barriers, or that the future guardian of her journal might not be able to keep it safe. My eyes search the room around me, just making sure no one has snuck in, before my eyelids flutter closed. The moments feel long as I feel nothing... nothing... I sigh. Clear my mind and try again. The longer I am patient.... slowly, I begin to feel it. Building out from my center in soft glowing waves of darkness, my body thrums with energy. Similar to how I see the aura of others, it's as if I am seeing my own aura and the inward connection it has to the shadows. No, not the shadows I realize. All shadows. I can feel all the shadows around me as if they were extensions of my true self, the kernel of dark energy within me vibrant and alive. There are other types of shadows too. I'll have to start naming them all to keep sense of them.

One of them has a slower pace to their thrumming, their darkness like a smudging of charcoal. Shade, I decide. They coo in response, their thrumming becoming a cresting wave within me as if in approval. Another is deep, green and.... cold. If a shadow can even be cold, but my mind recoils from it, as if on instinct. It reminds me of the shadows Sebastien wielded earlier. There is nearly a dozen different types of shadows connected to me, and the longer I listen to them, the worse I feel. It feels as if they are feeding on my very essence. I squirm, the discomfort from these powers warring against each other writhing under my skin like snakes. My shoulders heave as I force myself to breathe deeply, forcing myself to slow down and calm down. These new powers will take time to adjust to. After a moment, I laugh and realize I can just open my eyes and so I do. The immediate connection is gone, though I can still feel them to a degree. It feels like the sounds of the forest though-- I can treat it as meaningless background noise until I need it.

There is plenty more to read I am sure but reading this has drained me much more than I realized. The tome somehow makes its ways out of my hands onto a tea table nearby while I step closer to the fire pit. There's a little collection of iron pots for boiling water and tea pots and everything I need to make a hot cup of tea.

The soft patter of light footsteps alerts me to Sebastien's presence. I don't turn to see him walk through the doorway, but his presence is as familiar to me as my own.

"Sebastien."

"Rhea," he says. His voice is low, sensual, and sends shivers down my spine. I shrug the feeling off, keeping my nose turned down towards my book.

"Anything interesting in there?" he asks, as he settles into a chair opposite mine.

"A bit," I smile out of habit before letting it fall from my face. "Where's Bellum?"

"I helped him get settled in a room of his own... I've never seen that look on his face before. His nails were covered in flesh and blood."

"Good."

Sebastien looks at me and nods, but I can't say if it's in approval or some other emotion.

"Yes, but that doesn't make it any easier to watch. I suspect he will be atoning through his actions for a long time."

The comment feels weighted, but I ignore the subtle lash of his tongue. Ignore the way his gaze makes me squirm as he makes his way into one of the chairs around the fire. However, I fail to suppress the slight giggle that escapes me when he adjusts his position several times, apparently uncomfortable. My loveseat is quite large enough for two, maybe even three people. The little scalloped chair Sebastien is trying to prop himself up in is clearly meant for a singular person, and probably not designed for comfort.

"What?" he says, the agitation in his voice and frustration in his movements only making me laugh harder. "You would laugh at my misfortune?"

"Oh, yes," I beam, "Absolutely." Snapping the tome shut, I sit up and rub my eyelids.

After witnessing the emotions of the priestesses who died in the moments directly before their deaths..... well, laughter feels fantastic. The smile that breaks across his face in return is soft, genuine and breath-taking. His smile makes my heart pound with fear in a way I've only felt once before. When the smile slips from Sebastien's face, I know I've been projecting my thoughts towards him again, and I shrug a small apology.

"I'm glad it pleases you, my lady, as misfortune is a daemon's oldest friend." His tone remains light, but the words have a sharpness to them that doesn't match. A glimpse of memory bursts across the bond before he can contain it. The sadness in that small burst cuts me like a knife, it so akin to the grief I've felt every day since Sivan's death.

"When I was a child," I begin speaking in soft tones, "My cousin Janessa took me ice skating at the lake nearest the castle in Darrid. I don't remember how she convinced my parents to let me go. She's only a few years older than me, but she's got that sort of charm people just can't say no to." I smile at the memory, despite knowing how it ends. "Anyways, we're out there on the ice, right in the middle of the lake racing each other when there's this... haunting sound from below us. I don't know how else to explain it. I've never heard a sound like it since, but that sound taught me what fear truly is. Falling into the near frozen lake water was terrifying, but it was so cold it didn't really hurt."

I pause, shivering as the memory swells on my skin, shadows swirling like a fine mist. Sebastien's brows knit together like he can't figure out why I'm sharing this with him, but he'll understand soon enough.

"That was the first time the shadows did something besides protect my skin. They became solid for the first time. Strong and flexible. Without my asking, the shadows exploded from me, grabbing me and Janessa, pulling us up and across the ice. Saving us. Life always takes something from us. People think to fear death but dying is nothing. Dying is natural. Living in spite of the pain and challenges we face.... well, that is completely unnatural, but we choose to do it anyway. Death is all knowing and unescapable, and it is my closest friend."

"You would choose to remain in darkness, even knowing what it holds?"

"It holds everything I hold dear. It's as much a part of me as I am of it."

He nods at that, like he needs time to ponder my words.

Sebastien leans back, the firelight casting sharp shadows across his angular features. His eyes, usually so guarded, seem to soften as he regards me. "You speak of death as if it's an old friend. Most people speak of it with fear."

"Most people don't know it as intimately as I do," I reply, my tone even but edged with something colder. "You learn not to fear what you can't escape. Besides..." My fingers curl into the arm of the loveseat, the shadows around me shifting, restless. "The living are far more terrifying than the dead."

A faint smile tugs at his lips, though it doesn't reach his eyes. "That may be true. But I wonder..." His voice trails off, his gaze lingering on me as if searching for something he cannot name. "What would you do if you had the chance to let it go? The darkness. The weight of all you carry."

I laugh, the sound light but brittle. "Let it go? Do you think it's something I can simply drop like a cloak?" I shake my head. "No, Sebastien. The darkness is not a burden. It's my foundation. Without it, I wouldn't know who I am."

His expression darkens, and he shifts forward, elbows resting on his knees. The shadows ripple behind him, but they are not his; they are mine, drawn to his presence like iron filings to a magnet. "And yet," he says softly, "you keep people at arm's length. Even those who might understand."

The words hit harder than I care to admit. I clench my jaw, turning my gaze to the fire. Its flames dance in erratic patterns, mirroring the unease twisting in my chest. "You're assuming I want to be understood."

"Don't you?" His voice is quieter now, less challenging, more curious. "Don't you ever wish for someone who sees you, all of you, and stays anyway?"

My breath catches, and for a moment, I have no answer. The silence stretches between us, filled only with the crackling of the fire and the soft hum of the shadows. When I finally speak, my voice is barely above a whisper. "I wouldn't even know where to begin."

Sebastien leans back again, his posture relaxed, but his gaze still intent. "Maybe you don't have to begin. Maybe it just... happens. If you let it."

His words stir something deep within me, something I'm not ready to face. I stand abruptly, the motion startling even me. The shadows swirl around my feet like an eager tide, following me as I step closer to the firepit. I reach for the kettle, more to occupy my hands than out of any real desire for tea.

"I didn't ask for advice, Sebastien."

"No," he says, his tone mild, almost teasing. "But you needed it."

I glare at him over my shoulder, but his smirk only deepens, infuriatingly self-assured. The tension between us feels like a taut string, vibrating with unspoken words and emotions I'm not ready to name. I hate how he gets under my skin, how his presence draws out pieces of me I'd rather keep buried.

"Why are you even here?" I snap, pouring hot water into a teacup with more force than necessary.

He doesn't flinch at my tone, his smirk fading into something more serious. "Because you're here. And because, despite what you might think, you shouldn't have to be alone with your ghosts."

The vulnerability in his voice catches me off guard, and I freeze, the teacup trembling slightly in my hand. When I look at him, his expression is open, unguarded in a way that makes my chest ache. I want to dismiss him, to shut him out, but the words won't come.

Instead, I sink back into the loveseat, the shadows curling protectively around me. "You're persistent, I'll give you that," I mutter, lifting the cup to my lips. The tea is scalding, but the pain is grounding, pulling me back to the present.

Sebastien chuckles, a low, rich sound that sends another shiver down my spine. "You'll find I'm full of surprises, Rhea."

The way he says my name, soft and deliberate, makes my breath hitch. I glance at him out of the corner of my eye, but he's already looking at the fire, his expression unreadable. The silence between us feels different now—less like a barrier and more like a bridge, fragile but waiting to be crossed.

For a moment, I consider reaching out, letting him in, but the weight of my past holds me back. Instead, I sink deeper into the cushions, the shadows pulling tighter around me like a cocoon.

"Goodnight, Sebastien," I say finally, my voice quieter than I intended.

He doesn't move for a long time, his gaze fixed on the flames. When he finally stands, the shadows shift, reluctant to let him go. He pauses in the doorway, glancing back at me with an unreadable expression.

"Goodnight, Rhea," he says, and then he's gone, leaving me alone with the firelight and the whispers of the shadows.

I close my eyes, letting the warmth of the room seep into my skin. Despite everything, Sebastien's words linger, a quiet echo in the back of my mind.

Maybe it just... happens. If you let it.

CHAPTER TWENTY-ONE

MY breath comes out unevenly the next day as I once again ascend the stairs to the ceremony space from the day before. A cool breeze sweeps in from the ocean surrounding the sanctum, and dark clouds swirl above. Most likely a storm approaching from the sea for the breeze carries the scent of rain with it.

None of the others have arrived yet. I'm early. The sister suns have barely kissed the ocean line, barely dotted the night sky orange. I could scarcely sleep with Sebastien's words floating in my mind. My nerves got the best of me last night after flirting with Sebastien. Even now, my heart pounds unevenly, off kilter and out of rhythm. The loss of my husband still aches in my soul. Sivan saw me when no one else did. He did not care about my title or heritage, nor did he care about my powers of death. The shadows did not frighten him-- instead, they were soothed by him. As if the golden purity of his own magic were a balm to my own.

Sebastien will not be like that. His magic is as heady and dark as my own. I have the feeling when I finally give into these growing desires, the results will be explosive. Even now, my body tingles and aches in long forgotten places. My breasts feel heavier. Anxiety is not the only feeling making my breathing accelerate. And yet... there is much to discuss, many secrets to sort through before I can be intimate with him.

As I look out at the water, Sebastien arrives. I cannot see him, but every part of my being feels drawn towards him. The shadows on my skin urge me go to him. As I turn towards him, I catch him staring at me. His eyes flash as he devours the sight of me, his breath catches for a moment.

"What?" I ask, heat flooding my chest.

"You look absolutely divine bathing in the sunrise," he says, voice low. Voice sexy. Very very sexy.

I loosen a deep breath and lick my lips. Our eyes cannot part from one another's, the very space between us charged.

"Thank you," I quietly reply. My hair is in its usual braid, little black tendrils escaping in the humidity. My clothing is nice but unremarkable. Megara had a selection of clothing for us to browse through and I chose a set of loose white pants that are tight at the ankles but a long slit down the legs allows the breeze in, as well as a tight white cropped top with loose flowing material over my belly. I wasn't sure if we'd start with weapons today, but I figure there's a good chance my newly enhanced shadows will protect me better than any armor anyways. Anyways, there's nothing spectacular about my outfit, and I look down at myself a bit puzzled.

"Yes, you. You are beautiful, my goddess," he compliments me again and this time, the tingling reaches my very core, turning it into molten lava.

I wave him off with a small laugh, and tell him, "You flatter me. I was not sure what to wear, or what we might begin with."

He considers my words for a moment before analyzing the space around us. It's large, open, and as the suns climb higher and higher, they fill the terrace with golden light.

"We don't have much in the way of equipment," Sebastien says thoughtfully as he looks around, "so we'll need to use our bodies and the environment to train." He walks to the middle of the space and crouches low, reaching out a hand and touching the hard stone flooring. He grimaces at the floor as if it's offended him somehow and my lips twitch slightly as I hold back a laugh. Probably best not to laugh at the one trying to help you.

"Can you transmute objects?" he asks me, looking up at me from the ground.

I shake my head, indicating that I cannot. He purses his lips, stands up, and leaves without a word. I'm not sure what that whole scene was about but I am both annoyed and amused. What is he so miffed about?

After several minutes, where I choose to be patient and enjoy the warming suns, Sebastien returns with several sheets in tow. He arranges them neatly and smoothly on the ground before nodding at his handiwork, slapping his palms together, and turning towards me with a satisfied look on his grey face. The sight is too much, and I absolutely lose it, laughing and laughing. His satisfied expression changes and he looks confused.

"I-- I'm sor--," I try to explain myself in between laughter but it feels so good to laugh that I can't stop. It's utterly ridiculous and a bit embarrassing, but it's cathartic. Sebastien seems anything but upset though. Once he realizes why I'm laughing, a gentle smile crosses his face.

"I was concerned the rough ground might hurt your skin," he says simply. I tilt my head at him and raise my eyebrows.

"We're about to fight and potentially injure each other. I am literally a goddess, and you are..." I wave a hand at the muscled daemon in front of me before continuing, "You look like *that*. I have magical shadows that protect my skin. And you're worried about stone on my skin?"

He chuckles at bit, as if he understands my sense of humor, but nods.

"Yes, I am. But I see your point."

Neither of us make any motion to remove it.

Brynn and Faye Walk up the stairs a few seconds later, a grumpy looking Luna trudging up behind them, her tail flicking angrily.

Faye has brought a myriad of things to occupy herself with while the rest of us train and learn. She arranges plush looking blankets off to the side of the circle, setting up an umbrella and a picnic basket. She has several dusty looking tomes with her, and she sets them gingerly on her blanket. She snaps her fingers, and a teapot made of leaves and a matching cup appears before her. Her green skin glitters faintly and she settles in with her books and tea. I envy her immensely.

Luna glares at the sun and glares at all of us. She doesn't say a single word, simply morphs into her cat form, and lays down on a sunny spot on Faye's blanket. I raise a brow at Brynn in question and she shrugs her shoulders in return. She's changed her hair today, wearing it in dozens of tightly coiled miniature buns. Her outfit is similar to mine though she's wearing the orange Megara prefers. She looks happy and healthy. It warms my heart.

Once everyone is settled, Sebastien guides me and Brynn through a series of stretches. Some of them I've heard of before, and some are difficult even for me. During one stretch, he has me bend low to the ground and touch my toes at the same time. It's slightly uncomfortable but I'm used to physical activity. After a while, the discomfort goes away and my limbs become looser. Sebastien gives us corrections like my old tutors used to, but he's very kind about it, which surprises me for some reason.

When Brynn overextends her knee, he gently points it out and asks her to watch how he aligns his ankle with his knee, and why it's important to do so. She thanks him and he nods approvingly once Brynn corrects it.

He comes over to me after and asks if he can touch my back to straighten it. I nod my permission though that familiar heat floods me again as he does so.

"Don't hurt yourself, little raven," he murmurs into my ear, pressing a kiss into it.

He turns away and strides across the makeshift training area, reaching for a pitcher of water. Brynn turns to me as soon as he walks away, and mouths "wow, hot." A blush spreads across my cheeks, and I try to focus on stretching. Just stretching.

Not his grey skin moving underneath his muscles or what his horns might look like in my hands. In between my thighs. It's been so long since I've been touched by the one I love.... my body aches with need. The exercise somehow makes it worse. Sebastien returns, looking amused, as if my feelings are spilling out into our bond.

He says nothing, however, as he returns and begins walking us through the basic points of self-defense.

"Use whatever magic you have to keep your enemy away from you," he says, voice insistent and demanding, "Prevent them from getting close to you and you will never have to use what I am teaching you. Once we get to the Under-Realm, most of the men you will fight will be larger than you. You don't want to be up close and personal if you can help it." Brynn and I nod in unison, indicating we are listening and that we understand. There's only so much that you can do when your opponent has a physical advantage against you. That's when intelligence will carry you to victory.

Sebastien then goes through various ways to get out of an opponent's grasp should they grab you. Again, some of his techniques are familiar to me, yet others are wholly new and require me to think more creatively. After that, he takes us through a series of rolls, dodges, and self-defense maneuvers. All of it geared towards giving us space between an enemy and time to think of a way to defeat that enemy.

Sebastien is patient and gentle in his approach which continuously awes me. Once he's satisfied that we can do the stretches and rolls and dodges sufficiently, then he announces we're moving on to actual combat.

"Do the two of you know anything about fighting hand to hand?" he asks, tilting his horns to the side.

Brynn and I exchange a glance full of mischief and I know exactly what she's thinking of. All the time we rough housed with her brothers and sisters, all the punches we've thrown at one another, and all the wrestling we did with weird creatures in the Hollow Forest. She's been well taught in that regard.

"Not necessarily..." Brynn intones rather unconvincingly and I playfully shove an elbow into her ribs. She pretends it hurts and holds her rib cage dramatically while pouting.

Sebastien laughs but his eyes remain mostly serious.

"Tell me what you know. What you can do," he says, and I get the feeling he's trying to accomplish more than just teaching us today. He's searching for information. But what does he want to know? Brynn answers him first while I process his question.

"I'm trained and skilled in many types of combat," she says, a twinkle in her eye, "And I can heal. Quite extensive wounds as well, so I can always be an emergency medic. I can also control water." She doesn't elaborate on her water powers, and I understand why. She may not be a goddess herself, but Brynn is goddess blessed. The only water user who exceeds her is Adeline.

Sebastien nods without expression and then glances at me.

"Daggers," I blurt out, "I'm good with a dagger-- up close or at a distance. I know some self-defense. But mostly, I rely on my shadows." Sebastien frowns at this answer, something about it bothering him.

"You head to war against a goddess-like queen, and you do not know combat beyond daggers?"

His question annoys me. I narrow my eyes at him, slightly offended.

"A lot can be accomplished with a well-placed dagger," I remind him with a sniff. After all, a dagger is what prevented him from attacking me in the tavern.

His demure expression expands into a smile.

"That it can," he says graciously, "But would you be willing to learn other forms of combat?"

Warmth and joy spread through my chest. I like him. Against my will, I can't help it, but I like him. He's giving and smart and thoughtful. He makes me laugh. Things I thought were lost to me. Maybe moving on isn't so bad. Sivan would want me to be happy, at any cost.

"Absolutely," I respond, and we begin.

CHAPTER TWENTY-TWO

SEBASTIEN, Brynn, and I spend the rest of the afternoon on the terrace together. Sebastien shows us different punches, kicks, rolls, and other methods of grappling with another person or how to escape various positions and traps. When he's satisfied with our progress in one area, he builds upon the knowledge he's given us. Brynn and I practice with each other for a while in near silence, content with building our skills together. Sweat rolls off my body in droves, but I don't care. All I care about is building my physical strength.

Luna saunters over as the sunlight begins softening and takes me through a series of exercises centered around feeling the flow of my body, it's connection to my magic, and how the two can work in tandem. The physical stress is much less compared to the mental stress of expanding my consciousness to include the shadows all around me.

When she's satisfied with my progress, Luna skips over to Faye, whispers into the fairy's ear and the two head inside, apparently tired of their impromptu picnic in the hot sun. Brynn eventually tells me she's too tired to continue and leaves us as well. Sebastien and I are totally alone as the sun begins to set. I bite my lip, suddenly feeling awkward. I want... more. I'm not ready for sex with him, or even solidifying our relationship, but it's been so very long since I've been kissed. Since I've been desired. Held and cared for. Curiosity stirs within me. I think it will feel strange kissing someone new. But I suppose, I won't know until I attempt it.

Sebastien picks up on the shift in my mood instantly.

His head tilts as he asks me, "Are you alright?"

My teeth dig into my bottom lip, a terrible habit when I'm nervous. Looking up at Sebastien, his grey skin and elegant horns... the desire and curiosity only continue to build. The space between us suddenly feels unbearable, the silence stretches with anticipation. Can he tell I'm thinking of how his lips will feel on mine?

"Sebastien...," I begin hesitantly, "I was wondering if you might... if we might..." My words trail off as I lose my nerve.

Sebastien takes one hand and gently grips my chin, forcing me to look in his dark fathomless eyes.

"What, sweetheart?" he asks, "Never be afraid to tell me what you are thinking." His eyes blaze with intensity and emotion, but I can't discern what. He waits with seemingly endless patience, staring down at me with my chin in his large hand.

If you want something, you have to ask for it. You can't assume others will read your mind. Yet here I am debating with myself if I am allowed to do something so simple as kiss my mate. He's given me no indication that a kiss would bother him, and in fact has encouraged me in small ways. What am I waiting for?

I step closer to him, looking up into his eyes. He drops his hand from my chin as I lean up towards his face, resting my hands against the hard planes of his chest. His breath seemingly disappears as my lips nearly reach his, the air between our mouths charged.

"I'm thinking about how lovely it would be to kiss you," I whisper into his mouth. A small groan escapes him, but he does not move.

"So, kiss me," he whispers right back, unmoving, letting me take the lead in this moment.

I gaze into his dark eyes again for a moment, savoring the moonflies in my stomach, before gently closing my eyes and pushing myself up, up, up until my lips press into his. The moment we kiss, it's as if a fire unleashed. He kisses me like he will die if he stops. I feel as if I will die if he does. I find myself pressed tightly against Sebastien, legs locked around his waist, hands clasped around his neck. His arms support me, gripping my hips and ass with care, but he makes no move to do anything other than kiss me. We kiss over, and over, and over again, until my lips are swollen and my body heavy with need.

I've never felt an all-consuming desire such as this. Like molten lava running through my veins. Like I've been sleeping all these years but am finally awake. Even the very power at the core of my soul trembles with need, like every part of me needs every part of him. Soul fated mates. Guilt nips at me for a moment, but I do my best to push it aside.

After a while, our kisses slow, until we stop, and Sebastien places a kiss at the top of my forehead. He sets me back down on the ground gently, before looking down at me and sighing.

This confuses me and I raise a brow in his direction.

"What's wrong?" I ask, suddenly bereft.

He clears his throat and the way he gazes down at me.... I know he intends to tell me something I'd rather not hear.

"Tell me. Delaying doing so will not make the words any easier," I spit out at him, anger surging as quickly as my passion did. He doesn't seem surprised by my ire, if anything it's as if he expected it.

"I know why Rhiannon holds so much hatred for you, as well as the secret that all death queens die keeping. You will read it in the journal Megara gave you, but I might be able to offer unique insight into the circumstances surrounding the lost age... if you'd like me to."

His dark eyes shine back at me in earnest. I cannot doubt the truth of his words and the fact he offers this information to me freely makes me think a bit more highly of Sebastien.

He swallows hard and slow, the muscles of his throat shuddering painfully. My breaths come slightly quicker in anticipation of his words, but I remain patient and quiet while he works his nerves up. Nervousness is not an attribute I would think Sebastien possesses, but it's clear whatever he needs to tell me means a great deal to him. He briefly closes his eyes, then opens them and looks right into mine and says, "I am the son of the original Under-King, and I know why Rhiannon has become the malevolent force you know her as today."

A little sigh escapes me. Sebastien expects this information to be shocking, but I cannot muster up a feeling other than weariness. "I know," I tell him demurely.

He raises his eyebrows at me yet again, and I realize I've paid far much too attention to his little habits. He scrunches his nose when displeased and is fond of raising a brow and shaking his head.

"You know?" He demands. Both a question and a statement. I simply raise a brow back at him and cock my head to the side, indicating that I can wait until he calms down. An expression akin to annoyance and joy combined crosses his face.

"Did you really expect that I would wait to read the journal until everyone else was good and ready?" I ask Sebastien, meeting his gaze with the full force of my own. Sebastien seems crestfallen at this revelation, but I wave a hand at him-- "Oh, do not fret about it. I would still like to hear, in your own words, what events occurred that led us here today."

Sebastien stares at me in awe. Clearly, I have stolen the wind from beneath his wings. He looks bereft but shakes his head, as if shaking away the feeling, and then offers a hand to me.

"Shall we retire somewhere more comfortable where I may tell you the whole story?"

I nod my acquiescence, and we begin walking back towards the stairwell, when he suddenly tugs me to a stop and asks, "Would you like anyone else to witness the conversation?"

"Yes, everyone. Especially Luna," I respond, giving him a pointed look.

"Ah, yes. Quite. Let us make haste then," Sebastien says in a rather droll tone if I do say so myself.

I find myself grinning from ear to ear as we descend back into the sanctum and seek out our companions.

CHAPTER TWENTY-THREE

SEBASTIEN and I find the hallways utterly barren of life in a way that suggest mischief may be afoot. How long had the two of us stayed out in the sunset, chatting away the day? If there's one thing I know about Brynn, it's that she never misses the opportunity to pull a prank on Sivan and me. Well—

I guess just myself now. Sebastien and me? Ugh, it's all horribly confusing.

Cutting a hand in front of Sebastien to stop him, I turn towards him and put my finger over my mouth in a gesture of silence. He nods, a smile playing on his delicate lips. The two of us move down the stone hallway, inch by inch. Candlelight flickers along the walls. Windows dot the hallway, letting in a night breeze. Everything is perfectly normal and yet I can sense something is amiss. A familiar scent hangs in the air.

A few more steps and--

The candles all go out, leaving Sebastien and I in total darkness. Sebastien shifts restlessly behind me, anticipating more danger, maybe another attack. I fear not, for I already know who is responsible for this.

"AYIIIIIIIIIIIIIIIIIIIIIIIIIIII--" a loud, albeit feminine, voice pierces the hallway, and I sense movement coming from my back left side. Tapping Sebastien gently on the arm in the darkness so that he moves away, I simply sidestep as a pocket of air rushes at me. My attacker goes sprawling out onto the dark floor in front me, and lands with a groan of pain. Rolling my eyes, I shuffle towards Brynn's body in the dark. "Well dear sister, you nearly had me that time."

I extend a hand towards her, and I hear Brynn's familiar huff of exasperation as she takes it. The candle lights return revealing Faye and Luna giggling at the end of the hall as I haul the little devil to her feet.

"This is normal then?" Sebastien asks, his dark brows quirked together in an odd mixture of amusement and confusion.

Brynn and I look at each other for a moment before nodding emphatically together.

"Yup." Brynn nods at the same time that I say, "Pretty much."

Sebastien's eyes soften as if he is deep in thought, but his smile remains. To me, he looks rather melancholy.

"Brynn never realizes that screeching is not the best way to sneak up on a person unnoticed," I explain to Sebastien with a teasing lilt in my voice. The more time we spend together, my feelings for him intensify, in a way that makes me care about that hint of sadness. In a way that makes me want to take his sadness away. His memories swirl around him, but I push them out of focus. When he tells me about those moments, I will listen. For now, I can wait.

His expression remains a tad solemn but all he says, in a soft voice is, "wonderful." The sadness in his voice takes my breath away from a moment. I care. I care about him. This daemon from the

Under-Realm. I care about his feelings, and I care about his well-being. The brevity of the feeling has me going absolutely still. Sivan will always own my heart but Sebastien.... He has claim over my soul. The thought sends shocks of pain through my heart. Will I ever get used to the world without Sivan? Maybe not... but with Sebastien, the burden will be lighter. Somehow, I know he will not begrudge me for my pain, my vulnerability. Perhaps I can even share stories with him of a time before the illness, before this impending war.

There are many more things we need to discuss though. Sebastien and I split off from the others once again, headed towards one of the many day rooms scattered about the sanctum. We walk silently at first, but soon I find myself unable to resist asking him more questions.

"If you could live anywhere, where would you go?" I blurt out. Sebastien raises his brows at me in question but then seems to ponder for a moment. His expressions always seem to change rapidly, every feeling walking over his face-- at least when we're alone together. Do the others read him as easily as I do?

We keep walking, our pace leisurely, but I can feel him mulling the question over. It's as if every part of him is familiar to me, despite our strangeness with one another.

"In a land far north of Echosia, in a small country named Quehu, there's a little fishing village on the eastern coast. There, the people live in harmony with their environment. The magic they have comes from the health of the land and so every man, animal, creature is given respect. They use everything, wasting nothing. The climate is tropical, and they enjoy safety from natural disasters due to the magical aura surrounding them. It's not an island per se but connected to the mainland by an isthmus and..." Sebastien looks over at me and blushes, his cheeks turning purple.

"I realize I have been rambling," he says abruptly and goes silent.

"I quite like hearing what you have to say," I respond, "Why would I ask a question and then not anticipate an answer? It's nice to hear someone's true thoughts. It is a rare treat in this world."

"I understand what you mean," he says huskily and my eyes dart over to him. The way he walks.... well, I never thought someone could walk sexily but stars be damned. Everything from those deep eyes like the obsidian surrounding the sanctum, to the long leanness of him, or those beautifully pointed horns atop his head... everything about him calls to me. I shake my head a bit as if I can shake myself from these thoughts. We have more important things to ponder than the way Sebastien's pants cling to his shapely ass.

"We're nearing the day room," I tell him, "But I have another personal question."

"Ask anything you'd like, my queen." Were it not for the teasing note in his voice, I might have thought him far too solemn for the conversation.

He slows to a rather lazy pace, and I follow his lead, eager to draw out our pleasant time together before diving into what information the black tome revealed to me.

"Why Quehu?"

A slight gasp draws from his lips, as if this question is more personal than the last. As if I've caught him off guard. He keeps walking, taking a few moments to gather his thoughts. When my curiosity grows nearly unbearable, he finally responds: "It was my mother's birthplace." His tone does not invite further questioning.

Suddenly, I feel a bit bereft. Like I've spoilt something.

"It's nothing to fret over," he adds because of course he can sense my mood. Yet fret I do. If there is anything I excel at, it's worrying. The more I worry over, the more I can prepare for.

We arrive at the dayroom, and though the sun has disappeared, the sister moons sit proudly in the sky lighting up the room beautifully via a skylight. The room, like many in Megara's sanctum, is simple and cozy. In the middle of the small circular area, a tea table sits laden with treats and kettles nearly spilling over to the sides. I eye one cup in particular that looks precariously close to tumbling to the floor.

"One gold mark says it falls," Sebastien banters, his attention on the delicate looking teacup. How quickly his moods change. Maybe we are well suited for one another.

An idea pops into my head, and it occurs to me that he might have had the same one, but I laugh and respond, "Two gold marks says it doesn't."

"Very well," Sebastien says as he pulls out a chair from the tea table for me. Bemused, I sit gracefully and thank him in an overdramatic fashion. As he moves to his own seat, I notice a slow curling tendril of smoke slide free of Sebastien's arm and subtly push the cup. The slight motion is too much for the little cup and it indeed begins toppling over the side of the table. Expecting this, I use a shadow of my own to rescue the poor thing before it falls.

Sebastien's dark eyes dance with laughter as he tells me, "A gold mark is in order, my lady."

I scoff at him, waving my hand lazily. "A poor attempt at trickery. Have you forgotten the mass of siblings Sivan left behind? I've learnt quite a lot of the ways one can tease another mercilessly with simple magic."

"Ah, but I believe we said the marks for it falling. It fell."

"Yes, but we never said anything about pushing it. Would the cup have done the same if not acted upon by an outside force? We may never know now thanks to your efforts," I respond with a firm tone. A sly smile makes its way onto my lips as I hope he gets my sense of humor.

He nods as if the thought hadn't occurred to him.

"Mm. Indeed." Gone is the playful teasing lilt to his voice and I frown. I gaze down at my hands for a moment, observing the tears in my cuticles and the calluses on my palms. Hands earned through hard work, through perseverance. I'm sure whatever he knows, or thinks he knows, is plaguing him. A tired sigh escapes me as I stretch my back and spine out.

Sebastien looks at me in earnest from across the small table, his gaze making the space feel impossibly smaller. His gaze devours me.

"If it was your choice, would you like me?" he asks suddenly. The question is light, casual, but there's a serious edge to his voice.

"I'm unsure," I admit, "Sivan was my whole heart and soul. He still is. If you and I had met, while Sivan was alive, then... it would be a very hard decision indeed." Pain stabs at my heart, a sensation that comforts me like an old friend. I have grown to like Sebastien. I respect and admire him, even if he is just a pawn in some god's game.

But Sivan? I chose him. He loved me despite not being required to. Soul bonded mates sounds nice, but at the crux of it lies a deep issue. What if I loved another? or despised my mate? Do my feelings and choices not matter then, is it all the decision of the moons? It always sounded suspicious to me, and with the journal of the soul queens at my disposal, I finally understand that soul bonded mates can be another form of control.

Love is not always enough.

Sebastien's dark eyes flare at my honesty, but he stays quiet. One thing I admire greatly about Sebastien is how he takes time to contemplate his feelings. He does not feel pressured to speak on someone else's timetable, or to speak in order to fill silence. He is often intentional with his words.

Sebastien smiles at me with a grim look on his face.

"Thank you for your honesty," he tells me as he rubs his chin. He does not speak for several moments, instead electing to pop his knuckles and stretch out his spine.

"Tired?" I ask. His answering yawn is enough evidence for me. Sebastien shakes his head lightly, his horns causing the light to shift iridescently.

"I want to finish our conversation. I want to know what you think and feel, even if it is not to my liking. And I want to tell you about the soul queen's curse."

I sigh inwardly as I debate how to inform Sebastien that I likely know a great deal more about the curse than he does.

"Sebastien...," I begin but he interjects--

"My father was the original King of the Under-Realm. And he made a terrible decision to save his people." The breath wooshes out of him, as if he had been holding the statement in for quite a bit of time.

My hands tremble slightly as I look at him, his dark eyes wide and full of nerves.

"I know."

CHAPTER TWENTY-FOUR

SEBASTIEN'S grey skin darkens oddly, his eyes widen as if he had not considered I would find out without his telling me. The muscles in his neck flex as he works out what to say next.

"You know?" he growls softly across the table. Sebastien leans over the table, his arms down against the wood. He doesn't sound dangerous, he has no intent to harm me, but I can tell he's bothered by this news. He wanted to be the one to tell me. Maybe he thinks that it would hurt me less, or that I would blame him if I found out another way.

"Let me clarify a few things, and then you can return the favor."

He nods and leans back against his chair again. The movement causes his muscles to ripple. I didn't know that muscles could actually do that. It's distractingly sexy and I find myself looking up at him through my lashes, a smirk on my face.

When we make eye contact, it feels as charged as the air before a storm. I feel flushed and hot, so I take my braid down and run my fingers through the long black waves. Sebastien continues watching me as I scratch the sore spots out of my scalp and debate how to begin.

Sebastien grants me his patience, however, and I find it easier to speak than I did before.

"The black tome is a record of each and every soul queen's memories. Each queen, from the beginning, up until Thania recorded her memories and stored them within these pages." I pause, gauging Sebastien's reaction but he appears calm. Thoughtful.

He deigns not to speak, so I continue: "The first queen, Thania, included memories of her original contract with the King of the Under-Realm. Your father tied her power to the very land of the Under-Realm. It infused the soul queen with powers beyond imagining. Those powers were abundant, so long as the realm was prosperous and cared for, the soul queen would reign for eternity."

"And yet none of them were able to claim their full power... until you," Sebastien says darkly.

I roll my eyes at his tone and shake my head a bit.

"Do you know why that is?" I ask, my voice gentle as night. He shakes his head, but his eyes move in a way that suggests he's thinking, putting some of the pieces together.

"Why do you think Rhiannon sent you, the son of the Under-King, to kill me, the promised soul queen?" I ask when he doesn't respond further.

"Rhiannon knew we would be mates. And so, she set you on a path to find me, set you right there in front of me so that we would have to experience the mating bond. All along, it's because she also knows the truth of the soul queen's curse." His dark eyes flash enough that I know he has already considered why Rhiannon sent him to me.

"There's more than what you've told me thus far? Isn't it enough that you would be dead if your body did not accept the raw power that now courses through you?" Sebastien eyes reveal a hint of anger, a hint of worry at the possibility of my demise.

I purse my lips but straighten my spine. He will not make me feel guilty about this when he does not know the truth. My eyes slide coolly over Sebastien, and I stare at him until he settles in his chair again. Only then do I speak.

"Not only is the queen's life force tied to the realm, but the curse also means that there will never be a true death queen until she is mated to the Under-King's heir. For a death queen to rise, without dying slowly over hundreds and hundreds of years, she must be the true mate of the Under-King."

Sebastien stares at me, unblinking, until eventually he reaches a hand up and scratches a horn.

"Does that mean...," he trails off, putting the pieces together.

I whisper back, voice soft and low.

"Your father cursed the original queen with madness, knowing she would never become a true death queen because she denied their mating bond. That's the real reason Rhiannon's become this monster. Her magic is slowly leaking out of her, returning to the land. When she weakened enough that the land was at risk, that's when the power chose me. As it did for Rhiannon and the queen before her. Because the mating bond did not fall into place with them."

Sebastien appears to mull over my words. An odd feeling slides over me as I realize that Sebastien's way of communicating is a gift. What must his life have been like, being little more than a slave to Rhiannon? He does not react outwardly, but I feel echoes of his frustration through our mental bond. I decide I like the bond-- I enjoy knowing how he feels and when. It soothes my anxiety to know that every word he speaks is deliberate and thought out.

He gazes at me, before speaking: "And how is this all impacting you? How do you feel?"

My lips purse as I decide what words to respond with.

"I think... that it changes nothing. Rhiannon is still dangerous, despite the source of her madness. We can look into alternate ways to depose her, but ultimately, she's a threat and she needs to be put down. Permanently."

His gaze turns approving.

"Bloodthirsty girl," he says, nodding his head as he does. A blush creeps over my cheeks.

"Well, death is my oldest friend."

That storm-like feeling charges the air between us again. We fall silent, his dark eyes pouring into mine. My tongue darts out, swiping over my lower lip involuntarily.

"I would very much like to kiss you again," he says suddenly, standing up and moving around the table. He angles his body over mine, then grabs my chin delicately. My breath catches in my chest as I look over the long, hard planes of muscle above me.

"If you'll have me," he whispers as he leans in. He keeps a bit of space between our lips, and I decide I can no longer tolerate the distance.

I don't give him the chance to finish. He can be at least a little less respectful. My body surges up, the desire to touch and feel burning through me. I tangle my hands in the hair around his horns, pulling his mouth to mine even as he does the same. We clash together in a passionate, near violent kiss. He nips at my lips with his fangs; I respond in kind by sucking on his tongue.

A feeling I haven't felt in forever courses through me. Desire, like molten liquid, flows freely through our bond, back and forth, amplifying the lust we've been suppressing for each other. The shadows surrounding my skin are at peace and silent. This type of peace.... I haven't felt it since before Sivan died.

We find ourselves on the floor, not knowing how we got there. I wrap my legs around Sebastien's waist, sitting in his lap, as he pulls me even closer, his fingers tracing over my ribs. My fingers tangle in the dark hair curling around his horns. I trace one horn lightly, feeling the grooves and twists in it as I do. Sebastien moans lightly into my mouth and a shudder runs through me. He kisses my neck, my cheeks, my forehead, before returning to my mouth again. We kiss like we need each other to breathe.

Finally, when the desire is less overwhelming, we simply sit there with our foreheads together in silence. After a few moments, the peace is ruined by the sound of footsteps rushing down the hallway outside. With a hefty sigh, we untangle ourselves from one another. Sebastien smiles at me as he stands, offering me a hand up. I take it, noting how much easier it feels to touch him and be near him. As if a question has been answered.

The footsteps get closer and Brynn bursts into the small room, her frantic energy replacing the delicate peace.

I take one look at her face and ask, "What's happened?"

She's breathing heavily and just lifts up a piece of parchment instead of speaking. I take it from her outstretched hand and read over the curling words.

* * *

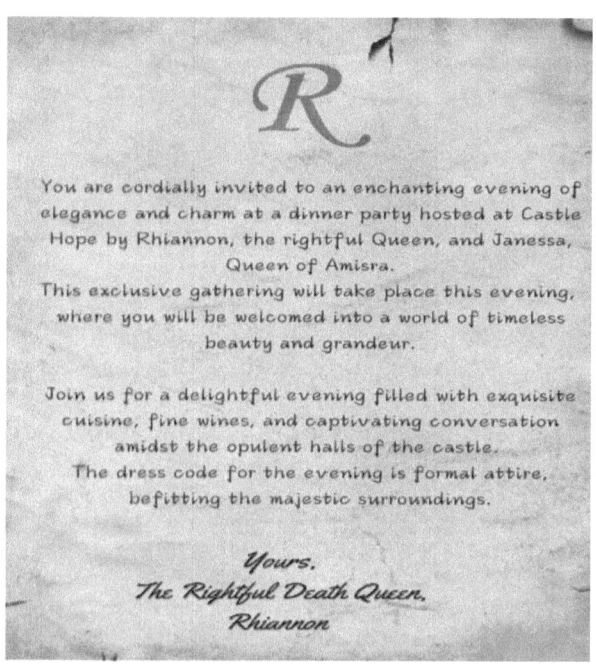

You are cordially invited to an enchanting evening of
elegance and charm at a dinner party hosted at Castle
Hope by Rhiannon, the rightful Queen, and Janessa,
Queen of Amisra.
This exclusive gathering will take place this evening,
where you will be welcomed into a world of timeless
beauty and grandeur.

Join us for a delightful evening filled with exquisite
cuisine, fine wines, and captivating conversation
amidst the opulent halls of the castle.
The dress code for the evening is formal attire,
befitting the majestic surroundings.

Yours,
The Rightful Death Queen,
Rhiannon

Sebastien watches my face; I can feel his eyes burning into me as I process the contents of the letter. I open my mouth to explain but stand there gaping like a fish instead. Instead of waiting for me to gather myself, he takes the letter with a gentle hand and reads it, a frown forming as he does.

"Who is Janessa?" Sebastien asks when he finishes. I slowly turn to him, the shocking words still rolling through me.

"My cousin," I finally spit out, "She lives at the castle here and oversees the Island as their current queen."

Understanding graces his face, even as the black and green swirls violently in his eyes.

"Rhiannon has taken control of the castle. She threatens your cousin," he seethes.

I nod. "Under the guise of a dinner party, no less." I pinch the bridge of my nose, desperately craving a break. It's scarcely been a few days since we arrived here. Reading between the lines of the message, it's easy to see the threat as it's intended. If I don't show up, I have no doubts she would kill Janessa.

"Are we going?" Brynn asks in an unusually solemn tone. Sebastien glances at her in surprise.

"We have to, don't we?" he asks, turning to me.

"Yes. Yes, we do. Sebastien," I turn towards him, "When Rhiannon says, 'formal attire,' do you know exactly what that entails?"

He frowns a bit. "She will expect nothing less than your finest. Which could pose a problem given our current state of affairs."

"Why's that?" Brynn asks, all nonchalant grace despite her earlier demeanor.

Sebastien appears confused as he tilts his head slightly, his horns glinting in the light. He looks at me questioningly, and I shrug my shoulder in response. Brynn sighs dramatically at our unvoiced thoughts. "Surely Megara has formal clothing in her closet. It's possible Faye does as well. Her bag contains much more than physically possible."

Honestly, it's a bit annoying I didn't consider either of those possibilities before but now my mind races with different routes.

"Sebastien, can you please gather Bellum?" I ask, "And see to both of your grooming needs while we find suitable attire for us all?"

He nods before slipping out of the room with nothing more than a heated glance at me. Brynn raises a brow at me but says nothing. The taste of blood floods my mouth and I realize I've bitten through my bottom lip. Janessa may be Queen of the island, but she has no magic powers to speak of. What had happened to the guards? They were loyal to the crown, treated fairly and seemed to love their positions as protectors of the realm. Rhiannon must have done something to them. Hopefully they're still alive.

I banish the dark thought from my mind when Brynn softly clears her throat, clearly intending not to startle me while she got my attention.

"Let's go. We can talk about it after we find something to wear. Or while we do it."

I nod. "I'd like that."

She turns and walks out the doorway, and I follow her after a deep sigh, on our way to dress up for that sadistic bitch queen. At least if we're going to kick her ass, we'll look like warrior queens doing it.

CHAPTER TWENTY-FIVE

MEGARA'S closet isn't a closet—it's an entire universe.

Every nook and cranny overflows with soft ethereal light that reflects off the oceans of silk and the galaxies of chiffon. Rows and rows of gowns line the towering walls of rainbow fabric. The scent of sea salt and chocolate fills the air. I wonder if Megara uses a spell for the scent. My companions grow giddy at the sight of so much finery, and I smile to myself as I finger a gown that looks like it's woven from moonlight. Luna runs up and down the rows, her tail bouncing behind her as she giggles.

"Is it wrong that I'm kind of excited?" Luna asks. "Obviously it's terrible that Janessa was taken hostage, but the chance to wear the goddess's clothes... I can't lie that I find the prospect enjoyable."

Brynn nearly shushes her. "It's okay to enjoy things, even if the circumstances are less than ideal."

"I'm more scared of picking the wrong dress and pissing off the bitch queen," Faye says with sugary sweetness, her arms deep in a pile of pink and orange fabric and tulle. She sparkles with glee as she searches for the perfect gown for facing our enemies in. Then, she pops into a cloud of sparkles and emerges in her fairy form. She uses it to dive in and out of piles of fabric.

Brynn and Luna turn to me, as if their feelings depend on my thoughts, which is more than a little uncomfortable. While I would prefer my cousin have not been kidnapped in her own home, I understand the thrill of dressing up and putting on a gown that makes you feel like you can conquer the five continents. I take a moment to respond, debating how I feel.

"Beauty is power," I tell my companions, "And a beautiful gown can make you feel powerful." Another poof of sparkles and Faye reappears nearby.

"Well said," Faye replies as she kneels devoutly into cascade of midnight blue chiffon, "Besides, if we're going to die, we might as well do it fabulously dressed."

I roll my eyes. "No one is dying tonight."

Brynn looks pointedly at Faye, as if communicating through eyesight alone. Faye nods in return before turning to Luna. "I think I spy a gown over there that would suit you quite well." She points a few rows over, to a spot where they can still see Brynn and I but won't be able to hear our conversation.

"Don't get lost!" Brynn shouts as Luna and Faye float towards said gown. When they are far enough away, Brynn turns to me, face serious. "Spill," she says. I sigh inwardly.

"We kissed," I say quietly with a glance at Faye and Luna. My fingers touch gown after gown; I avoid Brynn's gaze as my cheeks heat. Why does this feel so awkward to discuss?

"And?" Brynn asks.

"And what?"

"And," she says, voice impatient, "How was it? Was it a good kiss?"

I turn and stare at her in surprise. Of course. It was stupid of me to think Brynn would honestly mind anything that brings me happiness. She loved her brother, but she loves me too.

"Well, it might have been more than a kiss. Or two. Or three."

Brynn's eyes widen. "You didn't...." she asks, voice trailing off.

"No!" I blurt, "But it was definitely more like making out."

She waggles her brows at me. "Yeah? And was it good?"

The blush in my cheeks worsens. I bite my lip. "Yes. And it was fun."

Her eyes sparkle and she grins at me before looking over at the others. "Faye's good too. Really good."

"Did the two of you...?"

"Oh yeah." Brynn says, unashamed and unabashed. Her fingers skim over dress after dress, but she doesn't pick one up.

"I'm happy for you," I say, voice soft, "You deserve nothing less than everything."

She smiles at me. "Thanks... Was that all though? Just the kisses?"

"Well, it's possible that if I reject the mating bond that I'll slowly be poisoned by a magical contract signed centuries ago that will turn me mad and result in my inevitable death."

"You're joking." She stares at me, concern etched on her face.

I shake my head. "I wish I were. It's not that I mind the bond so much as I mind not being given a choice. I like Sebastien. I do. I just wish it wasn't something that was predetermined for me."

"I get that," she replies as she searches through another rack, "Especially after losing Sivan, you deserve to make that choice on your own. You still can you know."

I stop my search and turn to stare at her like she has sprouted an extra head.

She shrugs. "It's your choice. It's not your responsibility to fix everything. Despite my feelings about it, which you well know, no one can make you do anything."

"It's not a choice at all. But I appreciate you saying so."

She reaches out and squeezes my hand. "Don't worry. We've got this."

A companionable silence falls as we continue our hunt for the right dress. There are so many gorgeous options, but none of them feel like *me*.

Luna comes running over. "Look what I found!" she says with a mess of red and white fabric. She unfurls it and the rest of us let out the appropriate noises of awe. This gown was obviously designed to captivate, the perfect blend of vintage charm and modern grace. The bodice is fitted and structured, with slim straps and a romantic silhouette that hints at a timeless elegance. From there, the skirt unfurls like a blooming flower, its tulle layers fading from a deep crimson at the top to the softest blush at the bottom. The gradient gives the gown a sense of movement, as though glowing faintly with the last embers of the day.

"That dress was made for you," I murmur, still preoccupied by my conversation with Brynn, "I can't wait to see it on you."

Faye follows Luna shortly after, carrying a few choices over for us to discuss the pros and cons of. Brynn immediately pulls a silvery number out of the pile, declaring it the winner before the rest of us have a chance to even voice our opinions. It's not hard to see why.

This is no ordinary gown-- it's a celestial dream come true. It looks as if the stars took a dip at midnight, with silvery layers that shift like the surface of a quiet lake. The bodice is structured yet delicate with an array of tiny jewels and threads that catch the light as if they were kissed by the moons themselves. Thin straps frame the gown while the skirt falls in cascading layers of translucent fabric that I know will swirl like mist around Faye's feet.

Brynn whispers something into Faye's ears that has the fairy blushing.

"That gown looks fit for a queen," Luna says, staring at Faye with an odd look on her face.

"So it is," Faye chimes back. She does not elaborate. A weird tension fills the space between the grimalkin and the fairy. I look between Faye and Luna; suddenly sure I'm missing a vital piece of a puzzle. The moment drags on, before Brynn finally interrupts.

"I found a pantsuit!" she says, the excitement bursting out of her voice. A ghost of a smile plays on my lips. Trust Brynn to defy norms in the best way possible.

The suit she found is tightly fitted with a matching maroon jacket and pants. Underneath, black diamonds glitter from the bodice paired with the suit. Overall, it gives the impression of power and elegance. It also allows for plenty of movement should the need arise. We all take turns telling Brynn how amazing she'll look in the suit, gushing over her choice.

"Did you find anything Rhea?" Luna asks, her wide eyes settling on me.

Before I can tell her that I'm not sure, the shadows swirling around me slide away from my body. One tendril beckons me, as if telling me to follow. I trail after it. The shadows have never led me astray before. They lead me through a maze of racks and drawers, until we come to a series of cabinets lining one of the walls of Megara's gigantic closet. The shadows come to a stop in front of a glass case. My hand flies up to my mouth at the sight of the gown inside.

The gown is a masterpiece of artistry, a cascade of shimmering tulle that breathes with life. Peacock feathers sweep across the bodice, their iridescent hues glinting like stolen starlight under a faint beam. Dark green beads, like droplets of dew, weave intricate patterns along the one-shoulder neckline, creating a trail that dances in the light with every movement. The skirt fans out in soft, translucent layers, whispering secrets of elegance and power with every ripple, as if the wearer carries the essence of a peacock's regal beauty in their stride. Lace slithers around where my neck would go, creating the impression of movement.

Brynn catches up to us first. Her mouth drops open.

"That's the dress. You have to wear that. Not only will you be smoking hot, but I bet there's something special about the gown as well."

She's right. The gown seems to hide a shimmer of power, of my own powers perhaps. Maybe that's why the shadows harkened to it. They twist into tentacle like appendages, unlocking the case with ease and grasping the gown as if a precious child and delivering it into my hands.

"Thank you," I tell them, as it seems rude not to.

Choices in hand, we all set about finding shoes and accessories, including some that allow us to tuck in daggers and other weapons underneath our gowns. Luna locates a pair of pearl hairpins that are sharper than a goddess's tongue, and an excellent candidate for applying poison to. She claims that's all she needs. Brynn finds a few golden hair beads she wants to weave into her hair but insists with her pantsuit she has everything else she needs to conceal her own weapons. Faye uses no weapons and thus needs nothing besides a set of diamonds she finds.

"Megara did say we could use anything." She says, her desire clear on her face.

I shrug my shoulder. "Go for it. She keeps a private trove in her bedroom anyways." Faye squeals, the sound almost too high pitched to hear, and reverently scoops up the jewels. I'm amazed it doesn't my ears, though Luna winces slightly.

We all leave the closet wonderland with our hands full of borrowed wonders, a strange happiness emanating from us. Life really is about small experiences sometimes. I told my friends that I was brave, that I was sure we wouldn't die. But I'm not sure and I'm not half as brave as I'm pretending to be. Sebastien and Brynn sense it in moments, I can tell, but neither have fully called me out on it. Not really. If any of us perish, it will be me. I've always known I was lucky to find Brynn. Marrying Sivan was the best decision I've ever made. I didn't expect to love his family so much and then I did. Suddenly I fit in. Suddenly I could see a future and a family and children. Brynn was the sister I never had, the connection between us instant. While I get along with Sivan's other sisters, the connection has never been the way it is with Brynn. The world is not ready for her not to exist within it. Neither am I.

And Luna. I have no doubts fate brought me to her. I have no doubts I was meant to find her and remove her from that market. If we survive this, we might just have to go back there and see if any of the other animals in that shop are actually shifters of other kinds. Knowing there could be others like Luna out there makes me prickle with anger. I've come to love Luna as well, partially just from knowing her through her memories and partially because of her kindness in the face of potential war. I can't betray her trust. I will protect her at any cost.

I like Faye, but Brynn loves her, it's clear as a moonlit night. It would kill Brynn to watch Faye die and I can't make her go through that. My shadows and I will protect everyone. Sebastien will assist. My mind swirls with these thoughts and other darker ones even as I navigate the halls of the sanctum with my friends and return to our respective rooms to ready ourselves for the evening.

A few rooms away, I know Sebastien and Bellum are also preparing for the night, with a selection of appropriate formal wear sent to them by Megara. She didn't ask questions about Bellum's presence, but it seems she accepts it so long as she doesn't have to see him or hear him.

As Luna and I set about styling our hair, she looks me in the eye through the looking glass and says, "don't even think about it."

"Think about what?" I ask, pausing with my hands full of her long dark hair. It's not easy pinning her hair up around her ears and she squirms a lot. "You have a lot of hair, and we don't have a ton of time."

"You've been thinking your death would somehow right all the wrongs, save all of our lives and also prevent Rhiannon from winning. It's horse shit and you know it. I'm living proof that Rhiannon cares not for propriety or rules of engagement. If she wants to kill us, then she will try to kill us, but you getting yourself killed will do none of us any good."

I gulp, the guilt churning in my gut. "I'm not going to get myself killed, Luna." I grasp at random strands of her hair, somehow simultaneously styling her hair and not changing a thing about it.

"Do you know, I remembered my given name?" she says in a soft, dangerous voice. "You weren't far off the mark with 'Luna'."

I pause again, staring at her. "You did? Do you want to share it with me?" "Lunara Solis," she says, "or The Lonely Moon."

"You were named for the forgotten moon?" The lonely moon was a fourth, dwarf moon on the other side of the sky from the three sisters. One day, during the war, it disappeared entirely and to this day, no one truly knows why.

She nods, but her expression turns a little less grave, so I set about finishing my task. "My parents said it was due to the crescent mark on my face. It was the only mark like that in my family and so they said it reminded them of that little moon, all alone in the sky being forced to watch the sisters keep each other company. You can keep calling me Luna." Her eyes shoot into mine. "My point is that I know where you've been, and I can see where you're going. Dying tonight isn't the path forward."

"How do you know?" I say, looking down into her hair to avoid her penetrating gaze.

"Trust me. I know." Her aura flares out, as if commanding me to look at it though I haven't called on my powers. My shadows don't react, sensing Luna's goal is not to harm me. Her aura shows the same strange marks as before, but slowly the marks dissipate.

"They're called runes. Your people don't use them, but they were considered sacred to the grimalkin. Now, just to me I suppose. Usually, they're physical and tangible, but ever sense I was a kitten I have been able to call upon runes in my mind and shape them to my will. To my people, it made me a great seer. It was seen as a gift, especially for a royal family member to be granted it. I hated it, for a time, but now I think they're the reason I survived the slaughter. That I protected myself, even when I was in that river and unconscious."

When the marks fade fully, her aura bursts forth in a tidal wave of power. It is pure and deep purple, tinged with gold and blue. Not only is she incredibly powerful, but it's clear from her control over her rune marks and her aura that she is also meticulously controlled. I'm in awe of her power. She had taught me some of her mind focusing and mind clearing exercises but that was standing ankle deep in water, while her power feels like a tidal wave.

"You have much to teach me, it seems," I say with a slight smile. She visibly relaxes but remains serious in tone.

"I'm saying, you don't need to worry about me. I have my ways of taking care of myself. If we survive tonight, then I'll teach you everything I know."

She holds up her little finger. "Pinky promise me?"

I snort. "Really? A pinky promise at our ages?"

She says nothing, just raises her pinky finger again, insisting on my compliance. I sigh, mostly to be dramatic, but I entwine my pinky with hers anyways.

"I promise," I say, the lie convincing and easy on my tongue, "We've got this." I feign confidence I don't feel at all-- I've trained for all of a few days and now I have to go to dinner with my enemy who has dragons loads of experience more than I do.

Luna look like she believes me, and I don't feel guilty about the lie.

Not even a little bit.

CHAPTER TWENTY-SIX

A short while later, I am fully transformed into the visage of a goddess. My hair is swept into a half-up, half-down style, dark curls spilling artfully in every direction. Black kohl lines my eyes, accentuating their shape, while deep red graces my lips, bold and commanding. The gown chosen by the shadows fits me perfectly, hugging my curves in a way that makes me feel strong, supported, and utterly divine.

A girlish glee bubbles up as I admire my reflection. When was the last time I got to dress up like this? The reasoning behind tonight is grim, but moons be damned, I look ethereal. Sebastien better notice.

Ready far quicker than anyone else—yes, even Brynn with her efficient pantsuit—I wander the sanctum. My intent is to explore, but my steps instinctively lead me back to the moon terrace. Being outside feels freeing, a balm for my restless soul. Not only do I miss Sivan, but our home in the Hollow Forest lingers in my thoughts as well.

I walk to the railing, staring out at the ocean. Above, the sky stretches wide and open, the three moons gazing down like silent sentinels. Their silvery light calms me, grounding my spirit. Time blurs as I let the moonlight wash over me, waves crashing on the rocks below creating a soothing rhythm. My shadows swirl around me, more a part of me than ever.

For some reason, my thoughts drift to my parents. Would they approve of me taking up the crown? Would they be proud? The memory of my mother's sneer and my father's disdain crushes that fleeting hope.

"A lot on your mind?" a gravelly voice pulls me from my reverie.

Sebastien.

I turn to respond, but the words die on my tongue as he steps into the moonlight. He's taken the time to arrange his hair around his horns, each strand perfectly in place. His black silk shirt shimmers faintly, buttons adorned with subtle swirls I can't quite make out. The sight of his collarbone peeking from the open neckline makes my breath hitch. My gaze traces downward, lingering on the way his pants strain over corded muscles.

I shake my head, dispelling the altogether unholy thoughts invading my mind.

"Always," I reply with a wistful smile when my tongue finally obeys.

His eyes darken as they take me in. "You look beautiful," he murmurs.

"Beautiful? That's all?" I tease, leaning back against the railing.

He narrows his eyes, the predator in him awakened. In one fluid motion, he's upon me, pressing his body against mine. One hand tilts my chin up, the other pulls me tightly to him. His dark eyes smolder, igniting something deep within me.

I have the strangest urge to pant.

Leaning down, careful of his horns, he trails light kisses along my jaw, down my neck, and to my collarbone. My breath quickens as I press into him, craving more. His lips travel back up, lingering near my ear.

"You look utterly delectable," he whispers, his voice molten. "There has never been one as perfect as you. As beautiful as you. None could ever compare. If we didn't have pressing matters tonight, I would lock you away in my chambers and worship you until you understood just how divine you are."

A soft moan escapes before I can stop it. His lips brush my cheek before he pulls away, a mischievous glint in his eyes.

"Sebastien," I manage, unsure of what I'm trying to say.

"Rhea," he replies, amused.

Silence settles between us, heavy but not uncomfortable. When I finally speak, the shift feels natural. "Bellum?"

Sebastien's expression tightens. "He's ready to move at your command. The girls are almost done as well."

"The girls?" I ask, raising a brow.

He shrugs. "What else should I call the four of you? 'The four of you' feels clunky."

"That's fair," I concede with a nod. "It works, though calling us 'girls' feels strange considering we're all over twenty."

"You're still far younger than me," he says with a smirk. "But you're right. 'Girls' doesn't quite fit. How about 'the moon squad'?"

I snort. "The moon squad? Absolutely not."

"Fine. 'The moon court'?"

I groan dramatically. "Why do we even need a name? It's not like we're a traveling circus."

"Names hold power," he says, absentmindedly scratching a horn. "They command respect. Your court will transform the Under-Realm. A name that reflects your strength will cement your right to the throne."

His words, so serious, make my toes curl. How does he shift between playful flirtation and commanding gravitas so seamlessly?

"We have time to think about it," I say, ignoring the flutter in my chest. "Let's survive this dinner first, then we can talk names."

"As my queen commands," he replies with a sly grin, tipping a horn in mock salute.

We lapse into casual conversation, though unease snakes up my spine. Sebastien must feel it through our bond, but mercifully, he doesn't push.

The arrival of Brynn and Faye interrupts us. The pair walk in hand-in-hand, glowing despite their solemn expressions. My whistle cuts through the tension as I take in Brynn's jumpsuit.

"Moons be damned, Brynn, you look hot!"

She blushes, her deep brown skin darkening as she twirls with a grin.

"And Faye! Wow. You look like a queen straight out of a fairy tale." Her jeweled gown is something out of an ancient forest ball.

Faye waves me off, laughing. "None of us can compare to your ethereal beauty. Men will die at your feet tonight."

An honest-to-goddess giggle escapes me. "Where's Luna? Once she's ready, we can head out. Bellum's waiting."

Almost on cue, Luna appears, her steps silent. "Here I am," she says, fanning her dress. "It took a while to cut a hole for my tail. Does it look odd?"

Faye shakes her head. "Not at all. You look perfect."

Brynn nods. "It's as if the dress was made for you."

"You look beautiful," I add, noting her hesitation. Inspiration strikes. "Do you mind if I show you something?"

When she nods, I close my eyes and prepare the spell, one I had read about in the journal recently. Drawing from the core of my power, I push my admiration for Luna into her through our bond, push my memory of her walking onto the terrace tonight into her mind. When I open my eyes, hers are wide and shimmering.

"Wow," she whispers, tears spilling over. "Thank you."

Sebastien clears his throat, breaking the moment. "If everyone's satisfied, we should discuss our plan."

Before I can respond, Faye and Brynn whistle appreciatively at Sebastien.

"For a daemon, you look pretty hot!" Brynn says with mock drama.

"With you by her side, Rhiannon will die of jealousy," Faye teases.

Sebastien's eyes glint with amusement as he stifles a laugh.

"If I'd known we were holding a strategy meeting," I quip, "then I would've invited Bellum instead of making him stay outside like a dog."

"I can signal him if you'd like," Sebastien says, his words coming out like a question. I nod and wave a hand, indicating my agreement. Sebastien then taps a spot on his wrist three times.

"He'll be here in a few moments," Sebastien states. The girls and I share a look.

"That's... it?" Brynn asks. I shrug a shoulder when she glances at me, incredulous.

Sebastien appears sheepish as he explains that each of the riders can contact one another whenever they wish, even now that he is no longer apart of Rhiannon's court. Luna's eyes narrow at him in suspicion. Sebastien's look turns somber.

"It was a part of our soul contract with her," he tells us, "We were all forced to be interconnected. I no longer have access to the mind melding, but I can still contact the others if needed. Bellum and I have the strongest connection, since we are both bound to you Rhea."

I sit up a bit straighter and lean forward as much as my gown will allow. "Please, tell us everything we need to know."

Sebastien remains standing, and I take in the full length of him. Not in an "we just made out and I'm attracted to him" sort of way, but more viewing him from an enemy's perspective. He's tall, much taller than the average fae, and laced with muscle in a way that indicates he is not only strong but also has the endurance to back it up. Sebastien carries himself like he knows exactly how dangerous he is, that he's confident in his ability to defend, to kill. His horns that I've always thought of as elegant now fill me with apprehension-- he could use those to maim someone. The time's we've kissed he has been careful not to scratch me with them. Could he use them in battle? Would that hurt him? I'll need to ask.

"Rhiannon is the least of all the problems you will face at the castle," Sebastien begins, "Esuries and Victorum are lethal, and genuinely twisted. While Bell is often under command of the incubus within him, these two relish in death and gore. Each of us carries a special power, or plague as your people call them. Esuries is a vampyre. His fangs make mine look like the teeth of babes. He enjoys draining his victims dry, or if he is not in a position to do so then he leaves them with his plague. The famine. Which drains the victim of life over time. No food shall sate their hunger nor water their thirst. They just fade away, into the ether."

Brynn's eyes blaze with fury. "Like my brother? Is that what happened to my brother?"

Sebastien nods, ever pragmatic. "Yes. I'm not sure how Rhiannon managed it, but that is exactly why his death was so swift."

Brynn rolls out her neck and shoulders, loud cracking sounds occur. Faye glances around, the look in her gem blue eyes more like confusion than anything else.

"So, we kill the asshole, yeah?" Brynn demands, turning and making direct eye contact with me.

"Listen," Sebastien seethes, "Children. We have little time so please allow me to finish." Only when we are quiet to his satisfaction does he continue. "Esuries is skilled at all types of combat. Even I will have difficulty taking him in hand-to-hand combat without Rhea's assistance. We all know Rhea's main goal. Mine is to ensure her safety. My particular shadows will bolster your own," he says looking at me, "while Faye and Luna observe the other guests or provide distractions."

Faye raises her hand like a school child.

Sebastien blinks, the movement heavy and frustrated. "Yes, Ms. Faye?"

"Distraction from what?"

My small smirk grows at the sight of Sebastien trying to withhold a sigh. "I trust you to use your best judgment," he finally forces out. Faye nods solemnly, as if this is a very important concern, but the look in her eyes tells me she's just fucking with him for acting like we don't know what a dangerous situation we're going into, or maybe for assuming a role as commander without a discussion. However, he does have the most combat experience of any of us.

"Alright moon squad," I say dramatically, "Listen to Sebastien. He's correct that we don't have much time and only he knows our enemy. Knowledge is a virtue."

He perks up at that. "Brynn, your background and friendly nature make you an excellent fit for a negotiator. We can figure out courtly titles later, but during this dinner your focus should be on steering the conversation into Rhea's interests."

Bellum chooses that moment to arrive, wearing simple black leather armor and his blood red hair up in a braided bun. Everyone becomes silent as the air becomes charged with tension. He walks across the courtyard until he is standing before me and takes a deep bow.

"My lady," he says, his eyes low, "You sent for me?"
I roll my eyes. "Moons above, do not call me my lady. And stand up. You can look at me. This isn't that kind of court. Just don't go around murdering any more innocents or I will kill you." There's a slight sugary sweetness to my tone, but my message comes across loud and clear. He rises and makes eye contact, then goes and stands behind me. It almost feels as if he is... on guard. I catch

Sebastien's eye, and he nods as if to say "leave it." It has to be muscle memory then.

"Bell here will-- oh, sorry do you mind me using your short name? Bellum is a mouthful sometimes." When Bellum nods, Sebastien continues "Bell will be a silent but imposing presence, showing his new alliance with Rhea and will be ready to react if things go violently. I want Rhea sat between us at dinner.

Brynn's eyebrows rise so high they might fly away.

"Abso-fucking-lutely not. No. Over my dead body. She may sit between Sebastien and I, but she will not be sandwiched between two former members of that bitch's court. No sir."

Brynn's vitriol is understandable, and more-- I agree with her.

Sebastien shakes his head. "I understand your reticence but you three will sit together, across from us. If she tries to separate us, do everything in your power not to allow that."

"And what if her true goal is to kill us or capture us?" Luna asks, looking at her claws.

"Bell will defend Rhea with his life. He will summon his beasts if things become too intense. Faye and Luna, I need the two of you to plan an escape route once we reach the castle. Memorize everything you can about the layout and figure out the best exit. Rhiannon poses little threat to Rhea, with her magic waning, but Esuries is devoted to her. He will die for her if it becomes necessary. But he will kill for her first." Sebastien pauses and takes in the expressions on each of our faces before he glides over to me and extends his hand.

"My queen," he murmurs. Blood rushes into my cheeks as I take his hand and rise from the chair with his support. He lifts my hand

and presses a kiss to my knuckle, before asking "Are we ready?"

Sebastien's kiss lingers on my knuckles, a fleeting moment of calm before the storm. Around me, my court—my family—rises to their feet. Brynn's fiery defiance, Faye's quiet resolve, Luna's calm pragmatism, and Bellum's silent, looming strength—all of it fuels me.

"Let's go kill these moon fuckers," Brynn declares with a wicked grin, her energy crackling through the room. Faye's laughter softens the edge, but even her mirth has a steely undercurrent.

"Rear guard," Luna says firmly to Bellum, her commanding tone cutting through the tension. Bellum nods without hesitation, his hulking frame moving to her side like a shadow. There's an ease between them that I don't fully understand, but I don't need to—not tonight.

The weight of what's ahead presses into me as Sebastien guides me toward the door. The castle looms in my mind, its halls undoubtedly filled with Rhiannon's venom and traps. The thought of Janessa locked away, used as a pawn in this cruel game, tightens something deep in my chest.

But I push it down. No fear. No doubt.

The shadows within me stir, responding to my resolve, their whispers a reminder of the power I carry. I glance back at my court, the people I trust most in this cursed world.

"We walk in as guests," I say, my voice steady. "But we'll leave as survivors. And if Rhiannon underestimates us, she'll regret it."

The moons above glint like sharp teeth in the darkened sky, as if the heavens themselves are watching, waiting.

With Sebastien at my side, my court behind me, and shadows

swirling in my wake, we leave the sanctum and her walls behind.

Dinner awaits.

CHAPTER TWENTY-SEVEN

RHIANNON had spared no expense transforming my cousin's castle into the setting for a macabre mock ball.

Brynn lets out a low whistle, craning her neck to take in the spiraling towers that stretch into the night sky. The pale stone gleams under the light of the moons, its color washed out like seashells. Tiny windows dot the tallest spires, so high they're barely visible, giving the castle an eerie, skeletal feel. It doesn't seem stable to me—fragile, almost—but what do I know of architecture?

A rounded outer wall surrounds the castle, a protective barrier punctuated by a drawbridge gate at its center. The faint scent of salt and brine lingers on the breeze, carried in from the crashing waves below.

Brynn threads her fingers through mine as we approach the gate, her grip reassuring. I glance back to see Faye and Sebastien trailing us, their sharp eyes scanning the decorations with cool detachment. Behind them, Luna and Bellum walk side by side, Luna's tail twitching with what looks like curiosity—or amusement. I can only hope Rhiannon doesn't notice or question it.

Overhead, paper lanterns drift along invisible strings, their glow soft and enchanting. Some are shaped like animals—foxes, wolves, birds—while others resemble blooming flowers, petals carefully painted to mimic life. Each one is a miniature work of art, floating lazily in the night like a glowing menagerie.

The scent of jasmine and moonbells fills the air, soothing and almost cloying in its sweetness. It's a stark contrast to the sharp edge of unease coiled in my stomach. I shudder and shrug the sensation off. I don't need to be soothed—I need to stay alert.

As we cross the drawbridge, the castle proper comes into view. Up close, the pale stone isn't white as I first thought, but a soft, shimmering pink, like the scales of an exotic fish. Silken fabrics cascade from the windows, rippling in the cool breeze like waterfalls of silver and gold.

The courtyard is even more elaborate. Lush greenery spills from every corner, an explosion of life—towering ferns, flowering vines, and vibrant blooms in hues so vivid they feel almost unreal. Every step we take feels like an intrusion, as if we're walking through a surreal dream of abundance and decadence.

"Damn, but the bitch has good taste," Brynn mutters under her breath, her tone grudgingly impressed.

I shake my head. "This isn't her doing—it's Janessa's. She adores plants. She didn't marry because she'd rather talk to them than to people. The rest of the decorations..." I gesture to an array of lewd ice sculptures placed artfully among the flower beds, some of them dripping with what looks like chocolate sauce and orange candies. "That's pure Rhiannon."

Brynn snorts, stifling a laugh, and the sound causes my heart to swell.

Before we can reach the castle doors, they sweep open in perfect synchrony. A man steps out, his movements measured and practiced. He's dressed in formal evening wear, impeccably tailored, his salt-and-pepper hair combed back with precision. His tan complexion hints at Amisran heritage, but his sharp eyes—dark and calculating—are unmistakably Fieros.

"Good evening, most esteemed guests," he says, his voice smooth, with an accent that tugs at memories of my childhood in Darridean courts. "My name is Izhan. I have served this castle since before most of you were alive. Should you require anything tonight, do not hesitate to ask. I will do my best to accommodate."

His gaze lingers on me, his expression unreadable. "Miss Rhea," he says, inclining his head, "it is a pleasure to see you again."

It takes me a moment to place him. Izhan. He had once been a fixture at Janessa's side when we were children, a quiet presence in the background of our games. Now, his lined face and tense shoulders speak of years of wear.

I nod in return, careful to keep my expression neutral, though the tension in his eyes sets my shadows stirring uneasily.

"Thank you, Izhan," I say, my tone clipped but polite. "We'll keep that in mind."

He steps aside, bowing slightly as we pass. The doors open wider to reveal the castle's grand hall, bathed in golden light. Crystal chandeliers glint overhead, casting scattered rainbows onto the polished stone floor.

"Stay close," Sebastien murmurs beside me, his voice barely audible.

I glance back at my companions. Faye and Luna exchange a quick glance, their postures tense but composed. Brynn, still at my side, rests her free hand on the hilt of her dagger, her expression unreadable but ready. Bellum trails behind, his massive frame casting long shadows in the flickering light.

And somewhere in this gilded nightmare, Rhiannon is waiting.

Izhan steps aside, holding the massive door open for us. The castle interior is no less ostentatious than the outside. The grand hall is aglow with golden light reflecting off crystal chandeliers. Shadows dance on the walls, cast by the flickering flames of hundreds of floating candles. A table stretches the length of the room, set with enough precision to make even the most meticulous noble swoon.

The place settings are a study in decadence: plates of polished silver edged in delicate black filigree, goblets that shimmer like moonlight on the ocean, and folded napkins shaped like soaring doves. The table itself is carved from dark wood, each leg adorned with intricate engravings of serpents coiled around blooming flowers.

But it's not the elegance of the room that draws my attention—it's the figures seated at the far end of the table.

Rhiannon reclines in her chair like a queen awaiting her court. Her gown is a masterpiece of flowing crimson, slashed through with streaks of black that look like spilled ink. A faint crown of delicate black pearls glints in her hair, the effect both regal and menacing. No shadows surround her. To her left sits Esuries, pale and still as death, his piercing eyes fixed on us with unsettling intensity. To her right is Victorum, his ice-blue gaze scanning each of us as if measuring us for a coffin. His bow rests casually against the table, though I'm sure the relaxed posture is an act.

Brynn lets out a soft hiss beside me, her body tensing. I squeeze her hand before stepping forward, unwilling to let Rhiannon take the first move.

"Rhiannon," I say, forcing my voice to remain calm, "I see you've made yourself comfortable."

Her lips curve into a slow, dangerous smile. "Rhea. It's such a pleasure to see you again. I hope you'll forgive me for borrowing Janessa's home for this little... gathering."

Borrowing. My shadows twist inside me, their whispers of rage barely restrained. "I'm sure she's delighted by the company," I reply, careful to keep my tone neutral.

Rhiannon laughs, a low, throaty sound that echoes off the stone walls. "Oh, darling, you've always had such a sharp tongue. Please, come in. We have much to discuss."

Sebastien steps closer, his presence grounding me. Together, we lead the group to the table. Izhan moves quickly to pull out my chair, a courtesy that feels more like a warning. I glance at him briefly, searching his face for any sign of Janessa's whereabouts, but his expression remains impassive.

Rhiannon gestures languidly to the seats opposite her. "I've arranged for all of you to sit together. I thought it might be... comforting."

Brynn bristles. "Comforting? That's a word for it."

"Brynn," Sebastien warns softly, his tone enough to make her fall silent—for now.

We take our seats, the tension around the table crackling like a storm waiting to break. Servants emerge from side doors, carrying trays laden with food. They move like clockwork, setting plates before us with practiced ease. The scents are intoxicating—roasted meats, spiced wines, delicate pastries—but I have no intention of eating anything Rhiannon's hand has touched.

"Shall we toast?" Rhiannon asks, lifting her goblet. Her smile is all teeth.

"To what?" I ask, arching a brow.

"To peace, of course." Her tone drips with mockery. "Surely that's what we all want."

Faye leans forward, her voice cold. "You don't kidnap someone's cousin and invite them to dinner if peace is your goal."

Esuries chuckles, the sound low and guttural. "Perhaps not, but it's a start."

Victorum smirks, his fingers idly tracing the edge of his goblet. "It's so rare to have all the key players in one place. We couldn't resist the opportunity to... talk."

Rhiannon's gaze locks onto mine. "You could end this, you know. Surrender. Pledge your loyalty to me, and I'll release Janessa unharmed. You and your... companions can live out your lives in peace."

My shadows writhe, their whispers growing louder. Brynn's hand clenches into a fist, and Sebastien's jaw tightens.

"Peace?" I say, keeping my voice steady. "You mean servitude. You want us to bow and scrape while you drown the Under-Realm in plague and death."

Rhiannon shrugs. "Semantics. The Under-Realm is mine by right, Rhea. You're only delaying the inevitable."

I glance at my companions. Faye and Luna are carefully studying the room, likely memorizing escape routes, while Bellum sits like a stone at the end of the table, his gaze fixed on Rhiannon. Sebastien's hand rests lightly on the hilt of his blade, hidden beneath the tablecloth.

The air grows heavier, the tension thick enough to cut.

Rhiannon leans back, her smile fading. "Do you really think you can win, Rhea? That your little rebellion can stop me? You've already lost so much—your home, your family. Are you really willing to lose more?"

Her words hit their mark; a dagger buried deep. But I refuse to show it.

Before I can respond, Brynn slams her goblet down, the sharp sound echoing through the hall. "If you think for one second we'll bow to you, you're dumber than you look. And let me tell you, that's saying something."

Esuries growls low in his throat, and Victorum's hand moves to his bow. Sebastien tenses beside me, and my shadows curl protectively around my arms.

Rhiannon's eyes narrow, her calm mask slipping just enough to reveal a flash of anger. "Careful, little girl. You're in my house now."

Brynn scoffs. "You mean, Janessa's house?"

Rhiannon simply smiles, her lips stretching out like a snake. "Might makes right, dear ones." She waves a hand and Esuries rises from the table, disappears, and returns with my cousin in tow. She looks alright-- her tan skin unharmed and unmarked though her brown eyes are filled with worry. A snarl escapes me at the sight of Esuries' hand gripping Janessa's arm. She has no magic of her own; it isn't right for Rhiannon to bring her into this fight, though I suppose it's the least terrible thing she's done.

Bellum rises to his feet, the sudden movement shaking the table. Luna rises next to him and remains by his side, her claws sliding free and glinting dangerously in the candlelight. Plates rattle, wine sloshes over the edges of goblets, and the tension snaps like a bowstring.

Chaos erupts.

CHAPTER TWENTY-EIGHT

RHIANNON flies across the table, surprising me with a physical attack rather than the magical one I had prepared for. At the same time, Esuries eyes flit back and forth between Sebastien and Brynn, as if deciding, before he--

I don't get to see the rest. Rhiannon's blow hits me squarely on the nose, forcing tears from me as the white-hot pain spreads across my teeth, my jaw.

Toughen up, kid.

Blood gushes from my nose with alarming velocity, running down my chest and gown. Ugh. This is definitely going to bruise. My nose might even be broken. There's no time to worry about that right now, however, when my life is on the line.

"You got blood on my dress," I say through gritted teeth as I recover from her attack, "And I really love this dress." Shadows flow down my arms as I rebuild my defenses, and I let them flow all the way to the stone floor. They curl this way and that, spiraling around Rhiannon and I.

Goddess above, Luna better have gotten Janessa away from this mess.

She takes a step back, evaluating me like a predator analyzing its prey. We circle each other as the chaos around the room intensifies. Keeping most of my attention on Rhiannon, my eyes scan the room for my friends. Faye has vanished, from what little I can see. Across from us, Brynn and Sebastien are parrying with Esuries, each guarding one another and lashing out at Esuries quickly. Their movements are light, as if they are evaluating him as an opponent more than looking to seriously injure him. Yet.

"Never take your attention off your opponent, darling. Not even a bit." Her voice is smug. It pisses me off.

One tendril of shadows spikes out, gripping Rhiannon's ankle and tugging hard. She falls to the ground, but launches herself at me, her long nails scratching at my face. A wince escapes me, and I bite back a moan of pain as we tumble. My shadows affect her, but she can still injure me physically. How?

My eyes narrow in suspicion. She has still yet to summon a single shadow, not even her own which is a trick I mastered as a child after reading fairytales. My dagger is out and in my hand. As Rhiannon and I roll together, I stab her in the side of her abdomen, but before I can twist the dagger and finish her, a large hulking body crashes into mine and forces me away from the bitch.

"Forgive me," Bellum's voice is in my ear as he cradles my body. A whistling sound shoots pierces the room, and Bellum cries out as a sickening thud reverberates through him. Blood spatters out of his mouth, and he releases me.

"Oh, moons above," I whisper, "There's an arrow in your shoulder."

A long arrow, made of ice solid and cold, is lodged in his shoulder. The shot went all the way through, thankfully. If the arrow had been slightly longer, or I slightly taller, then I might have been impaled as well.

"Pull it out," he says, voice urgent.

"What?"

"Pull it out woman!" He whirls around, and points at Victorum, stringing his bow with another arrow.

I waste no time in cutting off each end of the arrow and pulling it through his shoulder. Bellum steps away from me, shielding me from Victorum's gaze. He does not pull his weapon from its sheathe. Instead, Bellum's hands raise in the air, and large black orbs emerge from his palms. They rise higher and higher, growing larger in size as they do so. From those black holes emerge beasts I have never seen before. They are all fang and claw and primal desire. There's at least a dozen of them.

Oh fuck.

Whirling back around to face Rhiannon, I see she has begun dragging herself away from me, a trail of blood following her. She rises unsteadily to her feet.

Now, I am the predator.

"What's wrong, your highness? Where are your shadows?" The question flows like sardonic wine from my lips. More and more, I can feel her shadows abandoning her as they answer the call of the true shadow queen. These are just the fae lands. I can only imagine how the shadows of the under will feel. It tingles, like the potion that prepared me for Sivan's funeral, though less warm.

"I suppose I grew lazy. Content. But all reigns come to an end, darling. You paid a price, but you do not know of the true cost. The story you were fed was but one version."

I scoff, impatient. "Yes, I'm aware that I must become Sebastien's mate to rule the Under-Realm. It's not as if I'm marrying him or anything."

"No, darling," she says. A hint of sadness lingers in her eyes. "When you agreed to die for your crown, did Ravenna explain to you the ultimate cost?"

"Was dying not enough?"

"No. It never is for those who crave power."

"Alright," I huff, willing to take the bait, "What is it?"

"Your soul will belong to Ravenna in the thereafter. Ravenna is the one who started the wars that decimated the fae, fairy, and daemon worlds. It was only a pact between the three that led to the contracts that stopped the war. Part of those contracts included the mate bond between the fae and daemon representative. Sebastien's ancestor and our pre-incarnations."

She stops for a moment, coughing a bit of blood up. I stand there, awkward and unsure what to do as my friends fight all around me for a future I am no longer sure I can give them. Patiently, I wait for her to continue.

"But other contracts were simply ways to amass power, like giving the soul goddess access over the shadows sacred to the Under-Realm. Ravenna snuck in one such clause where she would be granted the ability to rule over all souls in the afterlife, so long as she gained the required power. She did not explain what that power would be. It would be the souls of her later incarnations and those bonded to her. She would become eternal, immortal, more than even the goddesses. The secret ingredient was a freely given soul."

A shudder of horror goes through me as her words sink in. If this is true, then that means Ravenna is the strongest soul queen to ever exist. How much power it must take to rewrite history, to control the afterlife.

Rhiannon stares at me, as if waiting for me to speak or to finish her off.

"Why tell me all of this now?" My voice is low, sharp, but I can feel cracks forming beneath my anger.

She smirks, blood dripping from her lips, her face pale. "Because, darling... you should know what you're sacrificing *before* you decide to kill me." Her voice wavers, but the venom is still there. "You think you're ready to rule the Under-Realm? You're just a pawn, and Ravenna—"

I don't let her finish.

With a flick of my wrist, shadows explode from the floor and slam into her chest, pinning her to a pillar. The impact sends a tremor through the stone. She cries out, her eyes wide with real fear now.

Good. Let her be afraid.

The dagger hums in my hand, shadows curling around it like eager tendrils, urging me forward. My steps are slow, deliberate. The air hums with power, mine and hers.

But before I can plunge the blade into her chest, a scream cuts through the chaos.

"Brynn!"

The sound slams into me, turning my blood to ice. I whirl around just in time to see Esuries lunging at Brynn. His grotesque pale body moves with terrifying speed, a blur of claws and decay.

"No!"

My voice tears from my throat, but I'm not fast enough. His claws rake across her side, the sickening sound of tearing flesh reverberating through the room.

"Brynn!" I'm running, but my legs feel heavy, too slow, too far.

Sebastien is there, his sword already crashing into Esuries' side with a thunderous crack. Esuries roars, spinning toward him, his maw curling into a grotesque grin. Brynn collapses to the floor, her hands pressed desperately to her throat, blood spilling through her fingers.

"Brynn, hold on!" I shout, my voice raw, but she doesn't respond.

And then I see it: Esuries' dark form twisting as he rears back over her, his fangs descending. Time slows, every sound muffled except for the pounding of my heart.

I know what's going to happen. I can see it, like a terrible vision carved into stone. Brynn is too weak to move, and Esuries is too close. No one can stop him in time.

Except me.

The decision is instinctual.

I shove my legs into motion, ignoring the scream of my muscles, the pain in my chest.

Brynn's wide eyes lock with mine as I throw myself between her and Esuries.

The impact is instant. His jaws clamp down on my shoulder, and white-hot pain explodes through me.

I scream, my vision blurring as something vile seeps into my veins. The world tilts, the edges of my sight going dark. It's like a thousand needles stabbing into me, spreading from the bite, deeper and deeper, until I feel it in my very bones.

I can't breathe. I can't think.

But I can hear Brynn screaming my name.

"Rhea! No!"

Her hands grab at me, but it's like I'm drifting, floating away from her. My body feels heavy, like stone, but my mind—my mind is somewhere else, spinning through fragments of memory and shadow.

Sebastien's voice is distant, but it cuts through the haze. "Esuries!"

I blink, forcing my gaze to focus. Sebastien is there, his sword a flash of silver as he strikes. The blade sinks deep into Esuries' side, and this time he stumbles backwards. Black ichor sprays from the wound, hissing as it hits the ground.

Sebastien doesn't stop. He pulls the sword free and drives it into Esuries' neck, the blow so fierce it nearly severs the head. Esuries roars, thrashing, but it's already over. His massive body collapses as Sebastien keeps hacking, and hacking, and hacking.

It's over.

Or at least, it should be.

Brynn's hands are on my shoulders, shaking me. "Rhea, stay with me! Please!" Her voice is breaking, trembling, but it feels so far away.

"I'm... fine," I rasp, though the words taste like ash. My lips feel numb. Whatever the plagues are made of, the magic in it is ancient enough that even my goddess blood cannot heal.

"You're *not* fine!" she snaps, her hands pressing against the wound. The bite. The infection.

I glance down and see it spreading—black veins snaking out from the bite, curling up my neck and down my arm. It's moving fast, faster than I thought possible.

"No..." The word is barely a whisper.

Brynn's face is pale, streaked with blood and tears. "We'll fix this. We'll—"

"Brynn." My voice is steadier than I expect, even as the darkness claws at the edges of my vision. "You need to stop the bleeding. *Your* bleeding."

She hesitates, her hand going to her own throat, where Esuries' claws left deep, jagged gashes. Her blood is everywhere, staining the floor, her dress, her trembling fingers.

"But—"

"*Do it!*" I snap, the effort sending a fresh wave of pain through me.

Sebastien is suddenly there, pulling Brynn away, his expression grim. "She's right. You're no use to anyone dead."

Brynn resists for a moment, her gaze locked on mine, but Sebastien doesn't let her argue. He presses her hands to her neck and mutters something under his breath—a spell, maybe, or a prayer.

I try to sit up, but my body refuses to obey.

"Rhea." Sebastien kneels beside me, his face tight with worry. "We'll find a way to stop it."

I force a smile, though it feels more like a grimace. "You'd better." My voice is faint now, but I keep talking, if only to keep myself anchored. "I'm not... done with you yet."

The darkness is spreading faster now, consuming everything. I feel it creeping into my mind, my soul.

As my vision fades, one thought rises above the rest, sharp and clear:

I saved Brynn.

If this is the cost, I can live with that.

For now.

The last thing I hear is Sebastien's voice, low and fierce, swearing vengeance against a world that seems determined to take everything from us.

The last thing I feel is Brynn's hand in mine, her grip weak but steady.

The last thing I think is simple:

This isn't the end.

Not yet.

CHAPTER TWENTY-NINE

MY consciousness returns in slow increments. Someone carries me —Sebastien, if his scent is any indication—and my body sways, leading to an uncomfortable feeling in my stomach. My face curls into his chest automatically, holding on to the feeling of safety and comfort even as the burning in my veins heightens.

"You'll be okay. You have to." he murmurs, more to himself, than anything else. After what feels like an eternity, I'm carefully set down on soft bedding. Despite his attempt at being gentle, the movement sends a hiss of pain snaking up my spine.

I finally allow my eyes to open. Sebastien stares down at me, his dark eyes full of emotion.

"Hey," I say, my voice coming out as a hoarse whisper. Brynn shoves Sebastien out of her way and claps a hand over her mouth when she sees me. Tears well at the corner of her eyes.

"I'm so—," a sob escapes her, preventing her from speaking, "I'm so sorry."

"Shut up. You have nothing to apologize for," I respond after a few moments, "You're my sister." Her wound appears to have stopped bleeding. A clean white bandage covers the worst of the gouges.

Brynn sinks to her knees at the side of the bed, her hand trembling as it brushes mine. "I thought I'd lost you," she says, her voice cracking.

"You won't get rid of me that easily," I whisper, though the fire burning in my veins makes the words feel hollow. If I weren't already a goddess, I'm certain I would be dead.

Sebastien paces a few steps away, his broad shoulders tense, his jaw clenched. I don't have to ask to know what's weighing on him—Esuries, the shadows, the blood we spilled just to get out alive.

"What happened?" I rasp, forcing the words through the tightness in my throat.

Brynn glances at Sebastien, then back at me. Her lips part, but it's Sebastien who speaks first.

"Esuries is dead," he says flatly, his voice devoid of triumph. "I killed him after you..." His gaze flickers to my shoulder, where the infection still pulses beneath my skin. "After you fell."

The memory of Esuries' teeth sinking into me, the sickening sound of Brynn's scream, makes my stomach twist. I'd almost forgotten the image of Sebastien hacking away at Esuries' throat.

"And Victorum?" I ask, dread coiling in my gut.

Brynn's expression hardens. "He escaped. The bastard ran the second Esuries went down."

Sebastien nods grimly. "He fired at you—an arrow meant to kill you, not slow you down—but when Esuries fell, he realized he couldn't win. He used the chaos to slip away."

My chest tightens, frustration and fear battling for dominance. "He'll come back," I say softly, the words tasting bitter on my tongue.

"Yes," Sebastien says. "He will. But next time, we'll be ready."

I want to believe him, but there's more I need to know. My gaze shifts to Brynn. "And Rhiannon?"

The air in the room grows heavier, the tension thick enough to choke.

"She's gone too," Brynn mutters, her voice trembling with barely contained fury. "That coward ran and disappeared while you were..." Her voice cracks, and she swallows hard, unable to continue.

"She fled when Victorum did," Sebastien adds, his tone sharper now. "They must have planned it—both of them slipping away in the confusion. By the time we realized she was gone, there was no way to track her."

"Rhiannon always was clever," I murmur, the words tinged with bitterness. "And slippery."

Brynn slams her hand against the edge of the bed. "She was bleeding out when she ran! How is she still alive?"

"Because she's Rhiannon," Sebastien replies, his voice cold. "And because people like her always survive. No matter how much blood they lose, no matter how much pain they cause, they survive."

I close my eyes, letting their words sink in. Rhiannon escaped. Victorum escaped. Esuries is dead, but the shadows he left behind are still in me, poisoning me from the inside out.

"We'll find her," Brynn says fiercely, breaking the silence. "We'll find both of them. And when we do..."

Her voice trails off, but the promise in her tone is unmistakable.

"And Bellum?" I ask, forcing my eyes open again.

Sebastien exhales sharply, running a hand through his hair. "He stayed behind to cover us. When Esuries' shadows started lashing out, they turned on him. If Luna hadn't pulled him out..."

"He's alive," Brynn says quickly, cutting in before Sebastien can finish. "He's alive, Rhea. He's in the next room, but..."

"But what?"

Brynn's lips tighten. "He's in bad shape. The fight with Victorum nearly tore him apart. He needs time to recover."

"And Luna?"

"She's fine," Sebastien says. "She figured out how to stabilize you after you were bitten. Slowed the infection just enough for us to get you out. Without her..."

He doesn't finish the sentence, and he doesn't need to.

"She's with Bellum now," Brynn adds. "Keeping him from trying to get out of bed. You know how he is."

A weak laugh escapes me, though it feels more like a cough. Of course Luna is keeping him in line.

The silence in the room grows heavier, the weight of everything pressing down on me like a physical force.

"Bring them here," I say suddenly, my voice low but firm.

"What?" Brynn asks, confused.

"Bellum and Luna," I clarify. "I need to see them." My throat tightens as I force the words out. "If this is... if this is the end, I need to see them."

"Don't say that," Brynn snaps, her voice fierce.

"Please," I whisper.

Sebastien hesitates, his jaw tight, but he nods.

Minutes pass before the door opens, and Luna strides in, her sharp eyes scanning the room before landing on me. "You look like hell," she says flatly, though there's a note of relief in her tone.

"Thanks," I mutter, a faint smirk tugging at my lips.

Bellum follows her, his massive frame hunched but unyielding. His left arm is bound in a sling, and his usually stoic expression softens when he sees me.

"Queen Rhea," he says, his voice gruff. "You're awake."

"Barely," I reply, my voice weak but steady enough to make him huff a small laugh, "And you don't have to address me as queen. You almost died for us. I think that makes up for your earlier sins."

The five of us sit in silence, the weight of everything pressing down on me like a physical force.

Rhiannon is out there, bleeding but alive. Victorum, too, has escaped, slithering back into the shadows like the snake he is. Esuries is dead, but his bite left its mark—on me, on all of us.

Sebastien's voice breaks the silence, quiet but unyielding. "We'll find them. Both of them. And when we do, we'll finish this."

Luna nods, crossing her arms. "You don't get to die yet, Rhea. We still need you."

I look at each of them in turn: Luna, sharp and pragmatic, her mind already calculating the next steps; Brynn, her hands trembling, but her eyes blazing with determination; Bellum, battered but unbroken, his silent strength anchoring us all; and Sebastien, his gaze steady, the bond between us stronger than I want to admit.

Their belief in me is unshakable, but the infection pulses beneath my skin, a dark reminder of how little time I might have left. Sivan was no match for this disease. How can I hope to stand a chance? I shove aside the negative thoughts swirling within me.

I force a smile, the corners of my lips tugging upward even as my body feels like it's breaking apart. "If Rhiannon and Victorum want to play gods," I say softly, my voice cutting through the stillness, "then it's time they learned how gods fall."

The room is silent for a beat, and then Sebastien's lips twitch into a smirk. "That's the Rhea I know."

It doesn't feel like resolution—not yet—but for now, it's enough. The sickness hums low in my veins, quiet as a lullaby. Thoughts dissolve, drifting out of reach. And as the darkness folds around me, I surrender to it—calm, waiting, unfinished.

Acknowledgements

This book wouldn't exist without a small army of wildly patient, deeply supportive, and occasionally enabling people —and animals—who got me through all the long nights filled with anxiety and tears.

First, to my husband Jordon: thank you for editing, formatting, and handling every terrifying business thing I couldn't wrap my creative brain around. You made this book possible and kept me (mostly) sane in the process.

To my best friends—Salem, Sydney, Shelby, Chelsey, and Katelyn—you listened to my ramblings, read early drafts, and endured hours of me whining about commas. I am eternally grateful for your love, support, and tactical deployment of memes during writing crises. Thank you for believing in me.

Chipmunk and Sweetroll, my cats and co-editors: your presence on my keyboard was both a comfort and a hindrance. Thank you for the purring, and sorry for all the startled yelps when I accidentally rolled my chair too close.

This story was born during one of the hardest chapters of my life. To my therapist—thank you for helping me find light in the dark, for believing in my words before I could, and for teaching me that vulnerability on the page isn't a weakness, it's power.
To my mother, who handed me my first fantasy novel and never took it back—thank you for giving me the gift of story.

And to my overactive imagination: you are both a blessing and a menace. I wouldn't have it any other way.

To you, dear reader, for choosing my book. Thank you, thank you, thank you.
Finally, to SNHU and my creative writing program—thank you for giving me the tools to shape chaos into narrative, and for reminding me that "writer" is not just a dream, but a title earned word by word.

Here's to many more terrible, wonderful ideas.
—Ripley Shaine

www.ingramcontent.com/pod-product-compliance
Lightning Source LLC
Chambersburg PA
CBHW050013120726
47903CB00006B/1747